T3-BHN-208

INSEPARABLE

NEW YORK TIMES AND *USA TODAY* BESTSELLING AUTHOR

BRENDA JACKSON

INSEPARABLE

ISBN-13: 978-1-61793-044-7

INSEPARABLE

Printed in U.S.A.

To the love of my life, Gerald Jackson, Sr.
My one and only. Always.

To everyone who enjoys reading about
those Madarises, this one is especially for you.

To the 1971 Class of William M. Raines High School,
Jacksonville, Florida, on our 40th year class reunion.
And to all Raines Vikings everywhere. *Ichiban!*

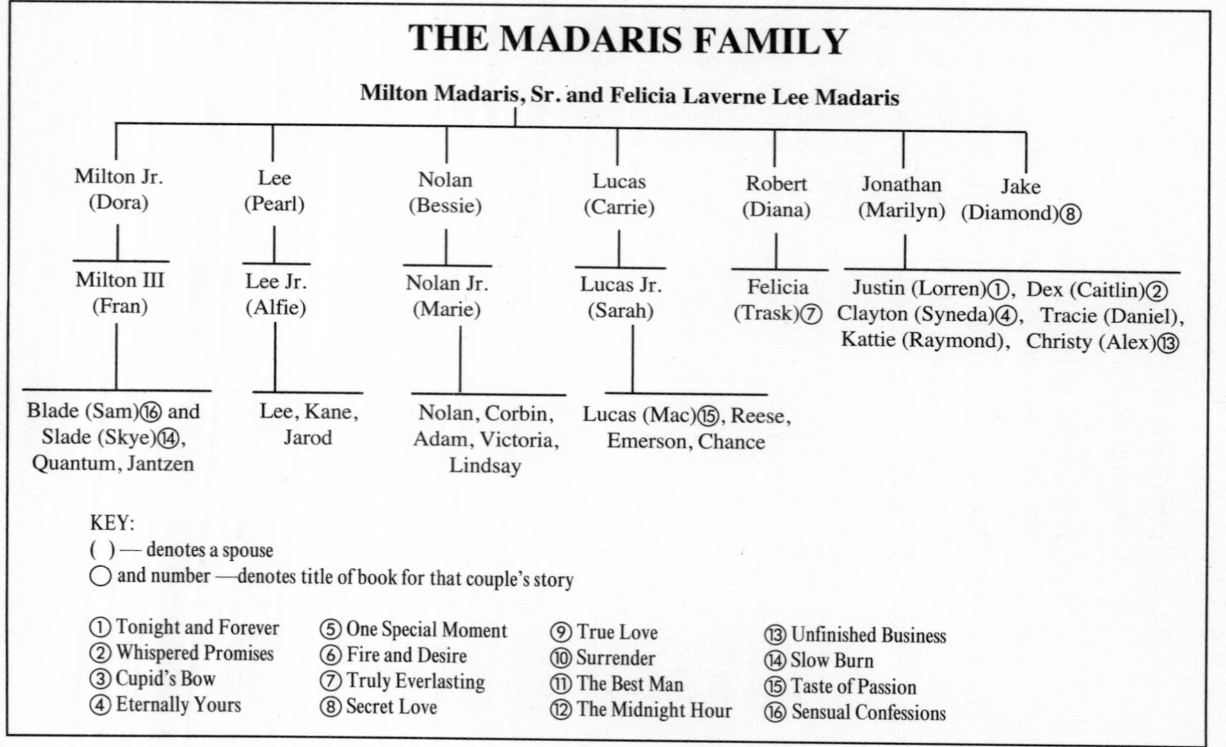
THE MADARIS FAMILY
Milton Madaris, Sr. and Felicia Laverne Lee Madaris
Milton Jr. (Dora)
Lee (Pearl)
Nolan (Bessie)
Lucas (Carrie)
Robert (Diana)
Jonathan (Marilyn)
Jake (Diamond)⑧
Milton III (Fran)
Lee Jr. (Alfie)
Nolan Jr. (Marie)
Lucas Jr. (Sarah)
Felicia (Trask)⑦
Justin (Lorren)①, Dex (Caitlin)② Clayton (Syneda)④, Tracie (Daniel), Kattie (Raymond), Christy (Alex)⑬
Blade (Sam)⑯ and Slade (Skye)⑭, Quantum, Jantzen
Lee, Kane, Jarod
Nolan, Corbin, Adam, Victoria, Lindsay
Lucas (Mac)⑮, Reese, Emerson, Chance
KEY:
( ) — denotes a spouse
◯ and number —denotes title of book for that couple's story
① Tonight and Forever
② Whispered Promises
③ Cupid's Bow
④ Eternally Yours
⑤ One Special Moment
⑥ Fire and Desire
⑦ Truly Everlasting
⑧ Secret Love
⑨ True Love
⑩ Surrender
⑪ The Best Man
⑫ The Midnight Hour
⑬ Unfinished Business
⑭ Slow Burn
⑮ Taste of Passion
⑯ Sensual Confessions

THE MADARIS FRIENDS

Maurice and Stella Grant
|
Trevor (Corinthians)⑥,
Regina (Mitch)⑪

Angelique Hamilton Chenault
|
Sterling Hamilton (Colby)⑤,
Nicholas Chenault (Shayla)⑨

Kyle Garwood (Kimara)③

Ashton Sinclair
(Netherland)⑩

Drake Warren
(Tori)⑫

Trent Jordache
(Brenna)⑨

Nedwyn Lansing
(Diana)⑭

KEY:
( ) — denotes a spouse
◯ and number —denotes title of book for that couple's story

① Tonight and Forever
② Whispered Promises
③ Cupid's Bow
④ Eternally Yours
⑤ One Special Moment
⑥ Fire and Desire
⑦ Truly Everlasting
⑧ Secret Love
⑨ True Love
⑩ Surrender
⑪ The Best Man
⑫ The Midnight Hour
⑬ Unfinished Business
⑭ Slow Burn

Dear Reader,

I never imagined when penning my first Madaris book that I would still be going strong sixteen years later.

The Madaris family is special, not just because it was my first family series, but because over the years you've made them your family. The Madaris men have become your heroes because they represent those qualities you desire in a man—someone whose looks take your breath away, and who has the ability to make you appreciate the fact that you are a woman.

In *Inseparable,* Luke's brother Reese takes center stage as a man who believes he has a best friend for life in LaKenna James. But things begin to heat up when she temporarily moves in with him while her condo is being completed. But Reese is a Madaris man through-and-through. And like all Madaris men, once he finds a woman he truly desires, he can't seem to walk away. But is Kenna the one woman who can claim his heart and soul? And for Kenna, an even bigger question looms...can a hot and heavy attraction ruin a great friendship?

I hope you enjoy reading *Inseparable,* the seventeenth book in the Madaris Family and Friends series.

All the best,

Brenda Jackson

A merry heart doeth good like a medicine:
but a broken spirit drieth the bones.
—*Proverbs* 17:22

Prologue

His eyes quickly moved from his plate of food to the flat screen as he followed the closed-captioning scrolling across the bottom of the television. He used the remote to raise the volume to hear the details of the breaking news story. As the anxious reporter stood in front of an abandoned warehouse, he listened with great interest.

"This is the sixth woman in a year's time who has been murdered in the Twin Cities area in what police believe may be the work of a serial killer. The latest victim was raped and then brutally tortured before being killed in the same manner as the other women. Each body has been found with one shoe missing." The reporter's face looked grim, shrouded in disgust and shock. "The killer, who has been dubbed the 'Shoe Killer' by police, is still at large and has been linked to similar murders in other states," the reporter continued. "So far there have been no leads. And police admit they aren't any closer to arresting a suspect, but they vow to bring whoever is responsible to justice.

Personally, I hope so—and soon. Just knowing he's out there somewhere means that no woman in the Minneapolis–St. Paul area is safe."

He shook his head at the newscaster and chuckled softly, amused by the reporter's last line, about no woman being safe. The observation was certainly an understatement.

The Minneapolis police were smart, but he was smarter, which was why he had eluded them for over a year. But then he hated taking chances. And he knew it was just a matter of time before he made a mistake, played a bad hand…like he'd almost done last night.

His tongue flicked across his lower lip as he remembered what had happened. Hell, she hadn't fought hard enough. Eyes that should have shown fear revealed nothing. When he'd finished, he had stared into her dark eyes and for a second had thought of sparing her life. But then the mere idea of such a thing brought out the beast in him. In the end, her death had been more brutal than the others because she had almost made him break his one steadfast rule: no survivors.

He drew in a deep breath as he pushed away from the table and stood up. He glanced around the house he'd called home for the past two years. It was as neat as a pin, which suited him perfectly. At times it provided emotional warmth, something that he hadn't been able to understand. It was only during those times when the house seemed dreary and cold that he'd known it was time to kill. But now it was time to move on. Another city. Another state. Another woman.

He smiled at the thought. He would be patient, blend in and gain the trust of those he met. Then when they least expected it, he would become who he really was.

Shaking his head, he turned off the television and walked across the room to a cardboard box and lifted the lid. Shoes—more than a dozen of them in all shapes, styles and sizes. Each one was a souvenir—not from a sexual conquest but rather from a kill. In his mind, one complemented the other. And both were just as important.

He sighed and glanced out the window. It was time for him to move on.

Chapter 1

Blade and Samari's wedding reception, New York City...

"What's this I hear about you and Kenna moving in together?"

Reese Madaris tightened his hold on the wineglass and met the intense gaze of the older woman staring back at him. She was his great-grandmother, Felicia Laverne Madaris—*the first,* since she'd had the honor of having a granddaughter named after her.

The elderly woman stood as straight as she could for someone in her nineties. She was quick to tell anyone that her cane was strictly for appearances' sake and not because she ever used it, although most people knew better.

You would think that since it was his cousin Blade's wedding day—an event his great-grandmother had worried might never happen given Blade's reputation as one of Houston's most notorious bachelors—she'd be happy. Reese couldn't help thinking, *Why isn't she in the middle of the ballroom floor doing a happy dance?* Instead, she was harassing him about his best friend, LaKenna James.

He knew his great-grandmother wouldn't give up until she'd gotten an answer. "Yes, Kenna's moving in with me for a while," he said. "She found out that her condo won't be finished for another month after she'd already packed up her stuff to leave Austin."

A smile touched his great-grandmother's lips. "That was nice of you to offer her a place to stay."

He shrugged. "I'd do anything for Kenna. You know that."

Felicia Laverne Madaris nodded. "Yes, I know. The two of you have a special friendship. I just hope it will survive the coming months."

He lifted a brow. "The coming months?"

"Yes. Since Blade is no longer Houston's most eligible bachelor, you are," she said.

"Which means?"

"You're a Madaris. And although you work for a living, most people know you don't have to. Whether you want to admit it or not, you're pretty wealthy. And thanks to your uncle Jake, you all are."

Reese took a sip of wine and acknowledged that what his great-grandmother had said was true. Thanks to his uncle Jake Madaris who was one of the area's most prosperous ranchers and a savvy businessman and investor, Reese, along with the rest of the Madaris clan, was extremely wealthy. If Reese never worked another day in his life, he would still be able to live comfortably. But the bottom line was he *did* work for a living and he enjoyed it.

"I still don't follow you, Mama Laverne. What does my being a bachelor with money have to do with anything?" he asked.

His great-grandmother shook her head. "Blade has been the

most eligible single Madaris man for so long that now you and your cousins have to assume the obvious."

"Which is?"

"Women will turn their sights toward another Madaris—you, Lee, Nolan and Corbin, but especially you."

He lifted a brow. "Why *especially* me?"

"Because you're the oldest Madaris bachelor, even if it is by just a few months. And because you're a loner, you date whenever it pleases you and not according to anyone else's timetable. They'll see you as a challenge—not only in pursuing you, but as the ultimate catch in marriage."

A scowl quickly appeared on Reese's face. His great-grandmother was right about him in that he only dated when it pleased him. He was more than comfortable being serially monogamous—dating one woman at a time. He didn't want any woman in his pocket and didn't intend to be in any woman's pocket either. In other words, he liked being in control. Unlike Blade and his older cousin Clayton, who had both enjoyed having plenty of lovers before they'd finally settled down, he was never interested in getting involved with a bunch of women just for the sake of doing so.

He had a habit of being up-front with any woman he dated. He much preferred relationships to one-night stands and casual affairs. However, the length of time the relationship lasted depended on how well he and his partner connected.

He had dated Alyson Richards for close to a year before she began showing signs of jealousy toward Kenna. That was the one thing he did not tolerate from any woman—Kenna would always be in his life. *Whoever came between them was wasting their time,* he thought.

He glanced across the room to where Kenna was dancing with his uncle Jake. She was his best friend and had been since college, and he refused to put up with any woman who had a problem with that. He refused to be a trophy for any woman who pursued him just for the thrill of it or for the Madaris status—that wasn't going to happen.

"Just thought I'd warn you," said his great-grandmother, her voice interrupting his thoughts. "You also need to consider how being the most eligible bachelor in Houston is going to affect Kenna."

His gaze moved from his uncle Jake and Kenna back to Mama Laverne. "Affect Kenna in what way?"

"Kenna being your best friend is one thing. But now that she'll be living under your roof for a while, it will cause a stir. She'll become the envy of every single woman in town."

Reese couldn't help but laugh. "Really, Mama Laverne, I doubt women will start coming out of the woodwork. Besides Kenna's and my relationship is strictly platonic. You and the family know that, and frankly it's nobody else's business."

"That might be the case, but I can see some women trying to drive a wedge between you and Kenna."

Reese shook his head, thinking their friendship was too rock solid for that to happen. "Thanks for the warning, but don't worry. Kenna is the closest friend I have and she always will be."

"Yes, and that's a good thing as much for Kenna as it is for you," his great-grandmother added.

He knew he shouldn't ask, but he couldn't resist. "And why is that?"

Resting both hands on top of her cane, she responded, "Because Kenna is a nice-looking girl who will be new in town. There will be plenty of men vying for her attention. There will probably be just as many men checking her out as there will be women knocking at your door."

She paused a second, glanced around and said, "Well, I might as well mosey on over and chat with May Lois to see what she's been up to."

Reese pondered his great-grandmother's words. After all,

Felicia Laverne was the matriarch of the Madaris family. She had outlived her husband, whom she readily admitted to being deeply in love with. She had raised seven sons and buried only one of them. She was close to her sons, *and* their wives, her grands and great-grands. She was a good mother—the best.

But she had one major flaw. She had a tendency to stick her nose where it didn't belong when it came to family. She knew it. They knew it. But she had a heart of gold that couldn't be traded for anything in the world. Since it was her only flaw, the family figured they'd overlook it.

After the song had ended, Reese glanced across the room and found Kenna again. She was back on the dance floor, this time with his brother Luke.

For some reason his great-grandmother's comment about Kenna being hotly pursued once she moved to Houston seemed to annoy him. Over the years she'd had a number of steady boyfriends, a few hits and a few misses. Some he'd liked and some he hadn't liked. But he knew for a fact that she hadn't been head over heels in love with any of them. She'd guarded her heart after her college boyfriend Terrence Fairchild had played around on her with another girl on campus. At the time Reese had been involved with someone else, but that hadn't stopped him from providing Kenna with the shoulder she needed to cry on.

Although she'd dated steadily after that, it was years before Kenna got involved in a serious relationship again. That guy was Lamont Cotton, whom Reese hadn't much cared for. She and Lamont had been involved for eight months before they'd gone their separate ways. Then she began dating again, but didn't get serious with anyone until Curtis Purcell. She'd mentioned last month that she and Purcell had split, but she hadn't said why.

Personally, he didn't need to know the details. What he did know was that another man she'd gotten involved with had broken her heart yet again. Over the years his protective instincts for Kenna had grown stronger. In a way, that was what had made them closer, and made their relationship seem what some considered more than friendly. For Reese and Kenna, it was normal. It was the way things were naturally supposed to be.

The very first time he had brought her home from college one weekend to introduce her to his family and explained to them that she was his best friend and nothing more, they had accepted her as such. But every once in a while someone would try to insinuate that there was more between them. It had gotten to the point where he let them assume whatever they wanted to.

He took another sip of cabernet. For some reason he couldn't stop staring at Kenna as she moved around the dance floor. He tried to see her as other men did. Not as his best friend, but as a woman—and if his great-grandmother's predictions were true—who would attract dozens of men once she moved to Houston.

Her short, medium-brown curly hair was stylishly cut and framed an attractive, warm-brown face. No doubt men would be mesmerized by her soft brown eyes, her full lips, creamy, flawless, chocolate-brown skin and the soft curves of her body. Although most women assumed a tall, slender frame was the only body type that could catch a man's eye. Reese knew that men were strongly attracted to a full-figured, voluptuous woman like Kenna, who was stacked in the most delectable ways. There was no doubt in his mind that any man would think she was beautiful.

Just like there was no doubt they would lust after her, he thought as he took another sip of red wine. Even Reese had to admit to lusting after her himself, *once*—the first time they'd met when she had shown up at his dorm room one day. He had been twenty and in his junior year at Morehouse and she was eighteen and a sophomore at Spelman. She was whip-smart and an ace in physics. She had been recommended as a tutor, and that had been the start of their friendship. That was eleven years ago.

"Any reason you're standing over here staring across the room watching Kenna dance with Luke?"

Reese blinked before looking around to meet his cousin Nolan's eyes. He, Nolan and another cousin, Lee, had all been born the same year. Nolan's brother Corbin trailed them by ten months. "I wasn't aware I was staring."

The corners of Nolan's lips lifted into a smile. "You were. There's nothing wrong, is there?"

He glanced back toward the dance floor to see that his brother Luke had been replaced by his cousin Corbin as Kenna's dance partner. "No, there's nothing wrong."

"Well, if you're waiting to claim a dance with Kenna you'll have a long wait on your hands. We're all waiting our turn," his cousin said, grabbing a champagne flute off a passing waiter's tray.

He couldn't help but smile at that. Kenna liked to dance and his brothers and cousins enjoyed the challenge of keeping up with her on the dance floor. "No problem."

He polished off his cabernet, thinking it really wasn't a problem. She was enjoying herself. From across the room he saw the huge smile on her face and the sparkle in her eyes. *His Kenna. His best friend.* She glanced in his direction, met his gaze and smiled.

He smiled back before looking over at Nolan to find his cousin staring at him strangely. "What?"

Nolan chuckled. "Nothing."

He tensed at his cousin's one-word response, wondering what was going on in Nolan's mind. He eyed him suspiciously before saying, "I'm going to dance with Kenna."

"Sorry, pal, you'll have to wait your turn" was Nolan's reply, before he began drinking his champagne.

Reese chuckled and said over his shoulder as he walked toward the dance floor to cut in on Corbin, "No, I don't, since I have an inside connection."

"Darn, Kenna, I can barely keep up with you. Are you sure you haven't taken more dancing lessons since the last time?" said Corbin.

Kenna couldn't help but smile. Besides painting, dancing was her favorite hobby. Growing up, she had envied the girls who had been able to take dance lessons, something her grandmother hadn't been able to afford. She'd made a promise to herself that once she finished college and had a job, she would take dance classes. And she did.

She enjoyed everything from ballroom to Latin to hip-hop. She did it all, including belly dancing and tap, which wasn't an easy feat for a full-figured woman. She blamed it all on her hips, which wouldn't go away no matter how hard she danced or worked out. She'd gotten used to them and accepted her curvy figure as something she'd have to live with.

"Come on, Corbin, it's not like you to whine." She laughed. "The music just started, so don't conk out on me now. It's just the tango." They snapped their heads around in perfect sync and stared at each other with feigned smoldering passion.

"Just the tango?" he said, as their heads swiveled back and forth in tandem. Corbin's thick, neatly coiled dreadlocks went flying over his shoulders. "Look around. We're the only ones left on the floor now. All eyes are on us."

He quickly glanced over Kenna's shoulder as he twirled her around. "I think Reese is coming to cut in. Of course he wants to be the center of attention."

Kenna threw her head back and laughed as Corbin dipped her body low to the floor. Anyone who knew Reese knew that the last thing he wanted was to be the center of attention, of anything. No doubt he was coming to sweep her off the dance floor since he probably thought that the long slit on the side of her gown revealed too much leg—one of the dangers of dancing the tango.

Reese could be a little overprotective at times. But she could deal with it. He had been her best friend for as long as she could remember, and she loved him like a brother. She quickly repressed the thought, which she knew was a lie. She did love him, had always loved him, and *not* as a brother. He was the man she would never have, and as her best friend he'd always looked out for her. She no longer fantasized about "what might have been," but accepted the role he played in her life now—the part he would always play.

She picked up his masculine scent long before he reached her. He tapped Corbin on the shoulder and took over as her dance partner. She couldn't help but smile at him. Like always, he dreamily smiled back.

Reese had no idea that whenever he smiled at Kenna—even though they were just friends—he had a way of making her feel beautiful and special. Even though their relationship was far from intimate, she knew him better than anyone. She knew his likes, dislikes, his innermost secrets. She knew when things were bothering him without having to ask. She could feel him. She could decipher his mood, and could even pick him out of a crowded room. It was like she had radar, a sixth sense, where Reese was concerned. They were simpatico.

Without saying a word, they danced the tango like contestants on *Dancing With the Stars.* When she had needed a partner for her ballroom dance classes a few years ago, he had obliged, but after much complaining. There was never any doubt that they were great dancing together, but they also *looked* incredibly good together.

The tango ended and the band began playing a swing dance number. The swing dance was another favorite of hers. And as she and Reese stood facing each other, hand in hand, moving their feet in rhythm to the beat, they couldn't help but laugh. Reese was the only man who could keep up with her on the dance floor and do it with such style.

As they danced, she couldn't stop her eyes from roaming over his body from head to toe. He was handsome in his tuxedo, but then he looked handsome in everything. He was one of the hottest men she'd ever laid eyes on, and in a room filled with good-looking Madaris men that said a lot.

Reese was tall, almost six foot three. And as far as Kenna was concerned, he was the epitome of masculinity at its finest. His deep, rich copper skin tone only deepened the most gorgeous pair of brown, bedroom eyes any man could possess. Then there were his dimples and his generous lips that beckoned women to want to lick them for days.

She swallowed hard, suppressing such thoughts, and reminded herself that although she secretly loved him, their relationship was based on friendship, nothing more. But that didn't stop her from appreciating him as a man—and seeing him through the eyes of a woman sexually attracted to a man—every once in a while.

The swing dance ended and the band began to play a slow song. Kenna turned to leave the dance floor when Reese tightened his hold on her hand and pulled her closer to him. She went willingly.

When he wrapped his arms around her and drew her closer to his muscular frame, she put her head on his chest and closed her eyes. It wasn't the first time they'd slow-danced together, but it was so rare that she relished the times they did.

After three dances with Reese she wondered why no one had cut in. She tilted her head away from his chest and took in the curious looks that were focused on them across the ballroom. Although she and Reese weren't the only ones on the dance floor, his family standing on the sidelines of the ballroom had their eyes glued to them. *Why?*

She tilted her head upward and met Reese's gaze. "Is something going on that I should know about?" she asked softly.

He smiled at her. "Why do you ask?"

"Everyone is staring at us."

He glanced around the room and returned his gaze to hers. "They always stare at us when we dance together."

"Yes, but this time it's different."

He shrugged. "You know how my great-grandmother is. She heard you're moving in with me and has probably gotten everyone thinking that there's more than friendship between us."

"But why would she say something like that? Everyone knows we're nothing more than friends," Kenna said.

"Yes, but I'm sure she reminded them that in the beginning Syneda and Clayton had been friends, too."

"Yes, but things between us are different. Surely they know that."

He smiled. "They do. Don't worry about it. They're just trying to mollify the old gal."

Kenna sighed softly and rested her face on Reese's chest again. She couldn't understand why his great-grandmother would say such a thing when everyone knew the kind of women Reese was usually attracted to—tall and slender, which was something she definitely was not.

The song ended much too soon, but instead of leading her off the dance floor, Reese tilted her chin upward to meet his gaze. His brown bedroom eyes scanned her face with concern. "Hey, you're okay?" he asked in a voice that was so low it was barely audible. It was lower than she'd ever heard before.

She nodded and smiled. "Yes, I'm fine. What about you? Are you beginning to think my moving in with you isn't such a good idea after all?"

"No, I still think it's a good idea. What kind of friend would I be if I didn't let you stay with me? And don't worry about my great-grandmother. We know the real deal regardless of what others believe is going on between us, right?"

She nodded, keeping the smile plastered on her face. *Yes, he was right. They knew the real deal. He would never look at her the way he looked at other women. They would never be anything more than best buddies.*

"Right," she said, smiling. "We know the real deal even if they don't."

He returned her smile. "True."

She drew in a deep breath as he led her off the dance floor, and she wondered how she was going to remain level-headed living under Reese's roof for thirty days.

Chapter 2

A month later...

Reese leaned in the doorway with a cup of coffee in his hand and looked behind Kenna to the moving truck parked in front of his ranch house. It was a truck he knew was loaded down with heaven knows what.

He had offered to fly to Austin and help her make the drive to Houston, but that independent streak in Kenna—which annoyed the hell out of him at times—had refused his help. She claimed she needed to do things herself, since it was her way of turning another page in her life. A part of him understood that, mostly because he understood her.

"So how was the drive?" he asked, offering her the cup of coffee in his hand. Like him, she needed the caffeine, especially during the early morning hours, and it was early. At four in the morning most of Houston was still asleep, including the men who worked his ranch. Kenna preferred driving at night, although Reese had been concerned about her safety.

She took a sip, closed her eyes and drew in a deep breath. She opened her eyes and met his gaze with sparkling eyes. "I hope you never lose your knack for making coffee. Starbucks has nothing on you, Reese Madaris."

"Glad you think so," he said, chuckling, taking the cup back from her and taking a sip himself. "There's a pot inside, waiting for you."

She smiled and he couldn't help but chuckle again. Kenna was easy to please. Before walking inside she glanced over her shoulder. "Do you want me to move the truck and park it somewhere else instead of right in front of your door?"

"It's fine right there. My men and I will unload it after breakfast," he said, pulling her into the foyer and closing the door behind them.

She turned to face him. "Aren't you going to work today?"

"No, I took the day off to help you get settled." He could tell from her expression she didn't like that. It was that independent streak again.

"You didn't have to do that, Reese," she said, frowning. "Remember our agreement? I don't want to disrupt your life or your lifestyle by moving in."

"You're not. Now go into the kitchen and pour yourself some coffee. You're usually in a bad mood until you've had your first cup."

"I'm not in a bad mood."

He grinned. "Yes, you are."

Her mouth curved in a smile. "Okay, maybe you're right."

"As usual. And while you're getting your caffeine fix, I'll be in my office checking my emails. After that I'll join you in the kitchen." He turned and walked down the hallway, headed toward his office. Kenna's gaze followed him as he walked away.

The foyer opened up to a spacious living room that had a spiral staircase leading to a second floor where most of the bedrooms were located. As Kenna made her way through the dining room and into the kitchen to get the cup of coffee she so desperately needed, she took in the decor.

She loved Reese's home and remembered when he had purchased the land for it. They had talked about it endlessly before he finally made up his mind to build his house. He had shown her the floor plans for the design of the house that his cousin Slade—the architect in the family—had drawn up. She had fallen in love with it immediately. It was a sprawling two-story ranch-style house surrounded by more than seventy-something acres of land. Reese was down-to-earth and enjoyed being in the great outdoors. He could never be happy living in a condo in Houston.

Kenna had been the one to pick out the furniture for every room. It was at a time when Reese had been out of the country working for Remington Oil. When he'd returned to the States, it was to find the house completely furnished and ready for him to move in.

In the kitchen were sleek granite countertops and sparkling stainless-steel appliances. It was a huge, spacious kitchen compared to the one she had in Austin. As she reached for the coffeepot, she couldn't help but think about how happy she'd been to see Reese when he'd opened the door. The moment he smiled, all the problems she had encountered on the road from Austin had faded away.

She'd gotten so sleepy while driving to Houston that she decided to check into a motel to get a couple of hours sleep. Although Reese had volunteered to help her drive from Austin, she felt she needed the time alone to think. She wanted to be sure the decisions she had made had been the right ones.

She would be the first to admit she was nervous about her new job. She had gone to work for the Austin Police Department right out of college, and for the past seven years the place had practically become her home. The people she worked with had become her family and she had enjoyed being a part of that. Now she would have to start over, meet new people, make new friends, and get used to her new environment.

She knew accepting the job in Houston had been a smart move, especially since she'd be earning almost double the salary she made in Austin. The Houston Police Department hadn't just considered her value as a sketch artist, but they had taken into account her ability to gather details others might overlook. With all the new technology, she figured it was just a matter of time before her job would be done by a computer. But there were some things computers just couldn't do, like factoring in things that required more than just sketching a suspect's face. Kenna was adept at obtaining seemingly inconsequential details from witnesses and victims—clues to solving crimes that might be missed. She had a way with people. And she had the ability to understand the human psyche in subtle ways.

She was good at what she did and very thorough. With Kenna, the typical three-hour interview was more than just a way to make a composite sketch. She had the ability to draw out subconscious details from witnesses that were important to the investigation. She had received several commendations from the police department for helping to crack a few cases. That was one of the reasons the Houston Police Department had wanted to hire her, making an offer any sane person couldn't refuse.

She didn't.

That had been a few months ago. She had come to town and found the perfect place to live. Her condo should have been ready by now, but bad weather had delayed completion of construction on the building.

Temporarily moving in with Reese had been his suggestion. And it had been a no-brainer, since she'd crashed at his place whenever she came to town anyway. She considered him family, especially after her grandmother—who'd raised her after her parents were killed in a car accident—died while Kenna was still in college. After that, the Madaris family adopted her as one of their own.

She leaned against Reese's kitchen counter as she took another sip of coffee. The other reason for her move from Austin was to be near Reese. Although he visited her fairly regularly in Austin, the need to be closer to him had been a motivating factor in accepting the job.

It was a decision she was already beginning to regret.

She knew how she felt about him. But he didn't have a clue, and she intended to keep things that way. Lately, she had begun seeing him through different eyes. And she knew why. This was the first time in eleven years that neither of them was involved with someone else. For her, that meant she had too much idle time on her hands and no man to keep her occupied. With Reese, she was nothing more than a dear friend, someone he could trust completely. Someone he could share anything with….except his heart.

She took another sip of coffee trying to recall just when she'd realized she was attracted to him. She'd been attracted to him since college, but her feelings had escalated when they'd taken a trip to Las Vegas together. It had been his present to her on her twenty-fifth birthday. *Had it been almost four years?*

She shook her head remembering that weekend. It was a couple months after she'd broken up with Lamont. Although she'd never told him, her relationship with Lamont ended after he'd questioned her friendship with Reese one too many times. She had warned him that if he brought it up again that would be the end of things between them. He hadn't taken her seriously, and in the end she'd shown him she meant business.

Reese figured she needed cheering up after her breakup, and to this day she'd never told him about Lamont's accusations. But Lamont wasn't the only man who had thought that something more than just friendship was going on between her and Reese.

"You're tired. I can tell."

She glanced up as Reese entered the kitchen. A smile touched her lips. "I am tired."

He angled his head and looked at her. "I'm going to be real upset if I find out you didn't take my advice and check into a motel for the night when you hit the halfway point."

She rolled her eyes. "It was only a two-and-a-half-hour drive. It was nice with no traffic. However, I did get sleepy and pulled into a motel for a few hours," she admitted.

"I'm glad. So, do you want to go to bed before or after breakfast?"

She smiled, knowing he hadn't meant it the way it sounded. But she could hope. "It's too early for breakfast, and I could use a couple of hours' sleep."

"Go on up. Your room is ready."

"Thanks." She took another sip of coffee, thinking the room he was referring to was just that—her room. And it had her signature all over it. She had decorated it to her liking and it was the one she always slept in whenever she came to visit. It was right across the hall from his.

She placed the cup in the sink. "I'll be up before the ranch hands are ready for breakfast."

"You don't have to. We can handle things without you. Your luggage comes in the house and everything else gets stored in the barn, right?"

"Right."

She didn't have to tell him that most of the stuff in the truck was what she didn't trust the moving company to take care of. They were keepsakes—things that had sentimental value and had once belonged to her grandmother but were now hers.

"Thanks for letting me stay here, Reese."

He glanced over at her as he poured another cup of coffee for himself. She felt his gaze and it stimulated something inside her. "You don't have to thank me, Kenna. What's mine is yours."

Something stirred deep within her again and she drew in a sharp breath before nodding her head. She turned to leave the kitchen and had almost made it to the dining room when Reese called out to her.

"Kenna?"

She stopped and turned around with a practiced smile. "Yes?"

"I'm glad you're here."

Something in Kenna's chest tightened and a part of her wanted to race across the room, throw herself into his arms and declare that she was glad to be anywhere he was—always. Instead she said. "I'm glad I'm here, too."

Before she could say something else, something she would later regret, she quickly walked in the direction of her room.

Reese slid his hands down his face as he watched her leave. They were both tired, and maybe that was the reason he had picked up on the tension between them. He knew there was something going on. He could tell by the firm set of her lips and her body language.

He took a sip of his coffee and tried replaying everything that had happened since she'd arrived. For some reason he needed to clear his mind of a few things and make heads or tails of the situation. She had arrived at his door a little past four o'clock in the morning. He hadn't been able to sleep knowing she was on the road at night and driving a rented U-Haul truck alone, so he was relieved when he'd heard the sound of the truck pulling into the yard.

Even though it took less than three hours to drive from Austin to Houston for most people, he knew Kenna wasn't like most people when it came to driving at night. When she was tired and sleepy, she couldn't stay awake. She had promised him that she'd get plenty of rest before making the trip, but he knew she hadn't done that. When he had talked to her before she'd left Austin, several friends were still at her place seeing her off.

The original plan was for her to leave Austin around six o'clock in the evening. That way she would have arrived by nine o'clock that night. But instead she hadn't left Austin until well past midnight, which had annoyed the hell out of him. He had been ready to bite her head off when he'd opened the door at four in the morning. However one look at her and he had been so glad to see that she had arrived safe and sound that he had pushed his anger aside. But now he was getting mad again.

Taking another sip of his coffee, he moved away from the counter to glance out the window. The sun was just starting to rise, which meant that the ranch hands would be up and stirring soon. Although he worked full-time for Madaris Explorations, he still maintained a working cattle ranch. His spread wasn't as big as his uncle Jake's or his brother Chancellor's by any means, but a part of him would always be a rancher.

His foreman, Joe Seaborne, had been with him since he'd built the ranch five years ago. Before that Joe had worked for his uncle Jake, and he had come highly recommended. Joe was a good man and kept things running smoothly. His uncle Jake was using Reese and Chancellor's land to expand the breeding program for his Red Brangus cattle.

He turned away from the window when he heard the key being inserted in the lock and wasn't surprised when Joe walked in smiling.

"I saw that big truck out front. I guess that means Kenna has arrived."

Reese shook his head, grinning. Of course most of his men knew Kenna and knew what a fantastic cook she was. Whenever she came to visit, she'd spoil them by preparing whatever they liked to eat. Even the ranch cook, Tanker Jones, enjoyed eating Kenna's food every once in a while.

"Yes, Kenna is here, but that doesn't mean she'll be at anybody's beck and call."

Reese knew it was hard for the big bear of a man to look sheepish, but he managed to do just that. "Of course not, Reese, but I'm sure one Sunday dinner won't hurt, will it?"

"You'll have to ask her." And there was no doubt that Joe would ask, like there was no doubt Kenna would prepare more than *one* Sunday dinner for his men. "Just remember she starts her job with the HPD in a couple of weeks. Until then she has to get settled in here."

Joe smiled. "I understand. And speaking of new jobs, that guy we hired starts today. He's already here."

Reese nodded. "I'll meet with him later. You did check him out before bringing him on, right?"

"Yes. He came highly recommended by his last employer."

"Good. We don't want a repeat of the last guy we hired."

Last year a new hire ended up skipping out with Joe's favorite saddle. Luckily they were able to catch him when the police stopped the culprit as he was speeding out of town.

Reese decided now was as good a time as any to meet with his new hire. He had a feeling Kenna would sleep longer than she intended, which was fine with him. Her schedule had been hectic the last couple of weeks as she packed up and moved from Austin to start a new life in Houston. As far as he was concerned she needed the rest, and he was going to make sure she got it.

Chapter 3

Kenna ran her fingers through her short curls once more before sliding her feet into her sandals to go downstairs. She had only meant to sleep a few hours, but a quick glance at the clock showed it was almost noon. The luggage Reese had put in her bedroom was proof that he and his men had unloaded the truck without her help.

Hearing voices outside her bedroom window, she walked over to the sill and saw Reese talking to a few of his men on the ground below. She recognized all of them except one, so she figured he must be the new guy Reese had mentioned he was hiring. He was a pretty nice looking man. But the woman in her couldn't help but appreciate Reese, especially in the looks departments. He was eye candy of the most luscious kind, and he epitomized what tall, dark and handsome truly meant. As far as she was concerned, no other man looked as good in a pair of jeans as Reese Madaris. But then he cleaned up rather nicely too, she thought, remembering how good he'd looked at Blade's wedding last month.

She and Reese usually talked two or three times a week. It wasn't unusual for him to tell her what was happening around the ranch. Sometimes he'd ask her opinion about certain things and she would do likewise. Whenever there was a problem she couldn't resolve—personal or professional—he was the first person she called. And no matter what he was doing, no matter whether it was day or night, he would make time for her.

When she saw Reese head inside the house, leaving the group of men behind, she closed the curtain and proceeded to go downstairs. But before she reached the doorway, the phone rang.

Kenna and Reese had come to an understanding years ago that their friendship gave them the right to answer the phone at each other's place. If the caller took issue with it, then that was *their* problem.

She picked up the phone in her room. "Tall Oaks Ranch."

There was a pause.

"Yes, I'd like to speak to Reese," said a woman's voice.

Kenna immediately knew it was Alyson Richards, Reese's ex-girlfriend, the one he'd dated for almost a year. Everyone had assumed that Alyson might become Mrs. Reese Madaris. But a few months ago, Reese had called and surprised Kenna when he casually mentioned that he and Alyson were no longer seeing each other. Kenna had every reason to believe it had been Reese's decision and not Alyson's. He hadn't given her an explanation for the breakup, and she hadn't asked for one.

"No problem. Hold on a minute."

"Wait! This is Kenna, right?" the caller asked.

Kenna's mouth curved into a smile that all but said, *like you didn't know.* Instead, she said, "Yes, this is Kenna."

"Hi, Kenna, this is Alyson. Reese told me you were moving to Houston. How nice."

"Yes, it is nice."

"And he mentioned you were moving into a town house."

Kenna really didn't want to get involved in a long conversation, since Alyson had never liked her and they both knew it. "It's not finished yet."

"Oh."

A smile touched Kenna's lips. She could imagine the wheels turning in Alyson's head. It wouldn't take her long to figure out that she was staying with Reese until her condo was finished. "Hold on, Alyson. I'll get Reese for you."

"Fine."

Kenna put the phone down and went to the edge of the staircase. "Reese, you have a call. It's Alyson."

He appeared at the foot of the stairs and stared up at her and smiled. She drew in a deep breath at the way his lips curved and how his dimples seamlessly appeared. She couldn't help but wonder if he was smiling at her or if he was smiling because Alyson was calling. *Of course it's because of Alyson and not you,* a mocking voice said in her head. *Get real, LaKenna James. Reese has no reason to smile at you that way.*

"Okay. I'll grab it down here. Did you get some rest?" he asked.

"Yes, but you should have woken me up, Reese."

"No, you needed to sleep. You missed breakfast, but come join me for lunch."

"Okay." She went back to her bedroom, and when she heard two voices on the line she hung up the phone.

Alyson Richards.

Kenna couldn't understand why Alyson didn't like her when she had been more than friendly to her. Alyson, who worked as an executive administrator at a local hospital, was beautiful and had everything going for her—including being the daughter of a Texas senator. The few times Kenna had seen Reese and Alyson together she'd thought they looked good together, and if they married, they would have beautiful babies. The very thought hurt, but she'd been honest about it anyway.

"If I had a man in my life I wouldn't have time for such thoughts," Kenna muttered as she made her way down the stairs. When she walked into the kitchen Reese glanced over at her and then said to Alyson over the phone. "Here's Kenna, why don't you ask her?"

She lifted a brow. Reese shrugged his massive shoulders and handed her the phone. "Alyson wants to ask you something."

Kenna continued to hold his gaze. "Yes, Alyson?" she said evenly.

"Kenna, now that you're moving to Houston you probably don't know a lot of people and I've come up with this wonderful idea," she said in a cheerful tone.

Was this the same woman she'd spoken to earlier? The one who'd acted cool and reserved? "And what's that, Alyson?"

"That Reese should give you a welcome-to-town party this weekend."

Kenna shook her head. "He doesn't have to do that."

"I think he should, since you're his best friend. And I've volunteered to help and host it at my place. It's more than big enough, and since it's in town it will be convenient to everyone. Reese said it's okay with him if it's okay with you. I think it's a wonderful idea."

A part of Kenna felt she should appreciate the gesture, but she had an uneasy feeling about Alyson. Drawing in a deep breath she turned her gaze away from Reese to look out the window.

She wasn't sure why the two had split. But from the sound of things, Alyson intended to use this party as a way to get back together with Reese. There was nothing wrong with Alyson trying to patch things up, even if it was with Reese—the man Kenna loved. And because she loved him, she wasn't about to stand in the way of someone who evidently was trying real hard to get a ring on her finger. Especially since it was a ring that Kenna would never wear.

She turned around to see Reese still leaning against the counter, watching her. She knew what he was doing. He was trying to read her, trying to figure out what she was thinking. Their eyes held for a moment before she lowered her gaze. "A party sounds like fun, but I wouldn't want you to go to any trouble."

"No trouble. Just let me handle everything. Goodbye."

"Goodbye."

She handed the phone back to Reese. "That's nice of her to do that."

Reese didn't say whether he thought it was a nice gesture or not. Instead, he said, "Go ahead and sit down. A couple of PBJs with cookies and milk are coming up."

Kenna smiled as she eagerly plopped down in one of the chairs at the kitchen table. At heart she was a simple girl who liked simple things. Though most women preferred gourmet food, a peanut butter and jelly sandwich topped off with cookies and milk hit the spot better than anything. The same was true for Reese. That was one of the first things they'd discovered they had in common.

She watched Reese as he made the sandwiches and thought the same thing now that she did whenever she saw him, no matter what he was wearing. He was more good-looking than any man had a right to be—gorgeous beyond words, ruggedly handsome and sexy to a fault. Plus he was the most wonderful friend in the world.

When other women saw him, they only looked at what was on the outside. She knew him inside and out. He was hardworking, honest and caring. He had this protective side when it came to her that set her teeth on edge one minute and made her feel like the most adored woman on earth the next.

She studied his hands as they spread peanut butter across the slice of bread. They were large hands—callused, even scarred in some places. She had begun imagining those same hands touching her in places a friend's hands didn't dare go. She probably should have hung her head in shame. But right now, she preferred sitting there and watching him through the lustful eyes of a woman who *wasn't* his best friend.

He was humming one of Drake's songs in a deep, velvety voice. He was certainly in a good mood. Had Alyson's phone call done that to him? She knew she shouldn't be envious of her if it had. Kenna knew she needed to put her feelings for Reese in check over the next few weeks and stop dreaming about something that wasn't going to happen, something that could end their friendship if Reese ever found out. She wasn't going to let her out-of-control libido jeopardize her relationship with the best friend she'd ever had.

She turned away and looked outside the window, instead. He had insisted that she stay here while her town house was being finished. Maybe she shouldn't have been so quick to jump at his offer. But then, she always stayed with him whenever she came to Houston. But a month was a long time to live under someone's roof. They'd never been together that long before. Was he up for it? Was she? He liked his space and she liked hers. But for some reason they had no problem sharing with each other.

Moments later, Reese brought the sandwiches to the table along with a plate of chocolate chip cookies and a pitcher of milk. She glanced over at him when he sat down. "You never did say why you and Alyson broke up," she asked as she poured a glass of milk.

He glanced over at her. "You never asked."

Point taken.

Had she asked, he would have told her, since there were no secrets between them. The fact that he didn't know that she was attracted to him didn't count. "Okay, I'm asking now."

He poured a glass of milk. "She was becoming too possessive, and after a while she became jealous of you."

Kenna winced. "Of me?"

"Yeah. She started questioning our friendship. Said she didn't believe we were just friends."

Kenna nodded. "But she does now?"

"We'll see."

For a moment Kenna couldn't do anything but stare at her milk. Did that mean Reese was giving Alyson another chance? Was she going to reclaim the spot she'd once held with Reese? He *had* hung in with Alyson longer than any of his past girlfriends. A part of Kenna knew she should be glad he was on the verge of possibly getting back together with Alyson, but…

"I need to meet with Dex later today at the office. Do you want to come with me?" he said, interrupting her thoughts.

A few years ago Reese had accepted a position with his cousin Dex's company, Madaris Explorations, and a couple of months ago he had been promoted to foreman. He had been ecstatic, elated and honored. He also knew he had big shoes to fill—those of Trevor Grant, the previous foreman. Trevor and two of his Marine buddies had decided to open a tactical operations firm.

In college, Reese had followed in Dex Madaris's footsteps and had gotten a degree in geology. And like Dex, he began working with Remington Oil right out of college. He'd traveled extensively when he'd worked for Remington, and had gotten the chance to work alongside some of the world's most renowned scientists and researchers.

Kenna glanced up and couldn't help but stare at how his mouth had widened to take a bite of his sandwich. She could just imagine that mouth touching her body in a number of places. She took a sip of her milk, not liking the way her thoughts were going. But how could she make them stop moving in that direction?

"Kenna?"

She glanced up at Reese. "Yes?"

"Do you want to go with me to the office?"

She shrugged. "Sure. I can unpack later. Besides, I need to stop by and see Clayton and Syneda. Now that I'm living in Houston, I want them to handle all my legal affairs, especially the foundation I've established in my grandmother's honor."

"Okay. I have a couple more things to do around here and then I'll be leaving around three," he said.

"I'll be ready."

He leaned back in his chair and looked at her with his deep, piercing brown eyes. "Something is bothering you, Kenna, I can feel it. And I want to know what it is."

Kenna swallowed hard. There was no way she was going to come clean and tell him what was really on her mind. It was her problem and not his. And truthfully, it shouldn't have been her problem either. He wasn't a fantasy she should be entertaining. She decided to feign nonchalance. "Nothing is wrong with me, Reese, other than I'm anxious about my job. You know how I am about starting something new."

She saw his body relax a little. "But that was one hell of an offer the HPD made," he said.

"I know," she said with a heavy sigh. "But still, change isn't easy for me, and other than you and your family I don't know anyone here."

He nodded slowly. "That's why Alyson thinks the party is a good idea. Are you sure you want one?"

She shrugged. To be perfectly honest, she didn't, but she wouldn't tell him that. He worried about her enough as it was and she didn't want to come off as ungrateful. "I don't want to put anyone out by having them throw a party for me. But if that's a way to meet people, then yes, I'm fine with it. It might be fun."

"First of all, you aren't putting anyone out. I should have thought of doing it myself, but I didn't. So maybe Alyson has the right idea after all."

She took a sip of her milk. If for one minute he thought Alyson wanted to throw this party for anything other than her own selfish reasons then he needed to think again. And now that she knew why Alyson and Reese had split, Kenna figured the woman had a good reason for wanting her to meet other people.

Fortunately for Alyson, her little plan just might work. In order for Kenna to rid herself of all these crazy, far-out fantasies she'd been having about Reese, she needed to meet someone, and the sooner the better.

She glanced up at him. "Yes, maybe she does have the right idea."

Reese bit into his cookie. It shouldn't have come as a surprise that Kenna was having second thoughts about moving to Houston, even though, like he'd said, the offer had been a good one.

He of all people knew how Kenna felt about change. When she'd told him about the offer, he had all but talked her into taking the job, mainly for his own purely selfish reasons. She was his best friend and he wanted to have her close by. Why? So he could look after her, of course. Without him around, she would work fifteen-hour days and not take care of herself. Being only a few miles away and in the same city was a lot better than being a hundred-fifty-plus miles away in another city. He'd never regretted the times he'd made the drive or took a flight to Austin to see her. But still…

"Want some more milk?"

He glanced over at her. "Yes. Thanks."

He watched as she lifted the pitcher and poured the milk into his glass. "So what about that guy you were seeing, Curtis Purcell?" he asked. "The two of you didn't want to do the long-distance romance thing?"

He wondered why he was asking her about it when he hadn't asked about him for months. She hadn't brought up Purcell either, which had been just fine with Reese, since he didn't care for him. Come to think of it, he'd stopped liking him the night when he had shown up at Kenna's house to surprise her, only to discover she was out on a date with Purcell. Reese had let himself in, made himself at home and had been there when Purcell had brought her home.

The man had kissed Kenna good-night when she got out of the car, but hadn't bothered walking her to the door. How tacky was that? As far as Reese was concerned, a gentleman not walking a woman to the door after a date was downright disrespectful.

She glanced over at him. "No. Why do you ask?"

"Just wondering." It was on the tip of his tongue to ask why, but he decided he would ask another time. He finally realized that for the first time in eleven years, neither of them was involved with anyone else.

He glanced at his watch as he stood. "I've got a few things I need to take care of before we leave for town."

"All right. I see you've got a new guy working for you. I looked out the window and saw him earlier."

"Yes, his name is Clark Lovell and he started today," Reese said. "Already I can tell he's one that keeps to himself. He doesn't have much to say, but he can handle a horse and can rope a cow and that's what Joe needs."

He paused a moment. "And just so you know, Joe is going to ask you about fixing Sunday dinner."

She smiled. "I don't have a problem with that."

He chuckled. "I figured you wouldn't. You're such a soft touch when it comes to the ranch hands. I'll be back to pick you up at three."

"Okay."

He headed for the door and then turned back after grabbing his Stetson off the rack. "I know you're still wondering if you did the right thing moving to Houston, Kenna. If you ask me, I think it was the right decision."

He walked toward the door, hoping that on that particular subject she believed him.

Chapter 4

"I'm ready, Reese."

Reese turned around, and Kenna's knees nearly buckled from the force of his gaze. Why was he looking at her like that, she wondered, as his eyes roamed over her from head to toe. "Is anything wrong, Reese?"

His gaze returned to her face. "No, nothing's wrong. Is that a new dress?"

"No."

He inclined his head. "I've never seen it before."

Kenna chuckled as she reached for her purse off the table. "Probably not. You don't go shopping with me, so you've never seen my entire wardrobe. Is something wrong with it?"

"No. It looks nice on you."

Her heart thumped in her chest at his compliment. "Thanks."

Her heart kept right on thumping as she followed Reese to his SUV parked out front. She breathed deeply, trying to get a grip. It wasn't her that had attracted Reese's attention, but the dress itself. Usually she wore slacks, and that was probably the reason he'd been taken aback by the dress.

He opened the door and she eased inside. When he hesitated, she glanced up at him. "Okay, Reese, what's wrong now?"

"Nothing."

Kenna frowned slightly when he closed the door and then walked around the front of the SUV to get inside. He backed up and pulled out of the driveway without saying a word.

"I'll introduce you to the new guy when we get back," he said, interrupting her thoughts.

She glanced over at him. He had changed his shirt and was wearing another pair of jeans. As always, he looked good. "Okay," she said. "I went out to the bunkhouse earlier and got a chance to talk to Joe a little, but he wasn't there."

"Who?"

"Your new guy."

"Oh. I guess he was out tending the herd or something."

Usually when Reese wasn't attentive it meant his thoughts were elsewhere. She decided to give him time to sort out whatever was bothering him. There was probably something going on at the ranch that needed his undivided attention.

While he was quiet, she would use the time to think about the phone call she'd gotten from Leon, one of the police officers she'd worked with in Austin. According to him, Curtis Purcell had shown up at the station looking for her. He claimed he had dropped by her house and found it empty and wanted to know if she'd left a forwarding address. She had, but Leon wouldn't give it to him, not until he checked with her first. She instructed Leon not to give Curtis her new address or her new cell phone number if he returned. How long had it been? Three months? He hadn't tried contacting her in all that time. Why did he suddenly want to see her now?

"You okay? You keep sighing over there."

Kenna glanced over at Reese. "Yes, I'm fine. But a friend of mine, a police officer back in Austin, called to let me know someone was looking for me today. He went by my place and saw that I'd moved out."

Reese's brow lifted as he glanced over at her. "Who?"

"Curtis."

Reese trained his eyes on the road ahead, but not before Kenna saw his expression tighten. "What did he want?"

"Not sure" was her response.

"Let me guess. He wants to be the comeback kid."

Just like Alyson. She bit down on her lower lip. "I'm not sure what he wants, Reese, and I don't plan to find out. I told Leon not to tell him anything. Besides, if he really wants to find me you'll be the next person on his list. He knows how close we are and that you'll know where I am."

"I would just love for him to contact me about you."

Kenna frowned slightly, tilted her head and looked over at him. "What did Curtis ever do to you?"

"Nothing. But he treated you like crap."

"He did not! He didn't walk me to the door that one time and you were ready to hang him up by his toes for it."

"Damn right. And you never said why the two of you called it quits," he continued, bringing the SUV to a stop at a traffic light.

"You never asked," she said, giving him the same response he'd given her about Alyson earlier that day.

He glanced over at her. "Okay, now I'm asking."

She looked straight ahead out the windshield for a few moments while nibbling on her bottom lip. She turned back toward Reese. "He pulled a Terrence Fairchild on me." She hated bringing up the guy who'd been her boyfriend in college. The one she'd assumed she would marry one day.

A deep frown settled on Reese's face. She knew he was

remembering the incident. He had been there for her. "You caught Curtis in bed with another woman."

She shrugged. "Not exactly."

His frown deepened. "Then what exactly?"

She paused a second. "I caught him in bed with another man."

Reese's hands gripped the steering wheel so tight he felt it might crumble in his hands. When he suddenly hit the brakes to avoid hitting the car in front of them, he pulled off to the side of the road and killed the ignition. At that moment he wished he could kill someone else instead—namely Curtis Purcell.

Furious, he unbuckled his seat belt and twisted around in his seat to face Kenna. "Why in the hell didn't you tell me? And don't you dare hand me that crap about me not asking."

He figured his tone along with the anger etched in his face painted a real good picture of just how mad he was, and that now was not the time to get cutesy on him. He was definitely not in the mood.

She nervously licked her lips and his gaze was automatically drawn to her mouth. Why was his gut clenching and why did he suddenly feel this hard lump in his throat?

"I didn't want to bother you about it. It was around the time you got your promotion to foreman and I didn't want to say anything that would rain on your parade, Reese," she said in a soft voice that pleaded for understanding.

His anger subsided somewhat. "So you went through all that alone?"

She shrugged. "Once the shock wore off, I could have kicked myself for not picking up on it earlier. I ignored all the signs that he was on the down-low. He was a former pro football player, for Christ's sake. He acted really macho and he had dated lots of women before. I was mad with myself as much as with him for falling for his line. In the end, I asked myself the same question I'd asked myself a number of times before. *Why me?*"

Reese took in a deep breath. *Yes, why her?* He could only shake his head as he recalled the men who, over the years, hadn't appreciated what an incredible woman she was. He would hate to think that more than a few of them had a screw loose, but seeing was believing. He couldn't understand why any man didn't appreciate Kenna. She was a good woman—the best. And he wasn't just saying that because she was his best friend. He knew it was true.

"So you want to give me any dating advice?" she asked.

He snorted. "Dating advice? Hell, I'm not totally together either, when you consider the number of girlfriends I've had over the years myself. But then you wear your heart on your sleeve."

She frowned. "I wasn't in love with Curtis, nor was I in love with Lamont. I believed I was in love with Terrence during the two years we dated. But the older I got, the more I realized I wasn't really in love with him. I liked the idea of being in love, if that makes any sense."

No, it didn't really, he thought. But he'd talked to enough women in his family to know that they sometimes looked at things differently than men. "What about Lamont? The two of you dated for more than a year. I didn't ask before, but I'm asking now. Why did the two of you split?"

She did that lip thing again with her tongue and the same as before, seeing her lick her lips did something to him. *Crap! What was wrong with him?* Granted he hadn't been with a woman since his breakup with Alyson five months ago, but still, this was Kenna for crying out loud. He'd seen that nervous habit plenty of times over the years, so why was he suddenly lusting over the one woman he shouldn't have the hots for?

"He was jealous of you. Like Alyson, he didn't believe the 'we're just friends' line either. The first time he brought it up

I gave him the benefit of the doubt, since I'd be the first to admit our relationship is a bit unorthodox. But I warned him that if he accused me again that things were over between us. Unfortunately, he didn't take me at my word."

Reese slowly shook his head as he buckled his seat belt again and started the car. He really didn't know what to say. When he glanced over at Kenna, he immediately knew what she was thinking. He cut off the ignition again.

"Look, Kenna, don't even think it. We agreed years ago that if we met someone and it got serious, if that person couldn't deal with our friendship it would be their loss and not ours. Are you having second thoughts about that?"

"No, but a part of me can't help but sympathize with Alyson. The two of you would still be together if she hadn't gotten it into her head that I was a threat."

"Maybe and maybe not. It's a bad idea for any woman to get it into her head that she can decide who my friends are. And as far as Lamont thinking we had something going on, then he was a fool. I never liked him anyway."

"Have I ever dated a guy you did like?"

"No."

He waited to see if she would ask him why and then exhaled slowly when she didn't. Had she asked, he wouldn't have been able to give her a reason. He just hadn't liked them. "So what do you think Purcell wants with you?"

"Who knows? He might want to try to convince me that finding him in bed with another man wasn't all bad and that we can work things out and get back together."

Reese snorted. Purcell was really stupid if he actually thought that. He'd heard how some women would accept their man even after finding out they were on the down-low. But he knew for sure that Kenna wasn't one of them.

"After your meeting with Clayton and Syneda, and mine with

Dex, we can stay in town and grab dinner. And if you're up to it, we can also do a movie. How does that sound?"

"Sounds great," she said, smiling.

He smiled back at her. "Good."

Chapter 5

"Mr. Madaris is in court now, but Mrs. Syneda Madaris will see you in a minute," the receptionist said.

"Thanks." Kenna sat down in the plush chair and glanced around the office. She had been inside the Madaris Building several times, but this was the first time she had visited the law offices of Madaris, Madaris and Madaris. Since Blade had gotten married, his wife, Samari Di Meglio Madaris, had joined Clayton and Syneda at their law firm. Kenna could just imagine Clayton, the only man, having to deal with his beautiful, opinionated wife, who was a lot to handle, plus his cousin's gorgeous, exotic-looking wife, Samari, whose hot Italian temper could flare at a moment's notice. Things could get pretty damn interesting around here.

While she waited, Kenna recalled the conversation she and Reese had shared during the ride over. After asking if she was interested in dinner and a movie, things had got pretty quiet between them. They talked about attending Morehouse's homecoming in a few months, and about how Luke's rodeo school, which was scheduled to open in two weeks, was doing. Reese hadn't invited her to go with him, and she couldn't help wondering if he intended to invite Alyson.

Kenna had received an invitation to Luke's rodeo opening before leaving Austin, so if Reese made plans to take a date then she would do the same. There was no way she would be a third wheel with him and Alyson. Maybe it wasn't such a bad idea to make sure that happened. Having a date was one way to ensure that Reese wouldn't feel obligated to include her in his plans.

"Mrs. Madaris will see you now."

Kenna smiled at the receptionist. "Thanks."

Kenna thought the same thing now that she had the first time she laid eyes on Syneda Madaris. The woman was simply gorgeous. And from what Kenna had heard, in the courtroom she was equally impressive.

Long, golden-bronze hair flowed down her shoulders, and her sea-green eyes always seemed to sparkle with excitement. Her pregnancy was more obvious now than it had been a month ago, and she had a radiant glow about her. Reese had mentioned that Syneda and Clayton had announced that they were having a boy. Everyone was happy, especially the couple's eight-year-old daughter, Remington, who had been begging for a baby brother or sister, preferably a brother.

"Kenna, it's so good seeing you," Syneda said as she hugged her.

"Thanks. Same here."

That was one of the things she enjoyed most about Reese's family. They were good people, down to earth and as friendly as could be. "Reese had a meeting with Dex, so I thought I'd tag along and use the time to meet with you and Clayton. I understand he's in court."

"Yes, his court docket was changed, but I'll be glad to help you with anything."

"It's about the foundation I established a few years ago in my grandmother's memory. I would like your firm to take over handling it for me."

Syneda smiled. "It will be our pleasure. We handle a number of foundations and trusts already, including the one Trask has set up and the one Uncle Jake and Diamond established as well."

"Wonderful."

"It will only take a few minutes to complete the paperwork and then a couple of weeks to get everything notarized. We'll call you back to sign the necessary documents at that time."

"That sounds like a plan," Kenna said excitedly.

Less than ten minutes later, Kenna had completed the paperwork and returned the forms to Syneda. "Thanks, Kenna," Syneda said, sliding the documents into a folder. "So when did you arrive in Houston?"

"This morning. I sold almost everything I had in Austin, since I want to start fresh and buy new furniture. The things I didn't want to part with I loaded in a U-Haul truck and drove here." She chuckled. "I think Reese was a nervous wreck until I arrived at his place. He was afraid I'd fall asleep at the wheel and wind up in a ditch or something."

Syneda smiled. "I can imagine. He's very protective where you're concerned."

She nodded. "Yes, and I'm very protective where he's concerned as well. I think he's a wonderful person and a special friend."

"Yes, and you're in love with him."

Kenna went utterly still. *Was Syneda a mind reader?* "What did you say?"

A knowing smile curved Syneda's lips. "I said you're in love with Reese."

Kenna drew in a sharp breath, opened her mouth to deny it

and then stopped. From the look Syneda gave her, she wasn't buying anything Kenna had to say. The sea-green eyes staring at her were sharp, shrewd, confident, and for a moment Kenna felt like a deer caught in the headlights. Syneda was right, of course, and the only thing Kenna could do was come clean.

"Yes, I love him. But how did you know?"

Syneda chuckled. "I can tell whenever you look at him. I always suspected as much, but last month when you were on the dance floor, you only had eyes for him."

Kenna shook her head. "That's pathetic."

Syneda gave her a soft smile. "No, it's not pathetic. There's nothing wrong with a woman loving a man."

"But it's pathetic when he doesn't love you back. Reese only sees me as his best friend and nothing more. I'm so afraid he's going to discover the truth one day and that will ruin everything."

Syneda shook her head. "I don't think it will be that way at all. Making the move from friends to lovers was pretty easy for me and Clayton."

"Was it?"

Syneda's smile widened. "Yes, and it will be just as easy for you and Reese once he realizes he loves you as well."

"Trust me, he doesn't love me that way. In fact, he and Alyson are trying to work things out, and maybe that's a good thing."

Syneda rolled her eyes. "Alyson Richards?"

"Yes."

The mere mention of the woman's name grated on Syneda's nerves. All it took was for her to remember when she and Clayton had run into Reese and Alyson at a political fundraiser last year. Alyson, who evidently considered herself a fashionista, had pulled Syneda aside to tell her that her shoes weren't the same shade of purple as her dress. Syneda quickly let Alyson know that she was well aware of that fact, and hadn't meant for them to be exactly the same color.

"I wouldn't be so sure if I were you," Syneda said. "Alyson is too possessive, and Reese knows it." Syneda lifted a brow. "And why do you think working things out between them is a good thing if you're in love with him?"

"Because I can control my emotions a whole lot better if he's seeing someone and if I am, too. This is the first time Reese and I aren't involved with anyone else, and I figure that's the reason for my attraction. There's no one else to take my mind off him."

"Oh, I see."

"So I figure it's time for me to find someone and start seriously dating again. It won't be so bad if Reese decides to get back together with Alyson. I've gotten used to her being in the picture and I know how to deal with her. Heaven forbid if he gets serious about some other woman who can't accept the kind of friendship we have."

Syneda didn't say anything as she studied Kenna. Clearly, Kenna didn't know her own beauty or power. Granted, Reese was slow. But Syneda was certain he would eventually realize he loved Kenna. With some men you had to light a fire under them. That's what had had to happen to Luke to get him to see what he'd be losing if he didn't come to his senses.

"So you actually believe Alyson is the best person for Reese?" Syneda asked Kenna skeptically.

Kenna shrugged. "I don't know about her being the best person for him, but I think she understands our friendship and knows it's non-negotiable. She'll be fine. She's even agreed to throw me a party this weekend at her place so I can meet new people. I'm hoping there will be at least one guy there I like."

Syneda forced a smile, just imagining the party Alyson had planned for Kenna. Then her smile widened. She had a feeling those plans were about to backfire and Alyson would finally see just how protective Reese was when it came to his *best friend*. Mama Laverne had it all figured out, and Syneda had a feeling the family matriarch was right once again.

"Well, if you think meeting new guys and moving on without trying to win Reese over is for the best, then do what you have to do," Syneda said nonchalantly. She would give anything to be a fly on the wall at the party this weekend. Kenna might have thought she was being the sacrificial lamb by graciously stepping aside and letting Alyson have Reese, but she had a feeling that in the end Reese wasn't going to let that happen.

"Now if I can just find someone to take me to Luke's rodeo school opening in a couple of weeks without appearing desperate," Kenna said, interrupting Syneda's thoughts.

"You aren't going with Reese?" Syneda asked, somewhat surprised, especially since Reese usually brought her to all their family functions.

She shrugged. "I'm hoping he takes Alyson. And if he does, then I don't want him to feel responsible for me."

"So you figure you should have your own date," Syneda said.

"Yes. Usually when I date a new guy, I tend to take things slow. But I'm not sure I'll have that luxury this time."

Syneda studied Kenna and saw that she was dead serious. "Well, even if you don't have a date, I'm sure there will be plenty of single men there. Reese won't have to worry about you, which means he'll be able to give Alyson his full attention." *I'd like to see that happen.*

After Kenna left her office, Syneda leaned back in her chair, smiling. She was going to miss the show at Alyson's place Saturday night, but there was no way she was going to miss the one at Luke's opening. In fact, she intended to have a front-row seat.

"Hey, aren't you Reese Madaris?"

Reese turned to face a woman who'd just passed him in the hallway leading to his office at the Madaris Explorations Company. "Yes, I'm Reese Madaris."

The woman flashed what Reese figured was her sexiest smile as she closed the distance between them and extended her hand.

"Hi, Reese. I'm Camille Strickland."

He shook her hand and returned the smile. "Hi, Camille."

"I dated your cousin Blade a while back. I hear he got married."

"Yes, he got married a little over a month ago."

"Oh. What a shame. I understand you're available." She reached out and traced a manicured finger along his arm.

"Available for what?" he asked, annoyed by her boldness.

"Whatever comes to mind," she said seductively. She seemed to be pouting. "You're not like Blade. He liked flirting," she said in a sultry voice.

"Sorry to disappoint you."

"Don't apologize. Here's my card," she said, thrusting it into his hand. "Give me a call." She batted her eyelashes several times and then gave him a flirty wink before turning to walk down the hallway, swaying her hips in a body-hugging pencil skirt and killer high heels that looked like they could double as lethal weapons.

Okay, he would admit that she looked good—but he wasn't Blade. And when it came to women, his and Blade's tastes were completely different. It would take more than a tight skirt and stilettos to make him tongue-tied. Even five months without sex hadn't made him *that* hard up.

He continued walking, shaking his head as he stepped into an elevator at the same time another woman did. She glanced over at him and gave him a come-hither smile. "Excuse me for asking, but aren't you Reese Madaris?"

Reese stepped off the elevator thinking that some women had no shame. The woman had tried coming on to him, and way too strong. When the elevator stopped on the next floor to let other passengers on, he retreated all the way to the back, as far away from her as he could get. She had repeatedly licked her lips as if to give him a blatant come-on, letting him know just what she could do with her mouth. The combination of her words and actions had been a total turn-off.

When he exited the elevator, he glanced over his shoulder and saw that the woman was still following him. When he rounded the corner, so did she. *Probably not a coincidence.* Reese continued walking and heard her make some sort of growling sound, but he refused to turn around. Damn, had he attracted a stalker? His grandmother had warned him what would happen now that Blade was off the market. And it seemed the old gal knew what she was talking about.

He smiled when he saw Kenna sitting in the lobby waiting for him. When she saw him she smiled, eased out of the chair and began walking toward him with a graceful stride that he couldn't help but admire. He really liked the dress she was wearing, which showed off her curvy hips, her ample cleavage and the most gorgeous legs any woman could possibly possess. She was the kind of woman any man would want to have as his own. She didn't have to flaunt her beauty and sexuality. It came naturally. He was convinced that one day she would make some deserving man very happy.

An idea quickly popped into his head. When he reached Kenna he pulled her into his arms and kissed her on the forehead. "Thanks for waiting, sweetheart."

"No problem," she said, giving him a what-the-heck-is-going-on look with her eyes.

He glanced over his shoulder to see the woman leaving the building, and it was only then that he released a deep sigh.

"Okay, what was that about?" Kenna asked him, following his gaze.

He chuckled as he tightened her hand in his. "Mama Laverne warned me that with Blade out of the picture, chances are single women would turn their sights on me. I thought she was joking, but apparently I was wrong."

"Wow, you're in demand, huh?" she asked, grinning as he led her out of the building.

"I don't see anything funny about it. In fact, on our way to dinner I need you to give me some dating advice."

She lifted a brow. "Dating advice about what?"

"How to handle unwanted advances…"

Chapter 6

Kenna shifted in her car seat as she thought about Reese's request for dating advice. She couldn't help smiling. *Poor baby.*

"I hope you're hungry, because I am."

She glanced over at him and snickered. "I guess a man can work up an appetite eluding women on the prowl."

"Hey, watch it. You know how I am about stuff like that."

Yes, she did know. Reese wasn't like most men who were as gorgeous as he was. He didn't have a conceited bone in his body. He probably thought he was just a regular-looking guy, even though his looks alone could make a woman's panties wet.

She remembered just what she'd thought the first time she met him at his dorm room to go over his physics studies. She had taken one look at him and for a moment all thoughts of Terrence had been erased.

The first thing she'd noticed about him, besides the beautiful color of his skin, the darkness of his eyes, his chiseled jawline and kissable mouth, was that he had the manners of a Southern gentleman—one who knew how to treat a woman like a lady.

It didn't take long to discover that he was a loner. Although he had plenty of friends on campus, he pretty much stayed to himself most of the time, rarely allowing others into his circle. He was not a party animal. In fact, the more time they spent together studying, the more she got to know the real Reese Madaris, the one few understood or ever got close to.

"You never did answer my question," he said, glancing over at her when the SUV came to a stop at a traffic light.

"Your dating question?"

He shrugged. "If you want to call it that. I'm not interested in any of those women. Most of them were probably involved with Blade. Do they honestly think they can just move from one Madaris to the next?"

Kenna couldn't help but laugh. "Seriously, Reese, a woman hard up for a man will move from one *brother* to the next. They don't care. Like your great-grandmother said, with your cousin Blade out of circulation, that means you're next."

"Then I guess that means you and I need to keep on pretending."

She rolled her eyes. "Or you and Alyson need to hook up again."

He shook his head. "I doubt that will happen."

She wondered why he felt that way, but decided not to ask. She figured the only way to get rid of her attraction to him was to make sure he was seeing someone and she was seeing someone, too. "We'll see."

When he didn't respond she decided to flip through the pages of a magazine she'd found in his SUV—a tractor magazine. "You're buying another one of these?"

He glanced over at her. "I'm thinking about it. And you never answered my question."

She hadn't answered it because she didn't want to think about how it would feel being rejected by a man like Reese. "My advice to you would be to let them know you're not interested up front. The worse thing a man can do is to lead a woman on."

He nodded. "That sounds fair. But what if they don't get the hint?"

She glanced up, met his gaze and grinned. "Trust me. You have a look that lets a woman know when you don't have the time or the inclination. A woman would be crazy to try and take you on. But then...there are a lot of bold, brazen women out there, so beware."

"But if push comes to shove, you'll be my backup plan right?"

She didn't want to think what being his backup plan might entail. Inside the Madaris Building when he had leaned over and kissed her on the forehead, it had taken everything she could muster not to get weak in the knees. She could see women—plenty of them—coming on to him. Yet he hadn't been interested.

"You haven't answered me yet."

She glanced over at him and gave him a rueful smile. He was asking a lot of questions and it seemed she was evading a lot of answers. "Okay, if I must, then yes. I'll be your backup plan. I guess that's the price of being your best friend, right?"

He chuckled. "Right."

After midnight they returned to his house. Reese couldn't remember when he had enjoyed an evening more. They had eaten at Sisters, a restaurant owned by Netherlander Sinclair, a family friend.

The food had been delicious, the entertainment enjoyable. The only drawback was when he had excused himself to go to the men's room. He was approached by two women who tried coming on to him. He was sure they had seen him sharing a table with Kenna but still were bold enough, thoughtless enough and disrespectful enough to approach him anyway. Taking Kenna's advice, he thanked them but told them he wasn't interested. His bluntness didn't seem to dissuade them. He couldn't understand how Blade had dealt with that kind of aggressiveness. But for Blade it wasn't a big deal. His cousin had enjoyed being Houston's most sought-after bachelor.

After dinner, Reese and Kenna took in a movie. It was Denzel's latest and was directed by former actor Sterling Maxwell, a family friend who made a cameo appearance in the movie. By the time the movie ended, it was still relatively early, so they figured they might as well see another movie. Since Kenna hadn't complained about watching his guy flick, Reese agreed to see a romantic comedy with her. He hated to admit it, but he actually enjoyed it.

"I guess I'll spend tomorrow unpacking," Kenna said once they returned to Reese's place.

He glanced over at her. "You can sleep late if you want to. Do whatever you want at your leisure. In two weeks you'll be working again."

He followed her to the kitchen and sat down at the table. She started brewing a pot of coffee and then went to the cookie jar. She was comfortable in his home, just as he was in hers whenever he'd visited her in Austin. Just as he would be once she moved into her place in Houston after it was completed.

For a brief moment he sat watching her. He couldn't help but wonder how things would be if they were both married to someone else. More than once someone in his family had taken him aside and told him that it was unrealistic for him to assume any woman would understand and accept the relationship he shared with Kenna. He had been quick to tell them he disagreed. Any woman he married would have to accept Kenna as his best friend. He knew Kenna had the same expectation of the men she dated, so he didn't see a problem.

Alyson had been fine with his friendship with Kenna after

he'd explained how things were. At least he thought she had been fine with it. But after eight months, she began questioning why Kenna had a standing invitation to spend the night at his place when she didn't. Why couldn't Kenna just get a hotel whenever she came to town? At first he'd ignored her, and thought sooner or later she would wise up and stop asking questions. But she hadn't, and the more she whined about his relationship with Kenna, the more he began putting distance between them. Finally, he'd gotten fed up and ended things with Alyson.

Reese didn't know what Alyson had planned for the weekend, but he figured she thought it would be a way to make up for all the mean and hateful things she'd said about Kenna. Unfortunately, he wasn't in a forgiving mood.

"How many cookies? One or two?"

He grinned. "Why do you bother asking? You know I can't eat just one."

She put two cookies on a plate and placed a freshly brewed cup of coffee on the table in front of him. "It's late."

His eyes connected with hers. "Am I supposed to have nightmares or something if I eat a chocolate chip cookie past midnight?"

"Maybe," she said, taking the chair across from him. "You never know." She took a sip of her coffee and then asked, "What time do you plan on getting up in the morning?"

He shrugged. "I have a meeting at a job site at nine, so I'll probably leave here around eight to get there. Why?"

"I need to return the moving van and pick up a rental car."

"It's already been taken care of."

"What do you mean it's been taken care of?"

"While we were in town, Joe took the truck to the rental agency and picked up a car for you. You didn't see the moving van when we pulled up, did you?"

"No, I just assumed it was parked in the back or something."

"No, your rental car is parked out back."

"Thanks. That saves me a lot of time tomorrow."

He looked over at her. "You don't have to thank me. You should know by now I got your back."

She smiled and picked up a cookie. "Yes, I know."

That was another thing that he appreciated about his friendship with Kenna. She wasn't hard to please, and over the years she had been nothing but supportive. After he graduated from college, she had supported his decision to go work for Remington Oil for a few years instead of working for Dex right out of college. She'd agreed with his reasoning that since Remington Oil was a bigger company, he could acquire a lot of skill and knowledge that would be valuable when he did make the move to Madaris Explorations. While working at Remington, he'd gotten the chance to travel to a lot of exotic places and meet a lot of interesting people. When he finally did decide to work with Dex's outfit, his résumé had been impressive and he had a lot more to offer.

He and Kenna sat at his kitchen table talking while they drank coffee and ate cookies. When he finally looked over at the clock, it was almost two in the morning.

"It's late. You need to go on to bed, Reese. You have to get up early in the morning. Thanks to you, I don't," she said.

She was right. Even though he usually didn't leave the ranch until eight, he made it a point to meet with Joe every morning around six. He would usually be in bed by now but hadn't been aware of the time, since he had enjoyed sitting and talking to her.

"You're right. I need to get to bed. You know your way around this place, and if there's anything you need, just ask Joe."

"I will."

With great effort he stood up from his chair. He wasn't ready to end their conversation. "You're going to stay up a while longer?"

"Um, not too much longer. I'm not that sleepy, since I took a long nap earlier. I might check out a movie downstairs."

Like her, he enjoyed movies. When he had the house built, Kenna had convinced him to include a home theater in the basement. The room had been built to her specifications and was perfect for movie and sports enthusiasts. Whenever she would come for the weekend, Kenna ended up spending more time there than any other room in the house.

"Okay. Then I'll see you when I get home tomorrow."

"All right. Don't work too hard."

He chuckled as he turned to leave the kitchen. "I won't."

Suddenly it hit him as he walked toward the stairway. He was feeling something he couldn't explain, some emotion he was trying hard to make sense of. What the hell was wrong with him? Why did he feel the need to give her a kiss good night? They hugged all the time. Once in a while, he would greet her with a peck on the cheek or the forehead when they hadn't seen each other for a long while. But usually he wouldn't just kiss her for no reason.

The only reason he'd kissed her earlier that day was to give his stalker the impression that he was already taken. But for some reason he couldn't explain, he felt his night wouldn't be complete unless he tasted the softness of her skin on his lips, pulled her into his arms and held her tight, and smelled her tantalizing fragrance in his nostrils.

A hard knot suddenly settled in his throat. *Crap!* What on earth could he be thinking? Kenna was his best friend, for crying out loud. His protective side, the one that usually emerged where she was concerned, was somewhere hiding right now. Shaking his head, he quickly walked up the stairs, thinking that once he got to his room he needed to smack his head against the wall a few times.

There had to be a reason his brain was malfunctioning, like it had short-circuited somewhere along the way. Why on earth would he see Kenna through the eyes of a man filled with lust? Granted, it wasn't the first time he had thought about it. Like last month at Blade's wedding reception, when he'd been looking at her, listening to his great-grandmother's comments.

He would get a good night's sleep and wake up in the morning thinking like the Reese Madaris he knew—the one who would not, under any circumstances, get hot and bothered about his best friend.

He walked into his bedroom and closed the door behind him. He would get a good night's sleep, and he was convinced come morning he would be thinking straight once again.

Kenna inhaled a slow, deep breath as she watched the couple on the wall-to-wall movie screen and wondered why no man had ever kissed her like that—warm and sloppy wet. Tongues do more than just mingle. They stake claims over and over again in a passionate way. It was the kind of kiss that could steal the breath right out of your lungs, make your head spin a thousand times and make your heart pound hard in your chest. She shook her head and thought it could only happen that way in the movies.

She glanced around the huge, dark room at three in the morning and realized this was just the place she needed to be. She had showered, slipped into an oversize T-shirt and leaned back in one of several comfortable, soft-leather recliners in Reese's home theater that cushioned your backside like nobody's business. The huge movie posters on the wall, the popcorn-making machine and the recessed lighting helped create an authentic movie-theater atmosphere.

Kenna found the perfect movie to watch, a romantic thriller. One minute she was aroused by the intimate scenes, and the next she was sitting on the edge of her seat as the couple fought off the bad guys.

The house was quiet since Reese had gone to bed. Although she had enjoyed going out to the movies with him earlier that night, she hadn't been able to concentrate, since she'd spent most of the time thinking about him. His closeness had an unsettling effect, and she became more convinced that the plan she'd shared with Syneda was the right one. If Reese and Alyson were together, then she wouldn't be so focused on every move he made. Now that she would be living in Houston, the only way she could continue to look at him as her friend and not the most handsome man she knew was to become involved with someone, and to make sure he became involved with someone, too.

There was no doubt in her mind that Alyson would invite plenty of eligible guys to the party, since the sole purpose was to help her meet people. Indeed, Alyson's definition of *meeting people* was for Kenna to meet other guys so that she wouldn't be around Reese so much.

Chapter 7

"So how are things going with you and your house guest?"

Reese switched his mobile phone from one ear to the other as he opened the door to get into his truck. He couldn't help but shake his head. His cousin Blade was convinced that there was more to his relationship with Kenna than just friendship.

"Before I answer your question, how about answering mine? What the hell did you do to the women in this town? I can't believe how bold they are. Some can't seem to take no for an answer," Reese said, recalling the woman who had shown up at the worksite that morning. She was the same woman he'd seen in the elevator yesterday. She was becoming a nuisance, and he'd come straight out and told her so. But his frankness hadn't seemed to deter her, and he had the feeling he hadn't seen the last of her. He had gotten hit on by women before, but never in such numbers.

"Probably because I never said no to them," Blade replied

easily. "They understood me and I understood them. Usually all they wanted was a good time."

Reese frowned. "Then they need to look elsewhere, because I'm not interested."

"I don't see why not. You're not seriously involved with anyone, unless you're thinking of hooking up with Alyson again."

Reese shifted in his seat. Kenna had mentioned that same subject a couple of times. And from the way it sounded, she didn't have a problem with it. She was evidently willing to overlook the fact that the reason he'd split with Alyson in the first place was because of her negativity toward Kenna.

"And if I am?" he decided to ask.

"Then you need to make certain she's no longer jealous of Kenna. Don't forget I was there that day when she dropped by your place and I overheard her accusations."

Reese snorted. Blade hadn't exactly overheard anything. He had been deliberately eavesdropping and they both knew it. "I can handle Alyson."

"I hope you can. A woman with a jealous streak can cause more harm than good. Now answer *my* question. How is Kenna?"

"Kenna is fine."

A few moments later, after disconnecting his call with Blade, Reese sat quietly without moving in the SUV. If anyone knew how women behaved, it would be Blade. He'd certainly had his share of them. At times his cousin's condo had seemed to have a revolving door.

His thoughts then shifted to Kenna. She had been asleep when he'd left that morning, but he knew that she'd stayed up late watching a movie. He hadn't been able to sleep and had heard her tiptoe to her room around four in the morning.

He had lain in bed, pissed at himself because he still hadn't come up with a reason why he was suddenly beginning to see

Kenna in a different way. Hopefully, yesterday was a fluke and things would be back to normal today. The last thing he needed was for Kenna to pick up on anything and have a reason to feel uncomfortable around him.

He nearly jumped when someone tapped on his window. He rolled down the window when he saw it was Dex. "You okay?" Dex asked him.

Reese nodded. "Yeah, I'm fine. Why do you ask?"

"Because you're just sitting there, staring into space. Aren't you going to go grab lunch?" Dex said.

"In a minute. I just finished talking to Blade."

"Oh, what's he up to? Did he say how he's adjusting to married life with a baby on the way?" Dex asked, leaning against Reese's truck.

Reese couldn't help but smile. He figured Blade was adjusting to marriage like Blade's twin brother, Slade, and his own brother Luke had. It seemed they all enjoyed being married, and according to Luke, he couldn't imagine his life without Mac. "He's adjusting just fine. I just wish all his used-to-be's hadn't turned their sights on me."

Dex chuckled. "Hey, I heard about that. Unfortunately, you'll probably be *it* until you get married."

"Married? I don't even have a steady girlfriend, Dex."

"Yes. But there are some people in the family who won't give up on the notion that Kenna is your girl."

Reese rolled his eyes. "Kenna's my best friend."

"So we've heard, for a few years now. Look, I have no reason to doubt you and I think everyone else knows she's your best friend. But I think there's some speculation about what might be in your future."

"Because Kenna decided to move to Houston?"

"Yes, that did lift a few eyebrows," Dex admitted.

"It was a good job opportunity for her."

"Yes, but another way to look at it is the two of you have become even more inseparable."

He looked at Dex through the window. "And the problem with that *is?*"

"The two of you are going to have a hard time finding someone else who's willing to put up with your friendship with each other. But hey, I support whatever rocks your boat. As far as I'm concerned it's no one's business but yours and Kenna's."

Reese let out a deep sigh. He agreed with Dex on that point. It was no one else's business but his and Kenna's.

"May I help you, ma'am?"

The words, spoken with a slight accent, made Kenna turn around. An easy smile touched her lips when she saw it was Reese's new employee. Tall, lanky and probably in his late thirties, she thought there was an intensity in the darkness of his blue eyes. "No, I'm fine. I thought I'd take Rollins out for a ride," she said of the horse Joe had saddled for her earlier. "I'm LaKenna James, but everyone calls me Kenna," she said, extending her hand to him.

"And I'm Clark Lovell. I just started working for Mr. Madaris a couple of days ago." He paused a second and then asked. "Will you need an escort when you ride out?"

"An escort?" She chuckled. "Thanks, but no thanks. I'm used to the ranch. I'll be fine."

"You come here a lot?"

"Um, enough. Reese and I are good friends." She wondered why she'd said that, then shrugged and figured that since most of the other men were aware that the two of them were friends, she might as well set the record straight with Clark from the start about the nature of her relationship with Reese.

"That's what I heard—that you and the boss are good friends. Well, I'll be seeing you. Good day, Miss Kenna."

"Good day to you, too." She watched him walk off. Reese had

said the new hire didn't have much to say to anyone, and that he mostly stayed to himself. Well, he'd certainly been talkative with her just now.

She used a stepstool to get in the saddle on Rollins's back and led him out of the stables. It was a beautiful day, and she figured a horseback ride would do her good since it was something she enjoyed doing. Reese had given her her very first lesson years ago.

When she'd awakened that morning, her brain had felt sluggish from so little sleep, but once she got moving she was fine. She had slept until almost ten before going downstairs to prepare toast and coffee for breakfast. After breakfast, she went back upstairs to unpack the rest of her things. It didn't take long, since most of her belongings had been organized and labeled.

She had taken a break from unpacking to enjoy lunch with Joe, a widower whose wife had died almost ten years ago. He'd brought her up-to-date on how his married daughters were doing and had proudly showed her recent pictures of his two grandkids.

Joe said Reese usually came home around five o'clock, so she decided to prepare dinner. She had cooked lasagna—one of Reese's favorites. Luckily, she didn't have to buy groceries, since all the ingredients she needed had been in the pantry.

As she rode away from the stable, she waved to the men she knew who were out tending the herd. Compared to Whispering Pines, Reese's uncle Jake Madaris's spread, Tall Oaks ranch and all the land it encompassed was relatively small. But as Kenna rode farther and farther away from the main house, it didn't seem so small after all. Every so often she would look up at the trees, remembering when Reese had first brought her to his ranch and how the first thing she'd noticed was the oak trees that were so tall they seemed to touch the sky. She had mentioned it to Reese, which is why he'd named his ranch Tall Oaks.

As she rode, Rollins maintained an easy, comfortable gait,

which was probably the reason Reese had picked the horse for her. One day she would convince Reese to let her ride Blue Bay, his personal stallion.

When she'd first met the family she had been amazed that all the Madarises knew how to ride, and that a few of them, like Reese's brother Luke, were expert horsemen. Luke had been a big rodeo star and still competed from time to time. But since he'd gotten married, he'd devoted most of his time to his rodeo school.

Reese had yet to mention anything about his brother Luke's rodeo school opening, so she could only assume he was taking Alyson. And when he did get around to mentioning it to her, she would play it cool. She'd let him know that she would be meeting someone there as well—a blind date or someone. He didn't have to know the entire truth. But in this case, her explanation would have to work.

She checked her watch. By the time she rode back to the stable, Reese would be home or arriving shortly. He had texted her earlier and said he had a surprise for her. She couldn't wait to see what it was. He knew how much she liked surprises.

The party was in two days, and she had called Reese's cousin Christy to see if she wanted to go shopping with her. Christy's husband, Alex, a private investigator, traveled a lot but was available for babysitting duties, so their shopping date tomorrow was all set.

Christy was an award-winning investigative reporter who had cracked an international kidnapping ring that was smuggling runaways out of the country as part of a sex-slave trade. Christy herself had gotten captured during the investigation and Alex had rescued her. It had sounded like an adventure at the time, but now she was certain neither Christy nor Alex had thought so then.

"C'mon boy, let's go home," she coaxed Rollins, tightening

her hands on the reins to make him turn around and head back. "Let's go home and see Reese."

Talking to Joe, Reese heard Rollins before he saw Kenna, and turned to glance toward the open plain. He could make out the horse and rider in the distance. And then when the pair got closer he saw her.

Kenna was riding like the skilled equestrian he, Luke and Chancellor had taught her to be. Sitting straight in the saddle, head held high and looking forward with her hands holding the reins tight, she let the animal know who was in control. Rider and horse were moving together in almost perfect rhythm.

He could still remember that summer right after her grandmother had died. She'd had nowhere else to go, so he had invited her to come home with him and stay at his parents' house. Having a woman in the house besides his mother had been something he, his father and brothers had to adjust to.

Luckily, Luke was on the rodeo circuit and out of town most of the time. But his younger brother Chancellor—whom everyone called Chance—had been home on leave from army ranger training, and Emerson—who'd been away at college—was also home for the summer. It had been during the couple of weeks around the Fourth of July when the Madaris family held their family reunion. Everyone was home and the place was like a madhouse. But in the end, he'd known that with all the craziness Kenna had enjoyed her visit.

He leaned against a post and stared at her. The last time she'd ridden Rollins her hair had been flying in the wind. This new short haircut would take some getting use to, but he liked it. He especially liked the way it framed her face. She was wearing jeans and a halter top, with big hoop earrings dangling from her ears. He thought she looked hot and it had nothing at all to do with the temperature. The closer she got, he began to recognize the glint of mischief in her eyes. He almost held his breath when she brought the horse to a full stop in front of him.

"Did you intend to run me over?" he asked, smiling, gazing up at her as he helped her off her horse. Boy, did she smell good. She never put on too much perfume. It was always pleasing to his nose, never overpowering.

"Nah, I'm just glad to see you," she said.

Why did her words send his heart pounding in his chest? And why was her smile nearly stealing his breath? And where in the hell did that heated rush that raced up his spine come from?

"I fixed dinner," she said excitedly, and he tried not to notice how cute she looked. He swallowed. Was she even wearing a bra? He could swear he saw the outlines of her nipples pressed against her halter top.

Hell! Why was he staring at her chest? And after the mental beat-down he'd given himself today, why was he still looking at her with yearning in his eyes again? What happened to Reese, the man who was nothing more than her best friend?

He cleared his throat. "I heard you prepared dinner. I also heard you made enough to feed just about everyone within miles of here. I'm sure Tanker appreciates getting a night off. You couldn't wait for Sunday, uh?"

She threw her head back and laughed, and the sound seemed to float in the air on this incredible wave of clouds. It was the same air he was inhaling, and it was causing a shudder to rip through his body.

"I don't mind cooking. And besides, come Sunday I don't know what shape I'll be in after partying all Saturday night."

He hadn't considered that, he thought, walking her into the house after handing the reins for Rollins over to Joe. But then he'd never known Alyson to give a wild party. She'd given one last New Year's Eve and he would be the first to admit it had gotten a bit rowdy, but that was to be expected. The one she'd given a few months before that for her sister's birthday had been rather tame. Her parents, who were strict when she was growing up, had been there, which is probably the reason no one was bold enough to cut loose.

He picked up the aroma of lasagna the moment he entered the house. He'd had her lasagna several times before and she knew it was his favorite meal. "Hmm, something smells good in the kitchen," he said.

"I hope you like it," she said, licking her bottom lip with her tongue.

Why were his eyes following the movement of her tongue again today? He was tempted to tilt his head to the side and concentrate on it even more. "I know I will," he said, knowing he needed to escape her presence, to see why he still had a few screws loose somewhere in his head. "I'd better go get washed up for dinner."

"All right. By the time you get back, everything will be ready."

He headed toward the stairs, taking them in quick strides while thinking he needed to focus all his energy on making sure he kept all his immoral thoughts to himself.

Kenna moved around the kitchen trying to calm the frenetic energy that was making her heart beat like crazy in her chest. The horse ride was supposed to make her relax, but once she'd moved beyond the trees and seen Reese talking to Joe in the distance, all she could think about was that he was home and she couldn't wait to see him, to tell him about her day and to hear how his day had gone.

"I wasn't expecting this."

She spun around when Reese returned to the kitchen. Her eyes roamed over him and the first thought that entered her mind was that she wasn't expecting this either—at least not the way he was looking now. When he'd said he needed to wash up, she hadn't expected him to shower and change. But he had, and the results were impressive. Not that he'd looked bad before, since Reese was a good-looking man to begin with. But for some reason the rays of sunlight coming through the window hit him at an angle that accentuated the deep, rich brownness of his skin and the long lashes covering his dark eyes. Standing in his bare feet, he slowly slipped a shirt on over his bare chest, covering the low-riding jeans that braced his hips.

She'd seen him shirtless before, so that wasn't the problem. It was the total package that was throwing her hormones off balance.

Kenna did her best to suppress the rising heat as she turned back to the cabinet to retrieve the wineglasses. "I don't know why you weren't, Reese. You know I don't half-step when I do anything," she said. Since he had left that morning, Kenna had managed to make over his kitchen with an Italian-themed decor. Blade's wife, Samari, was a mix of Italian and African-American, and had been more than happy to drop off a few items to help with the transformation.

"You might as well sit down and dig in," she said, moving quickly across the room with the glasses in her hand. *For crying out loud, I need to find a boyfriend, and fast,* she thought, trying not to stare too hard at him.

With the grace of a man quick on his feet he crossed the room to take his place at the table. "Need help with anything?" he asked at the same time he began pouring wine into their glasses.

She gave him her best smile. "You're doing a great job at that. Just don't give me too much wine. If you do I'll sleep like a baby tonight."

"A far cry from what you did last night," he said, handing her the casserole dish filled with lasagna. "I hope the movie last night was worth it."

She shot one dreamy-eyed look his way. "Are you kidding? It was Idris Elba—who I can watch any time day or night—although

I've seen that movie at least three times already." However, now was not the time to tell Reese that Mr. Elba had nothing on him.

"A toast."

She glanced over at Reese and lifted her glass. "To what?"

"To your move to Houston, your new job and to our friendship, which will last forever."

Her stomach made a somersault at the last part of the toast as guilt gnawed at her conscience. *If he knew what her thoughts had been lately, he wouldn't be so quick to toast their friendship,* she thought. Before she could dwell on it, Reese clinked his glass to hers, sealing the toast.

The question that immediately went through Kenna's mind as she sipped her wine was how was she going to make sure their friendship *did* last forever?

Reese couldn't sleep. He had tossed and turned most of the night and now he felt thirsty, like his throat was dry and he needed water to quench it. He got out of bed and was about to go downstairs in the nude when he remembered he had a houseguest. How in the heck could he forget, when he had gone to bed with thoughts of Kenna on his mind?

He had enjoyed dinner with her and he thought her Italian meal had been great. They had talked during dinner and then later over wine had talked some more. He had shared with her how Madaris Explorations was teaming up with Remington Oil to do a major project that would take him out of the country for a couple of weeks.

Slipping into his jeans, he left his bedroom, but noticed the light from one of the spare rooms at the end of the hall. It was one of the rooms he hadn't furnished yet and he mainly used it to store his workout equipment for whenever he found the time to use it. Lately, it was easier to just join Blade, Slade, Clayton and several of his cousins after work at the fitness center that had recently opened on the ground floor of the Madaris Building.

He walked toward the room and noticed the door was slightly ajar. He glimpsed inside, and at that moment his breath caught. Kenna stood in the middle of the room wearing an oversize Houston Texan T-shirt he had given her last year, painting a canvas. The T-shirt barely covered the upper part of her thighs. And it was pretty damn clear she didn't have anything on underneath. No bra, no panties. Nothing. Her beautiful legs were long and smooth, complementing her rounded hips and luscious thighs.

His gaze moved upward to Kenna's upper body. She had nice breasts. Although he'd never seen them bare, he knew they were firm and ripe. And he knew they were the real thing. He couldn't say that about Alyson or some of the other women he'd been involved with.

Although his focus was on her, Kenna's focus was on her painting. When a lock of hair fell close to her eyes, she pushed it away, lifting her arm so that the T-shirt inched up higher on her thighs. *Gracious.*

He drew in a deep breath when the beat of his heart increased. Okay, this attraction to Kenna was utterly ridiculous—totally out of line. Wasn't it? In a way it was and in a way it wasn't. He was a man, after all. But it was only lately that he'd begun to look at Kenna through the eyes of a red-blooded, lustful man who had more on his mind than just friendship. And that was wrong, especially since she didn't expect or want anything else from him than what they already had.

He felt an erection, hard and tight, press against his zipper and slowly backed up and headed in the opposite direction toward the stairs. Not only did he need a glass of water, it had to be a tall, cold glass that would not only soothe his throat but also cool his body.

* * *

"So what do you think of this, Kenna?"

Kenna glanced over at Christy Madaris and the dress she was holding up to her body—a body that any woman would practically die for. Christy had gorgeous legs that looked good in anything she wore. But then the total package included a very beautiful young woman with naturally red hair and a vibrant smile.

"For me, or for you?" Kenna asked smiling.

"Does it matter?" Christy said, tossing curls from her face. Already the mother of a beautiful little girl, A.C., who looked just like her, Kenna had heard Christy and her husband, Alex, desperately wanted another child.

Kenna studied the outfit, a flattering soft blue dress. She had seen it earlier and noticed it came in her size…but she knew it would look so much better on Christy. "I like it but…"

Christy raised an eyebrow. "But what?"

"My hips might be too much for it."

"Nonsense," Christy said smiling. "You have just the right hips for it and with your small waist it will fit perfectly. Go ahead and try it on. I know it will look good on you."

Kenna hoped so, too. At first she didn't think she'd be excited about the party. But since it was for her, and she knew she would be the center of attention, she wanted to look her best. Knowing the way Alyson's mind worked, she figured there would be plenty of eligible men there, which was definitely what she needed. Hopefully, she would like at least one of them and would want to get to know him better. She desperately needed diversion from thinking so much about Reese.

She hadn't been able to sleep last night, so she had gotten up and painted instead. Even when she was wielding her paintbrush, she had thought of him in ways she should not have. She had awakened when he'd gotten up to get ready for work. She had been tempted to go down and join him in a cup of coffee before he left, but decided to leave well enough alone. Right now he was a temptation she'd rather not deal with.

A half hour later, she and Christy left the shop with the dress in a shopping bag. The short and sassy number had looked better on her than she'd expected. Even some of the customers had complimented her when she'd stepped out of the dressing room for Christy to see. There was something about the cut of the dress and the way it fit snugly around her small waist and hugged her hips that made her feel sexy without looking too provocative. It was a dress that would probably tease a man in a subtle sort of way. It wouldn't knock him across the head at first, but would chip away at his resolve until there was nothing left of his self-control.

Knowing she would be on the hunt for a man at the party on Saturday, the thought of any man losing self-control because of her only made her smile.

Chapter 8

"I'm ready, Reese."

Reese turned at the sound of Kenna's voice and immediately became transfixed. He stared at her totally mesmerized, wondering who in the world this gorgeous creature standing before him was.

They had gone out together a number of times and she'd always looked good, true enough. But tonight she didn't just look good, she looked ravishing—all five-foot-seven of her. From her head all the way down to her stilettoed toes. He couldn't recall the last time he'd seen her in heels that high, but he would be the first to admit that her shoes did awesome things to the shape of her legs.

Her outfit—heaven help him—had heat radiating from every part of his body. At that moment he was too awed to even try to rein in his sexual attraction. It was too intense. He'd always known she had delectable curves and a voluptuous body, but when had both become so alluring they would make a man's jaw drop to the floor and weep. *Lordy.*

She saw him staring, smiled, and then twirled around and said. "Well, how do I look?"

He swallowed. When she'd twirled around in the short blue dress he could actually hear the swish of soft silk against her skin. He was certain he hadn't imagined it. Instead of answering her question he had one of his own, but had to swallow again before he could ask it. "Where did you get *that* dress?"

Her smile widened. "I bought it yesterday when Christy and I went shopping. And you never answered my question about how I look. Do you like it?"

It definitely looked good on her and oh, yes, he liked it—a little too much. There was no doubt in his mind that any man who saw her tonight would like it as well. How could one dress make a woman look cool and elegant and hot and luscious at the same time?

"Reese?"

He blinked and she lifted a perfectly arched brow, something else that was new. Her eyebrows always had a natural curve but now they had a seductive slant over her eyes. When had that changed?

He decided he would answer her first question before asking another one of his own. "You look good as always. And yes, I like it."

She squealed with happiness and laughed before rushing across the room and slipping her arms around him to give him a hug.

Moments later he held her back, lifted her chin up to study her features and then asked. "Your eyebrows are shaped differently?"

She chuckled, pleased that he'd noticed. "Yes, Christy introduced me to the guy who does her brows. Don't they look neat?"

Yeah, they looked neat all right. What they did was emphasize her beautiful eyes, making them look soft and seductive. "Yes, they look neat." What else could he say?

"Come on, we don't want to be late," she said, tugging on his sleeve and pulling him toward the door. If only she knew how her touch was making him feel, hard and achy, she would let go of his arm.

"Why are you in such a hurry?" he asked, tempted to dig in his heels. He wasn't sure he was ready for anyone else to see her tonight. He knew the thought was crazy, but that's the way he felt. He not only felt protective but also downright possessive. It didn't make much sense, yet he felt that way.

"Because the party is for me and I shouldn't be late."

He thought he'd refrain from telling her that according to Alyson they were already late. She'd called twice. Evidently people had begun arriving early and were ready to party.

"We're taking your car instead of the truck," she said, interrupting him as she glanced at the vehicle parked out front once they were outside.

He frowned, not sure if it was a good idea or not, especially since he would have to watch her climb in and out of his Mercedes sports car in that dress. A few moments later when he opened the car door for her he knew it was definitely a bad idea. The moment her backside touched the leather seat, the hem of her dress raised an inch too high, showing a pair of gorgeous thighs. He suddenly had a fleeting thought about just what he could do with those thighs.

Something hard twisted his gut as he visualized it. This wasn't just any woman he was having lustful thoughts about. This was Kenna—his best friend. She was the one woman in the whole entire world he admired, trusted and respected. What kind of Kool-Aid had he been drinking lately, and whatever the flavor it had to have been spiked. A shudder rippled through him at the thought of how his mind had gotten warped ever since she had arrived on his doorstep a few days ago and he hadn't come to his senses since.

"Do you have a problem with my shoes, Reese?"

He blinked and shifted his gaze upward toward her eyes. "Why do you ask?"

"Because you're staring at them."

She thought the reason he was staring was because of her shoes. She had no idea he hadn't made it past her thighs. Besides, he had checked out her shoes earlier, and quickly came to the conclusion that on her feet they made her legs lethal. "No, I don't have a problem with your shoes," he said, deciding to leave well enough alone.

He walked to the other side of the car and slid inside.

"Then why were you staring at them?" she said.

He shrugged as he buckled his seat belt. "You usually don't wear heels that high," he said.

"Yes, I know," she said, giving him a conspiratorial wink. "Tonight I plan to enjoy myself."

"And those shoes are going to help make that possible?" he asked as he backed out the driveway.

"For what I have in mind, yes."

The words were spoken with determination, in a voice belonging to someone who had her mind made up. He struggled not to stiffen. *Just what were her plans for tonight?*

For the time being he was better off not knowing. He tried to concentrate on his driving as he maneuvered over mostly barren roads as he drove toward the interstate. The distance from his home to the hub of Houston was about twenty minutes. Usually, he enjoyed the ride, but tonight he was feeling tense, and all because of the woman sitting in the seat next to him.

She was wearing a different perfume, he thought. He had picked up on it. His gaze narrowed on the road. What the hell was going on with him? But the bigger question was what was going on with Kenna? He glanced over at her when he came to a stop sign. "Nice perfume."

A smile spread across what he thought was a pair of incredible-looking glossed lips when she glanced over at him. "You noticed?"

How could he not, when he wanted to inhale her right there? "Yes, I noticed."

Her smile widened. "Good."

He lifted a brow. "And why is that good?"

She chuckled. "Because when it comes to women you can be slow about noticing some things, Reese. That means if *you* of all people noticed my perfume, there's still hope."

Hope for what? It took all he could do not to swear under his breath. He decided to change the subject and not dwell on the party. "You haven't forgotten about Luke's grand opening next weekend, have you?"

She shifted in her seat and he heard silk rub against skin again. The sound made those lustful fantasies return to his head. He quickly shoved them aside.

"No, I haven't forgotten," she said in what he thought was a sexy and husky voice.

"I'll take care of our plane tickets."

He heard the swishing of silk against skin again. "Ours? Like yours and mine?"

He detected surprise in her tone and wondered why. "Yes, ours. Like yours and mine."

"What about Alyson?"

He glanced over at her as he exited the interstate. "What about her?"

"Isn't she going?"

"As far as I know, she wasn't invited," he said, coming to a traffic light.

"B…but I thought she would be going with you."

He cocked his head. "I don't know why you would assume

that when I told you a couple of months ago that Alyson and I aren't seeing each other anymore."

"Yes, but you're seeing her tonight."

"Because she's giving you a party. Um, let me rephrase that. *I'm* giving you the party. Only thing is that it's at her place and she's acting as hostess."

"And I'm sure you know the real reason why."

He couldn't help but smile. Evidently she thought he might be slow in some things but not in others. Instead of responding to her comment he concentrated on the road. Yes, he knew the real reason, and as far as he was concerned it was a wasted effort on Alyson's part.

They heard the boisterous partiers the moment the car pulled into Alyson's driveway. Kenna couldn't help glancing around at the many cars parked just about everywhere when Reese's car came to a stop. He glanced over at her. "Sounds like the party started without you."

"Yes, sounds like it," she said, letting go of her seat belt and wishing she could let go of her nerves as well. For the past five minutes her stomach had been twisting in knots, and she'd been trying to convince herself that she would be doing the right thing by coming to this party with the intention of finding a guy. This was the first time she'd gone on a manhunt, and if it hadn't been for some online dating advice, she'd be totally clueless now. *Rule number one: It's okay to flirt, but don't come across as too available.*

She smiled at Reese when he opened the car door for her. "Thanks."

He nodded as he closed the door behind her. She lifted a brow and glanced over at him as they walked toward the front door. She had been so busy trying to quell her nerves that it just dawned on her that Reese had gotten really quiet in the past few minutes.

She slowed when they reached the door and paused. "Hey, you okay?"

"Why wouldn't I be?"

She cocked her head to size him up, wondering why he'd given what she perceived as a smart-aleck answer, and was about to ask when the front door opened and a gorgeous-looking Alyson threw herself in Reese's arms and proceeded to place a huge kiss on his lips.

Jealousy ran up Kenna's spine and she realized at that moment that no matter what Reese had said earlier, he was going to have a hard time fighting off Alyson's advances tonight. The woman was on the prowl, and Reese was her prey.

Alyson turned to her, smiling brightly. "Kenna, you look great, girl. There are quite a few people inside dying to meet you."

Before she could open her mouth to respond, Alyson took her hand and pulled her inside and they immediately got lost among the crowd.

Reese didn't need anyone to tell him he was in a bad mood, because he felt his less-than-pleasant attitude all the way to his bones. By the time he got inside and made it through the crowd of people, several things became quite clear. He knew less than half of them, and eighty percent of them were men. What the hell was Alyson thinking?

He frowned because he knew damn well what she'd been thinking and he didn't like it. He paused in the act of taking a sip of his drink and glanced across the room. Kenna was surrounded by a group of men, as she had been most of the evening. *Who in the hell did they think they were, crowded around her like that?* They were flirting, and it was obvious she was flirting back. And he wasn't sure just how he felt about that.

He took a swig of his beer and knew it was a lie the moment the thought popped into his head. He did know how he felt about it. He didn't like it one bit. She was beautiful, damnit—a seductress in a blue dress. He knew it and every man in the room knew it. She looked beautiful. But it wasn't just the dress. It was the entire package. Not surprisingly, quite a few men had latched on to her and had no intention of letting go.

He glanced at his watch. It was past midnight now and he had a mind to leave and take Kenna with him. But it was her party, and so he figured doing such a thing wouldn't be a good idea. He glanced over at Kenna. It seemed some of her admirers had finally whittled away. And instead of being surrounded by a group of men, there was only one man who remained, determined to vie for her attention.

"Looks like you're ready for another one of these," Alyson said, suddenly appearing at his side. She took the almost empty beer bottle out of his hand and replaced it with a full one.

"Thanks."

"And sorry I had to leave you for a moment. I had to make sure the caterers kept the food coming. In other words, Mr. Madaris, I intend to make sure you get your money's worth tonight. I think the food is fantastic."

He nodded as he took another swig of his beer, even though the catering was the last thing on his mind. It was on the tip of his tongue to tell her that she didn't need to apologize for leaving him, since he'd needed the time alone. She'd remained tethered to him the entire evening, having left only briefly to deal with the caterers.

He glanced around the room but his gaze kept returning to Kenna. "Who is that guy who's practically breathing down her neck?"

Alyson's gaze followed his and she had the nerve to smile. "Oh, that's Dr. Wendell Thomas, a well-respected neurologist who recently joined the staff at Park Plaza Hospital last month. Umm, look how she's blushing. I think she likes him."

Reese decided not to share his thoughts about that. But he

would share his thoughts on something else that bothered him. "Why are there more men here than women, Alyson?"

She stopped sipping her glass of beer and looked at him. "The purpose of the party, Reese, was for Kenna to meet people."

He gave her a cold stare. "I'm well aware of that, Alyson. But she was supposed to meet people, not just men."

She frowned at him. "And why do you have such a problem with it?"

He couldn't answer that. So he denied it. "I don't have a problem with it."

She twisted her mouth in exasperation. "Yes, you do, Reese."

He was about to respond to Alyson's accusation, but he looked across the room and discovered Kenna was standing alone for the first time tonight. Evidently the neck-breather had gone to fetch her another glass of wine or something. It didn't matter where the man had gone off to. Reese refused to pass up an opportunity to snag Kenna's attention, if only for a second.

Not giving Alyson a backward glance, "Excuse me for a moment," he said, and then quickly walked across the room toward Kenna.

Chapter 9

Kenna glanced to her right just in time to see Reese heading across the room toward her—tall, dark and handsome, wide-chested and broad-shouldered. She couldn't help but admire what a fine specimen of a man he was.

He was wearing a pair of dark trousers and a blue shirt, and as far as she was concerned there was no man at the party who looked better than him. No man who could make her heart jump in her chest like he could, including the very eligible Dr. Thomas, who was determined that she spend the night in his bed tonight. Fat chance! She needed a man in her life, not a *sex* partner.

"Here," Reese said when he came to a stop in front of her. "You need this," he said, handing her his beer bottle.

She took a couple of sips and then handed it back to him. "Thanks. And how did you know I needed that?"

He looked down at her, giving her his best grin. "Because I know you."

She nodded. Yes, he did know her, and because he knew her it wouldn't be long before he figured out her problem and the part he played in it. She couldn't let that happen. "Are you enjoying the party, Reese?"

"No."

She glanced up at him. "Why not? I think Alyson did a fantastic job spending your money."

"That's not the point."

She waited to see if he would clarify the point, but he didn't. Instead he asked, "What happened to the good doctor?"

She lifted a brow. Was that irritation she heard in his voice? "Wendell was paged by the hospital and went out on the patio to take the call."

"And left you alone?"

She chuckled. "Don't pretend you're agonizing over it, Reese."

"But I am."

She drew in a deep breath. Yes, he was probably agonizing over it, mainly because of that overprotective side of him. "Well, now is not the time. Wendell is returning, so put on a smile so I can introduce the two of you."

"What if I said I didn't want to be introduced to him?"

"Then I'd tell you to retract those protective claws. Every man I meet isn't going to be another Terrence, Lamont or Curtis."

She didn't have time to say any more because at that moment Wendell returned. She smiled up at him. "Wendell, I'd like you to meet my best friend, Reese Madaris."

Wendell raised his chin in time to see Reese tighten his jaw. "Your best friend?" he asked as he held out his hand to Reese.

"Yes, her best friend," Reese responded, not giving Kenna a chance to do so.

Wendell studied Reese as if sizing him up. Reese did likewise. The man's handshake was strong, and Reese respected that even if he didn't like his obvious interest in Kenna.

"I've invited Kenna to go boating with me tomorrow," the doctor said smiling. "She's accepted."

Reese looked at her as he took another sip of his beer. "Is that a fact?"

Kenna glanced over at Reese, and from her expression he could tell she was probably wondering what in the world was going on with him. He glared down at her and in response she glared right back.

Alyson seemed to suddenly materialize out of nowhere. "Excuse me, but Reese, may I borrow you for a second?"

He blinked and then shifted his gaze from Kenna to Alyson. "Yes, for a second."

Kenna watched as the pair walked off toward the patio. She noticed Reese was striding powerfully, as if he was agitated. It was taking some effort for Alyson to keep up with him.

"They make a nice couple, don't they?" Wendell said.

She glanced up at Wendell's face. He was studying her expression as if to see what sort of reaction he would get from her. She smiled brightly, deciding not to give away the fact that her heart was slowly breaking. "Yes, Reese and Alyson make a nice couple."

"What in the world is wrong with you, Reese?"

His eyes flickered at Alyson. She looked genuinely confused. And he was trying to refrain from saying, welcome to the club. She looked beautiful; he would be the first to admit it. And more than a number of people had remarked that the two of them looked good together. But what they lacked, which she evidently hadn't picked up on in the ten months they'd dated exclusively, was chemistry.

He'd dated women before who'd been able to get his blood stirring, but not Alyson. Although they were okay together in the bedroom, whenever he thought of hot, sizzling sex her name never came to mind. He found her to be good company and someone who was fun to do things with…until she became jealous.

“Reese?”

“Yes?”

“I want to know what in the world is wrong with you? Back in there when you confronted Dr. Thomas you acted like a dog guarding a bone.”

He squared his shoulders, raised his chin and pierced her with dark eyes. “And what if I am?”

She crossed her arms over her chest and glared up at him. “Then I think something is definitely wrong with that picture.”

“Wrong in what way?”

“Kenna is supposed to be your best friend and not your woman. At least that’s what you’ve told me.”

“And that's what I meant.”

“Then explain your actions back there, Reese.”

He rubbed the back of his head annoyed. “I recognize the good doctor for what he is.”

“Which is?”

“A man on the prowl…” He’d been around Blade enough to know the signs.

“And what if he is? Kenna is old enough to take care of herself. Why can’t you accept that? Why are you playing the role of a jealous lover instead of doting best friend? Why?”

He blinked. *Jealous lover?* “I’m not playing that role.”

“Yes, you are. In fact, this whole relationship between you and Kenna isn’t normal. At times the two of you are almost inseparable.”

He ignored the fact that Dex had mentioned something similar. “We’re separated now, aren’t we?”

“Yes, but if you had your way, you would be right there by her side, making it impossible for Dr. Thomas to hold a decent conversation with her.”

The man might be holding a conversation with Kenna, but

Reese doubted it was anything close to decent. "Is this what you pulled me aside to say, Alyson?" He watched her close her eyes and breathe in a few times, a sure sign there definitely was more to come.

She reopened her eyes and stared up at him. She was no longer glaring. Her eyes had gotten soft and he recognized it for what it was—a manipulative move on her part. "I thought we were close, Reese, and that our relationship had gone beyond games and that we were even contemplating marriage."

"Marriage? That word never came up between us," he said in a surprised tone. He definitely wasn't expecting her to use that angle, since he knew for a fact he'd never brought the subject up before, although he'd picked up on her hints a time or two.

"I know, but I assumed that eventually we would get to that point."

He figured now was not the time to tell her she'd figured wrong, and although he was certain she would make some man a good wife, that man wasn't him.

"But I never had a chance. And although you might have cooled things between us because of my accusations about you and Kenna, I can now see that I was right all along. There's more between you two than mere friendship, and the sad thing about it is that I'm not sure either of you knows it."

He frowned. "What are you talking about?"

The glare was back in her eyes. "What I'm talking about, Reese, is that you never act protective around Kenna, you act territorial. There's a difference. And the two of you are so into each other it's obvious. You drank out of the same beer bottle, for heaven's sake. It's such an automatic thing, I doubt either of you realizes you're doing it. You've never even shared a glass with me like that."

His chest tightened as a sense of panic settled in. How far was Alyson planning on taking this? "Kenna and I have been best friends for over eleven years. We're used to each other."

"And you and I dated for almost a year—exclusively. You should have gotten used to me, too."

He drew in a deep breath. "Look, Alyson. I don't know what to tell you. Things didn't work out between us and I thought we had moved on."

"I tried but I can't. I want to get married, and you're the man I want, Reese. I'm used to getting what I want. How can you deny me?"

Easily. Thanks to her parents, she was pampered, spoiled rotten and selfish. He knew just how those traits worked together.

"Sorry, Alyson, but when I ended things between us that was it," he said.

"Just because you want Kenna."

"No. Because things didn't work out between us." He hoped she'd let it go and wouldn't ask for specifics. He wanted her to walk away with her pride intact, and she wouldn't be able to do that if he were to be completely honest.

She scowled at him. "No matter what you say, I'm going to think otherwise."

"That's your prerogative and there's nothing else I can say, is there? And I think it's time for me to leave. Take care of yourself, Alyson." He turned and walked away.

"Reese!"

He stopped and turned around. "Yes?"

"If you walk out of here, I won't give you another chance."

He didn't recall asking her for another chance. Instead of telling her that, he turned and headed back inside.

Dr. Wendell Thomas gave Kenna a long, searching look. "So what time do you want me to come pick you up to go boating tomorrow?"

Kenna flashed him a smile. "Any time after noon. I was planning on sleeping late."

"I was serious when I said you can sleep over at my place. I have several spare bedrooms," Wendell said.

Yes, and she'd bet her diamond earrings—the same ones Reese had given her last year for her birthday—that the bedroom he intended to put her in if she spent the night was his.

"We just met, Wendell. What makes you think I'd spend the night at your place?" she asked sweetly, keeping her gaze fixed on his face. He was handsome, and she knew a lot of women who had no qualms about sleeping with a man they'd just met, but that wasn't her style. She had agreed to go boating with him and that was as far as it would go for now.

"I was just being kind," he said.

Yeah, right. "Thanks for the offer, but I have a comfortable bed to sleep in tonight."

"The one at Reese Madaris's house?"

"That's the one."

"And what's your relationship to him again?" he questioned.

She frowned. The man had heard Reese loud and clear when he'd said that they were friends. But just in case he had hearing problems… "Reese is my best friend. I told you that when I introduced the two of you. *And* he told you that as well."

"Yes, but I wanted to be sure, since he seemed quite annoyed when I told him about our date tomorrow."

Yes, he had. "Reese and I have been best friends since college and he can get a little overprotective at times. He's the big brother I never had."

Wendell smiled. "I have a younger sister, so I know how that can be, and I'm fine with it, as long as that's all it is and goes no further."

Wait a minute. Didn't we just meet? Why is he trying to control things here? The last thing he should try to do is rattle my cage in order to bolster his ego. She leaned in close to him. "Are you questioning my friendship with Reese?"

There must have been something in the tone of her voice and the look in her eyes that alerted him that he was on shaky ground. "No, no. I just need to know where I stand. After all, I am an established neurologist."

She smiled and took a deep breath. This was the first time she'd ever shown interest in a doctor, especially one who evidently took a great deal of satisfaction from being an M.D. There was nothing wrong with being proud of your accomplishments, but he was becoming a bit too much. How many times had he told her tonight what he did for a living, like it would open all kinds of doors, especially the one leading to the bedroom? Red flags were going off in her head, and she had a tendency to pay attention when they did.

"And I'm a gifted artist," she said proudly. The handsome prince was turning into a jerk.

"Yes, I know. You're a police sketch artist who will start working for the Houston Police Department in a few weeks."

She frowned at the smirk on his face. Was he looking down on her, making light of what she did for a living? She was about to lean in closer and tell him she'd decided not to go boating with him after all.

"Come on, Kenna, we're leaving."

She swung her head around and met Reese's dark, intense gaze. "What?"

"I said we're leaving."

She studied Reese's features. He was upset about something. Had he been any other man she would have told him to go on and leave without her, she would find another way home. But this wasn't any man. This was Reese, and something or someone had ticked him off. She looked past him and saw Alyson hurrying in their direction. The look on her face was furious, mutinous—downright bitchy. Kenna held her breath when Alyson stormed across the room.

"Go ahead and go with him, Kenna, since he won't leave

without you," Alyson snarled, causing a scene. "And the two of you need to stop lying about your relationship, because you're more than just best friends."

Dr. Thomas cleared his throat and diplomatically said to Reese and Alyson, "Maybe the two of you need to take it outside."

"We already have, and he refuses to admit the truth," Alyson wailed.

Kenna blinked. There was nothing worse than seeing a grown woman whine. She figured a temper tantrum was next and Alyson would probably begin throwing things. She glanced over at Reese and caught his eye, read his thoughts and nodded. They were on the same wavelength. It was time to get out before the missiles start flying, especially since they both were targets.

"I think it's best if Reese and I left now," she said.

Dr. Thomas gave her a look that all but said, *smart move.*

Reese took her hand and was about to lead her to the door when Dr. Thomas said, "Umm, Kenna, maybe we should take a rain check on that boating date tomorrow."

She smiled. "No problem."

Reese tugged on her hand and together they turned and quickly left the party.

Chapter 10

Like two thieves in the night, they sped away from the scene of the crime. Reese made quick time getting to the interstate. It was only then that Kenna relaxed. "Am I wrong or did we just escape from *The Twilight Zone?*"

Reese shot her a quick glance. "Hell, I was thinking more like something from *Friday the 13th.*"

She chuckled. "What went down on that patio to get Alyson so hot under the collar?" Kenna asked, twisting around in her seat. "Talk about fireworks."

Reese wondered how much he should tell her and decided she deserved to know it all, especially in light of the accusation Alyson had flung at them right before they left. "You heard her. She's still not convinced we aren't lovers instead of best friends."

Kenna rolled her eyes upward. "Jeeze. What is it going to take for people to stop assuming that? Can't they see that you don't see me that way?"

Reese nibbled on the corner of his mouth, thinking if only she knew where his thoughts had been going lately she would hit him over the head a few times. "And you don't see me that way either. Trust me, I think you're beautiful, intelligent, smart as heck and successful. But we're just friends and that's all we can and ever will be," he iterated, for his benefit more than hers.

"I agree, and thanks for saying that, especially since Wendell doesn't share your opinion."

"I didn't like him," Reese muttered under his breath.

She mustered a half smile when she heard him. "I think your dislike of him was obvious, Reese. What I want to know is why. He didn't start acting like an ass until later, when he saw I wasn't going to jump into his bed quick enough to suit him. He figured being a doctor afforded him certain privileges. Too bad nobody told me about them."

He knew he should feel bad, but in all honesty he felt good knowing she'd found out about the man before it had been too late. He could tell she'd been taken with him. He had seen her flirt, which was something he'd never seen her do in all the eleven years they'd known each other.

"So, what all did Alyson say?" she asked.

He wasn't surprised she wanted all the facts. He drew in a deep breath, deciding not to mention Alyson's calling him a jealous lover rather than a best friend. "She thinks our relationship isn't normal and that we act like people in love do."

"In what way?"

"Like drinking from the same beer bottle without giving it a second thought..."

"Oh." Kenna didn't say anything else for a long while, which made Reese wonder if she thought there was something to it. He told himself there wasn't, but wondered how many other friends did that.

"We also eat off the same plate sometimes," she finally said. "Even share the same cookies a time or two."

He nodded. "Yes, we've even shared the same fork and spoon." *But never the same bed,* he thought quickly.

"Yes. But that only shows how much we trust each other."

"It does," he agreed.

"And that you'll do anything for me and I'll do anything for you."

He totally agreed with her there as well. He would do anything for her and believed she would do the same.

"So, we're into each other's lives to a point. Is that such a big deal?"

"No," he answered quickly, focusing his gaze on the endless stretch of interstate in front of him. Although he knew for some people it would be a big deal. But things were different for them, especially since they weren't dating other people. During the time they were dating others, they never went into any details about their relationships. He knew when she was dating a guy and could usually gauge how much the guy meant to her by how much time she spent talking about him. She rarely talked about any of the men who'd passed through her life other than Terrence, Lamont and Curtis. All the others had been out of sight and out of mind.

"I think we should continue and not let anyone dictate what type of friendship we should have," she said.

"I agree." She didn't say anything else for a while, and the more he thought about what she had said the more his mood lightened. Although he felt that Alyson didn't have the right to behave the way she had, she had said how she felt and what she believed.

He glanced over at Kenna. "So you aren't going boating tomorrow."

"Nope. I'm sleeping late as planned."

"When you get up will you ride with me over to Dex and Caitlin's place?" he asked. "I need to go over a few details for a project before he leaves town."

She smiled at him. "I'd love to."

She didn't say anything for a while and then she began laughing. Reese glanced over at her. "What's so funny?"

"Us, and the way we hauled ass out of that party. It reminded me of the other time we did something like that. You remember?"

Yes, he remembered and couldn't help but smile. "It was when you talked me into taking you to that party on campus in the frat house only to discover there was an orgy going on in one of the back bedrooms."

A smile touched the corners of Kenna's lips. "I'll never forget the look on your face. I stumbled on the naked bodies first and then went and got you to make sure I wasn't imagining things."

She hadn't been. Reese shook his head as a wry smile touched his lips. "All I could think about at that time was a police raid and what would happen once my family's name was smeared all over the newspapers."

They had quickly left the party, which was a good thing, since one of the neighbors eventually called the police and everyone at the party had gotten busted and hauled off to jail. They read about it in the papers the next day. Not only had there been an orgy, but the police had arrested some of the partygoers for drug possession as well.

"That's why if we're ever at a party together and you say let's go, I'm going," she said. "No questions asked."

"Like tonight?"

Kenna threw her head back and laughed out loud again. "Yes, all I could imagine were plates flying over your head and hitting mine instead."

Reese chuckled. "That was a good possibility. And I would not have taken too kindly to anything hitting that pretty little head of yours."

"Oh, you're so sweet," she said, giving him a glowing smile.

He smiled back her. "I am your best friend, and don't you forget it."

"We're just friends and that's all we can and will ever be."

"I'm your best friend, and don't you forget it."

Kenna moved her head on the pillow as the words Reese had said floated through her mind, keeping her awake. What he'd said only reinforced what she'd known all along, but she had needed to hear it anyway. In fact, Reese saying it had propelled her back on course, and she knew it was the right one. Now it was up to her to make sure she didn't veer off for any reason.

Okay, so she was back to square one. Reese didn't have a significant other and neither did she.

When Alyson first introduced Wendell Thomas, she'd felt a surge of excitement thinking he would be a good candidate. But once the man revealed his true colors—coming across as arrogant and self-centered—she was disappointed.

Kenna refused to believe there wasn't at least one man out there she could become interested in. All she needed was one. Especially now, since things hadn't worked out between Reese and Alyson. She figured he wouldn't be free for long, not with all the single women in Houston vying for his attention and affection. It was just a matter of time before one of them caught his eye. She drew in a deep breath, thinking she couldn't muster enough enthusiasm about that prospect, even though in the end she knew it was inevitable. Things would go back to being like they were before between them.

Feeling restless and frustrated, she kicked off the covers. She refused to be defeated. She still had Luke's rodeo school opening to look forward to next weekend, and chances were some of Luke's old rodeo buddies would be there. Thinking there was possibly hope after all, she found a comfortable position in bed and tried drifting off to sleep.

She forced back the tears that stung her eyes. Giving up the man you love to another woman wasn't easy, but it was something she had to do.

The man pretended to study the coffee in his cup while out of the corner of his eyes he watched as the woman grabbed her purse off the table to leave. She wouldn't get far. He'd see to that. He appreciated the friend who'd taught him something about auto repairs—namely, how to make a car work and how to stop it from working.

He studied his coffee and wondered what she was doing out this late anyway. It appeared she had been waiting for someone and had been stood up. Oh, well. Her disappointment wouldn't last long.

Deciding he had given her enough time, he put his money on the table and walked out of the restaurant. He never paid for anything with a credit card, since that could be traced.

Less than five minutes later he found her, standing on the side of the road next to her car with the hood up. He was about to slow down and offer assistance when he noticed another car parked in front of her.

Damn. Someone was already there. More than likely it was the same man she'd been waiting for earlier. Evidently he had decided to show up, which would account for him getting there so quickly. He was a husky guy, so the thought of taking him out and still dealing with the woman was pushed to the back of his mind.

He kept his eyes straight ahead as he passed both vehicles. He became angrier. Tonight wasn't going as planned. But he was convinced there would be other nights. He could feel it.

Chapter 11

"So what's this we hear about you and Kenna at that party Saturday night? I understand a lot went down."

Reese rolled his eyes. Leave it to Blade to bring it up, and of course he could count on his cousins sitting beside him to be all ears. It was Monday, and the five of them were seated at a table eating lunch at the deli located on the ground floor of the Madaris Building.

"Tell me what you heard," he said smoothly, deciding to put the ball back in Blade's court. There was no doubt in his mind that Blade had heard something. When Reese had arrived at the party he had run into a couple of Blade's cronies, all members of the Notorious Gentlemen's Club. He doubted that any of them could be called a *gentleman*. But they were all *notorious* bachelors with just one thing on their minds when it came to women. Blade used to be the ringleader before settling down with Sam.

Blade leaned back in his chair and held his gaze. "According to Carter, Alyson all but accused you and Kenna of being lovers in front of everyone."

Reese nodded, waiting to see if there was more. He figured there was.

"And Carter also mentioned something about you being in a bad mood most of the night, scowling from across the room at anyone who tried to get close to Kenna," Blade added.

"That sounds like something you would do," Nolan piped up, grinning.

Reese rolled his eyes. "I don't recall scowling at anyone."

"But you do admit to being in a bad mood?" Lee asked, leaning closer into the table and smiling.

Reese shrugged. "Possibly. Alyson deliberately invited more men than women."

Corbin chuckled. "Hey, man, I think that was the point of the party, wasn't it? To welcome Kenna to town and introduce her to people."

Reese frowned at Corbin. "Yes, but the key word is *people*. There were three times as many men as women there. It was not a party to put Kenna on display in front of every horny man in Houston. I didn't like that."

There was no need in telling them that things weren't any better since he was becoming more and more attracted to her each day. He knew it was crazy, but he couldn't explain it. Yesterday when they'd gone to Dex's and ended up staying for dinner he had watched how she had interacted with Dex and Caitlin, as well as their children. She loved kids. He'd always known that, just like he knew she would be a great mother.

"Well, the family is convinced there's nothing between the two of you, but your actions don't help matters. When you act like the big bad wolf whenever a man comes near Kenna, people will start wondering," Lee said.

Reese took a sip of water. "Let them think whatever they want. That doesn't bother me."

"Evidently," Blade said easily. "But what about Kenna? What if she meets someone she wants to become seriously involved with?"

Reese studied his glass. For some reason his heart nearly missed a beat at the thought of that. She deserved the best, and not the kind of man she'd dated in the past. He should be happy if she met someone and they got seriously involved, especially if he knew the man would be good for her.

"Reese?"

He glanced up to see four pairs of eyes watching him intently, waiting on his response. "If Kenna meets someone she wants to become seriously involved with, and if I knew the man would do right by her, I would give her my blessing."

Since this was the week Dex was out of town, Reese spent a lot of late nights at the office or on-site. Most nights Kenna was asleep when he came in, and she usually wasn't awake in the morning when he left.

In a way she needed the time to get her head back together and once again become the cool, confident, smart woman that she normally was. She figured what happened with Curtis didn't count. She bet even his former teammates didn't have a clue he was on the down-low. He wanted to keep things hush-hush and wanted her word that she wouldn't reveal his secret.

She got up from the table where she'd just enjoyed a PBJ, cookies and milk for lunch when the kitchen phone rang. She reached out and picked it up. "Tall Oaks Ranch."

"Hello, stranger."

The deep, raspy sound of Reese's voice had Kenna's heart hammering against her rib cage. "Do I know you?" she asked teasingly.

He chuckled. "If anyone knows me, it's you. What are you doing?"

She smiled. "I just finished eating a PBJ, cookies and milk. They were good."

"I bet. Joe mentioned you had to go into town yesterday."

She nodded. "Yes, I had a few more papers to complete at the HPD and to meet the people I'll be working with. Some had taken the day off, so I'll meet them on the first day." She would have told him all that herself had she seen him. But even though they were living under the same roof, she hadn't seen him since Monday, and today was Thursday.

"How did it go?"

"Good as far as I know. I have another week before I start work. I got to see my office, and it's a lot bigger than the one back in Austin. I can see downtown Houston from my window."

"Sounds like a nice setup. You need to tell me all about it when I see you later."

The hammering in her chest increased and she was convinced her heart skipped a beat. "You're getting off early?"

He chuckled. "No, I'm getting off on time. Dex's back. Like us, he and Caitlin are headed to Oklahoma City tomorrow for the festivities this weekend."

Kenna couldn't help but get excited at the thought of going away with Reese for the weekend, even if they would be doing so only as friends. She liked his family, felt like she was a part of them, and they always treated her with warmth and kindness.

"I'm looking forward to it. In fact, I'm going shopping again."

"With Christy?" he asked.

"No, Christy and Alex have already left for Oklahoma," she said. "A group of us are hitting the malls. The excursion is being led by your cousin Traci."

She laughed out loud when he moaned before muttering a word that all but burned her ears. She understood. Traci was one of his older cousins who everyone knew was a bona fide shopaholic. "Relax, you don't have to worry about me going on a spending spree and not being able to move out at the end of the month."

"That's the last thing I'm worried about. You know you can stay with me for as long as you want, baby. I'll see you later."

She tilted her head to the side. Why did the sound of his voice have to be so sexually charged? And he'd called her *baby.* Had he ever done that before? "Okay. I'll see you later," she managed to say before hanging up.

By the time she got off the phone she wasn't sure which thing had made her day. The thought that he wouldn't be working late and she would see him today, or the fact that he'd told her she could stay with him as long as she needed to or that he had called her *baby.* Although she was sure he didn't mean anything by it, it warmed her heart nonetheless.

Reese parked his truck at the side of his house. He had so easily become used to Kenna staying with him, and for someone who was a loner that said a lot.

Before leaving that morning he had scribbled a note asking that she meet him for lunch, but had tossed it in the trash before walking out the door. He'd missed seeing her over the past few days, but the strange thing about it was that when she'd lived in Austin he would sometimes go without seeing her for weeks, although he would often talk to her. What made this time so different? The only difference was that he had always been involved with someone. Did that mean that he was only turning his attention to Kenna because he was unattached?

He rubbed his fingers along his forehead. Attached or unattached, he had no right to be thinking of Kenna in the way he'd been thinking of her lately, and that wasn't good. Instead it seemed like everything Alyson accused him of was true. More than anything he was determined that no matter how much his body wanted to react whenever she was around, it was nothing more than a passing infatuation. Nothing had changed between them and nothing ever would.

As he opened the door to get out of the truck, what he'd told his cousins at lunch played in his mind. He knew that sooner or later some man would see Kenna for the kind, warm, loving person that she was. He didn't expect her to remain single for the rest of her life. She deserved marriage, and to have all the children he knew she wanted. She was entitled to all the happiness a woman could have with a man, and deep down he knew that. Still, the thought of her building a life with someone else, establishing a closer relationship with someone other than with him, drove him into panic mode. It was something he needed to figure out, and quick.

They had talked about it before, the possibility of meeting other people—like Alyson and Lamont—who didn't understand the closeness of their relationship. They had agreed not to become involved with anyone who couldn't accept the kind of friendship they had. He hadn't told her, but Alyson hadn't been the only one. Over the years there had been others. Most weren't important enough for him to care about. And he was sure there had been men who'd accused her of the same thing. He didn't question her every time she'd broken up with someone. Mainly because he felt it was best for her to handle her business like it was best for him to handle his. But Alyson had brought it all out in the open. She had made accusations, and they were the kind that couldn't be ignored.

Did he care?

Yes, he cared, more for Kenna's sake than his own. He wasn't interested in starting a new relationship with a woman right now. No telling when he would be. He liked being single and was in no rush to settle down. But Kenna might feel differently. Some women liked having a man around, and in the years that he'd known her, she had been in a steady relationship most of the time. He shouldn't expect anything to be different now that she had moved to Houston. He should feel comfortable with it if she met someone. Of course, after he checked him out.

He paused. Did he even have the right to check out Kenna's dates? Shouldn't he respect her judgment enough to let her choose the kind of man she wanted? Hell, she was twenty-nine years old. But the thought of another man breaking her heart didn't sit well with him. The thought of another man with her *period* gave him pause. What had Alyson accused him of? Being territorial and not protective? Could there be some truth to her claim?

He was thinking way too hard, way too much, and giving Alyson far too much credit. He opened the door and entered his house. A feeling of excitement coursed through his body just knowing Kenna was living under his roof. It was a feeling of warmth, the familiar presence of a woman who meant a lot to him.

He stepped into the foyer and glanced around. He didn't see her, but he certainly smelled her. The entire house was filled with her scent—vanilla and jasmine. He liked it. He'd always liked it.

Since she was probably in the kitchen he moved in that direction, only to take a few steps when he heard someone behind him. He stopped and glanced over his shoulder at the staircase above and saw her as she came rushing down the stairs. He turned around. "Reese! You're home."

There was something in the way she'd said it, something in the way she'd looked at him when she said it that made him feel welcomed, missed and appreciated. And at that moment it made him aware of her not as a friend but as a woman he hadn't seen in almost three days. He was also aware of what he felt upon seeing her, and that almost took his breath away.

"Yes, I'm home," he said. Their eyes remained fixed on each other for a long, sexually charged moment. He wanted to turn away, to look at something else, start some mundane conversation, but he couldn't. She was wearing another dress, one he'd never seen before, and she looked pretty. In reality, she looked better than just pretty. She looked radiant, gorgeous. His mind kept saying over and over, *Hey man, lighten up. It's just a dress.* But he thought she was beautiful in every sense of the word. Some women worked hard at being beautiful, but with her it came naturally. Just seeing Kenna made him aware of every nerve ending in his body, of every cell and molecule. Even his skin seemed to be on fire, tingling in a way it had never done before.

What in the hell was happening? What was making his emotions stir? What was wreaking havoc with his body and his mind? And what, at that very moment, was compelling him to move in her direction with an urgency he couldn't begin to define?

If he had been thinking rationally he might have had time to pull himself together and convince himself that he was about to make a mistake, or at least consider the consequences of his actions. Instead he kept walking and when she was within arm's length, he reached out and pulled her into his arms and devoured her lips.

Kenna felt Reese's mouth greedily consume hers. She could only moan in response. Not once did she think to pull away, even when she saw it coming. She had assumed until the last moment that he would stop, come to his senses and deny her the one thing she craved.

How many times had she dreamed of him kissing her this way, their tongues mating and tangling in a passionate exchange? At that moment her brain felt as weak as her knees, her breasts became heavy and ached against his chest. She continued to groan as the kiss, slow and steady, became more forceful, more intense and even more desperate.

Suddenly, he broke off the kiss. Disoriented and practically in a daze, she grabbed the front of his shirt to keep from falling as he pulled air into his lungs. She wasn't sure what had happened and knew from the dark, penetrating eyes staring back at her that neither did he. The one thing she didn't need right now, the one thing she couldn't handle, was for him to have regrets.

In the back of her mind, she saw more than them sharing a kiss. She could see her body underneath him, naked, with her legs spread wide open, her back arched, her hips raised—ready to receive him in the most intimate way. She wanted to show him just how much he was loved.

He would have been shocked by her thoughts, but at that moment she didn't care. After all this time she had finally gotten a taste of Reese Madaris, and fantasy paled in comparison to the reality.

"Kenna?"

Oh, no. He was looking at her with disappointment in his eyes when she'd felt only hope. But that hope was beginning to fade.

"Yes?"

Instead of answering, he covered his face with his hands and took a step back, putting distance between them. When he lowered his head she knew what he was going to say and she didn't want to hear it.

"I had no right to do that. I'm sorry. I don't know what got into me just now."

"Yeah," she said, raising her hand to her lips to touch them, feeling the wetness on her fingertips. "I know what you mean," she lied. "I don't know what got into me just now either." A girl did have her pride, and if he regretted kissing her she wasn't going to let him see how much it hurt her to know that.

"You're my best friend," he said in a low voice, like he was trying to remind himself of that fact. "The only excuse I can give for my behavior just now is because—"

"You're horny and haven't had a girlfriend in a while and—"

"No! That isn't it. I—"

"No need to explain, Reese, really. Look, I promise not to bring it up again if you don't. Come on. I fixed dinner."

And before the tears she was trying hard to fight back could flood her eyes, she rushed into the kitchen.

Trying to hold himself in check, Reese watched her hurry off. *Damn!* What had he done? Then slowly, by degrees, he remembered. He had kissed Kenna with a hunger he'd been holding in for days. He'd sunk his mouth into her, tasted her, and when their tongues had tangled and mingled she had kissed him back. Her response had turned him loose and he'd tried getting his fill and then some.

She had felt good in his arms—so perfectly right. And for a moment he had been so consumed that he could barely recall what day it was. The only thing he could remember was how good she'd tasted. And that was the crux of his problem, the root of this unwanted attraction he felt for the woman who was his best friend. Guilt surfaced. She didn't deserve to be mauled by him, although he distinctly remembered her kissing him back. But that was beside the point. He had made the first move, taken advantage of a woman who hadn't expected such behavior from him. She certainly hadn't anticipated it.

She was a woman who deserved more from him or any man.

He drew in a deep breath. She didn't want his apology. In fact she didn't want him to bring up what had happened ever again, so he had to join her in the kitchen and pretend nothing was amiss and things were as they used to be, when a part of him knew that things would never be the same again.

Kenna scurried around the kitchen as she began to set the table. She had to stay busy or else she would think about what had happened between her and Reese a few minutes ago. Oh, she knew he had kissed her. She still felt the effects down to her toes, not to mention the taste of him on her lips.

And as shameless as it sounded, she would give anything for a repeat performance. Unfortunately, Reese had other ideas. He never meant to kiss her and regretted doing so. Then why had he? Deep down, she knew the reason and had called it like she saw it. He was a man, a good man. But he was a man nonetheless, and men had needs. He'd tried denying it, but it was what it was.

When Reese entered the kitchen, she refused to turn around to acknowledge him. She needed a few moments to gather herself. "You can go ahead and sit down, Reese, I'll bring the food to you," she said over her shoulder.

"No, I'd like to help."

That's what she was afraid of. Although it was a rather large kitchen, she had a feeling it wouldn't be large enough for the two of them now. She was about to turn and tell him that she'd rather he didn't help her when she felt the heat of his body behind her just seconds before he reached around her to grab a couple of serving bowls off the counter.

"Excuse me," he said in a low, husky voice.

She closed her eyes for a second.

"You okay?"

How could he ask her that when she wasn't okay? Now that he had kissed her she was more aware of him than ever. His aftershave, which had always smelled very masculine, was now an aphrodisiac. She paused for a moment to breathe in his scent.

"Anything else you want me to do, Kenna?"

Yes, kiss me passionately a few more times, she thought. "No. Nothing else," she said, afraid to turn around and face him, especially now.

The sexual tension between them had moved from the living room into the kitchen, and she felt it. It was as thick as anything she'd ever known. Any other time she would have welcomed it with open arms, but not now, because it was for all the wrong reasons. She had dated enough to know how the male mind worked. He didn't want *her* per se. He just wanted a woman to fill the sexual void. As much as she loved him, she couldn't be that woman, because it would end up destroying their friendship. She knew it, and she felt deep down that he knew it as well. But temptation was temptation, just like hormones were hormones and testosterone was testosterone, and it seemed that all three were working against them.

Forcing a smile, she turned around and nearly wilted under Reese's dark, penetrating stare. "This is a new recipe I tried. I hope you like it," she said, moving away from the counter to head toward the table.

"I'm sure I will. But first I think we really do need to talk," he said in a voice so low she had to almost strain to hear him.

She shook her head. "Not if it's about what happened out there, Reese."

"But I feel I owe you an explanation—the right one. Because what you're assuming is all wrong."

"It doesn't matter. If you're worried about things changing between us because of what happened, they won't. And that's all I'm going to say about it. Please let it go. For both our sakes, you have to."

It was several moments before he responded. "Are you sure that's the way you want it, Kenna?"

What other way can there be? she wanted to scream. More than anything she would love to see him look at her the way she'd seen him look at other women who'd been by his side.

She met his gaze. "Yes, that's the way I want it."

He nodded slowly. "All right. Then that's how it's going to be."

He'd given in to her request. Reluctantly, he'd agreed to do what she'd asked. She avoided looking at him as she sat down at the table. She felt an uncomfortable silence surround them, and it nearly pierced her heart. For the first time in all the years they'd known each other, she and Reese were at an impasse, and there was nothing she could do about it.

Chapter 12

"Okay, Reese, what's going on with you and Kenna?" Mackenzie Standfield Madaris asked gently.

She had seen Kenna and her brother-in-law together enough times to know when something wasn't right between them. At family gatherings the pair had always been inseparable, but since they'd arrived in Oklahoma it seemed they were intentionally staying as far away from each other as they could.

Reese wasn't sure how to respond to his sister-in-law's question and was certain that others in his family had noticed the strain in his relationship with Kenna as well. It was eating away at him, and all because of a kiss. A kiss he'd initiated that should never have happened.

He gave Mac a look that all but said it really wasn't any of her business, but he was too polite to be so blunt. In response, she merely lifted a brow like she knew what he was thinking and wasn't having any of it.

Reese couldn't help but smile at the woman who had captured

his rodeo-superstar brother Luke's heart. In a way he could see how it had happened, since Mac was a beautiful woman who made men's heads turn when she walked into a room. But like him, Luke had been a loner, and the rodeo was his passion and his heart. Somehow Mac had entered his life and changed all that. Now it was Mac who took top billing in Luke's heart.

Although Luke had opened his rodeo school, everyone, including Mac, knew that eventually he would return to the rodeo circuit, if for no other reason than to make an occasional guest appearance.

"Go ahead and answer my question, Reese. I'm an attorney. I'll cross-examine you if I have to. Don't make me prove it."

He laughed. "Is that a threat?"

"No, I'm married to a Madaris. And I know you don't take threats lightly."

We don't take them at all, he thought, remembering some of the threats that had been made against members of his family. Mac had been threatened last year, and a few months ago Blade's wife, Sam, had been in danger.

"No, we don't," he agreed, "unless the person making the threat has a beautiful face." And she was definitely beautiful. But then so was Kenna.

He looked away from Mac and glanced across the room to where the object of his irritation was talking to some cowboy, one of Luke's friends from the rodeo. All he had to do was to study the man's expression and stance to know he was taken with her. Several of Luke's friends who'd met her tonight were. No surprise there.

He remembered how during dinner that night after they'd kissed, they had said very little to each other. He had helped her clean up the kitchen in an uneasy silence. Afterward, she'd said she needed to start packing for their trip, and she had raced off to her bedroom. He had retired to the basement to watch a movie. And there he had stayed most of the night.

She had been asleep when he'd left the next morning. When he got home that evening she had left a note saying she would be staying in town to have dinner with his cousins, who she'd gone shopping with that day.

He had been determined to see her and talk to her Friday night, but when she'd finally gotten home around nine, she claimed she was tired and rushed up to her room with her shopping bags in tow.

He knew she had deliberately been avoiding him, and the thought irritated him. By Saturday morning he was in a funk driving to the airport. His mood hadn't changed much since, especially when she was flirting with just about every cowboy at the party—and there were plenty of them.

"Flattery will get you just about anything, Reese Madaris," Mac said, interrupting his thoughts as she followed the direction of his gaze. "Except out of answering my question."

He turned toward her. He had always liked Mac, even before his brother Luke had finally realized his true feelings for her. She was his favorite sister-in-law, and then he smiled remembering that she was his *only* sister-in-law. But more important, he knew Mac was someone whom he could trust. And more than anything he could use a woman's perspective on a few things right now.

"I messed things up with Kenna, and I may have lost my best friend," he finally said, dropping his gaze from Mac to look down at the glass of wine he held in his hand. To Reese, his future seemed just as dark and murky as the red wine he'd been drinking.

"Messed things up how?"

Of course she would want details, he thought, glancing up at her and seeing how her dark penetrating eyes reflected her concern. "I kissed her."

He watched Mac expecting to see a look of shock. Instead, to his surprise, a smile touched the corners of her lips. "You actually kissed her?"

He frowned, wondering what she was smiling about. "Yes."

"Oh." Mac didn't say anything for a moment and then leaned in closer. "Was it a serious kiss? And by serious, I mean hot and heavy, or was it a platonic peck-on-the-lips kind of kiss?"

He wondered what difference that made when in either case it had been out of line. "It was serious—*very* serious."

And as far as he was concerned, it had been so serious his body still ached from the memory. When he remembered the way his tongue had explored her mouth, nearly drowning in her sweetness—a sweetness he should never have experienced—his heart literally skipped a beat.

"I'm going to ask you a question, Reese, and I don't want you to answer right now. What I want you to do is think about what your answer would be."

He was thoroughly confused, but he shrugged it off. "Okay."

She tilted her head at an angle that made her long, jet-black strands of hair brush up against his arm. "After the kiss—the very *serious* kiss—do you honestly want your best friend back, or do you want the passionate woman you now know Kenna is?"

Mac grinned at him before leaning over and placing a kiss on his cheek. She turned and then walked away.

Kenna remembered the last time she'd been to Oklahoma City. It had been to attend Sam's bridal shower a few months before. Reese had flown into Austin and they had rented a car to make the trip, taking their time to enjoy the sights along the way.

They'd had a lot to talk about. He was excited about his promotion and she was overjoyed about the job in Houston, even though she was nervous about all the pressure that came with the position. Reese had been able to calm her fears and boost her confidence, reassuring her that it was the perfect career move.

She quickly glanced across the room. Emotions overwhelmed

her when she caught sight of Reese. After arriving at the opening together, they'd gone their separate ways. Since they'd always acted as if they were joined at the hip when they'd attended his family's functions, Kenna was sure their behavior had raised some curious eyebrows. So far, no one had said anything about it. Not even Syneda, who knew her feelings for Reese.

Several women had flirted shamelessly with Reese, but Kenna had pretended not to notice. Now he was standing in a group with several of his cousins. They were all eye candy, every last one of them. But she only had the hots for Reese. The kiss they'd shared had ignited a passion that just wouldn't go away. So she avoided Reese as much as possible throughout the night.

"So tell me something about LaKenna James that I don't know."

The cowboy's question reined in her attention. His name was Ernest Keyes and he was on the same rodeo circuit that Luke had been on for years. He definitely was handsome, and had the word *cowboy* written all over him. But he had, through no fault of his own, one major flaw. He wasn't Reese Madaris. He didn't even come close.

Her attraction to Reese meant Ernest didn't have a fighting chance. "The list would be endless, since we just met tonight," she replied.

"Then I guess we need to do whatever we can to get to know each other better, sugar."

His deep, husky voice probably would have stoked sexual chemistry with any other woman, but not with her. There was no spark, not even a burning ember. Instead what she felt was sheer frustration. How in the world was she going to become interested in another man if she encountered emotional roadblocks at every turn?

"You don't believe in going easy on a girl, do you?" she said in response to Ernest's flirtation.

He winked at her. "No."

"I can't believe you're actually saying no to a woman, Ernest."

The deep, velvety voice made Kenna's heart pound in her chest as she braced herself for Reese, who came to stand beside Ernest.

Ernest's face broke into a smile of recognition. "Reese Madaris, it's been years. The last time I saw you, you were just starting college. Good seeing you again after all this time."

"Good seeing you as well," Reese said, smiling, even though anyone who knew him could easily see his smile didn't quite reach his eyes.

"And as far as me saying no—" Ernest grinned "—you came up on the tail end of the conversation. I was trying to convince this pretty little filly to blow this party with me."

"Really?" Reese said, staring at Kenna with eyes that seemed to see right through her. The even tone of his voice didn't fool Kenna. He was upset about something. "Well, before you convince her to do that, do you mind if I steal her for a dance?"

Not waiting for an answer, "Excuse us," Reese said, as he reached out and took Kenna's hand before leading her out to the dance floor.

A slow song was playing as Reese pulled Kenna into his arms. For the first time in their relationship he was at a complete loss for words. Nothing about his attraction to Kenna had made sense initially. He'd been so sure that seeing her through the eyes of an amorous man was a phase he would soon get over. But a part of him seriously doubted that he would, and deep down he knew it was more than just that kiss.

"The Madaris Construction Company did a great job building this place, didn't they, Reese?"

Her soft-spoken words heated something inside of him, and he tried concentrating on his surroundings instead of on her. She was right. The building that housed Luke's rodeo school was both massive and impressive, with two floors and several rooms. There was a classroom facility to help familiarize the students with all the rodeo equipment before moving outside to where the hands-on training took place. His cousins, who owned Madaris Construction, had been instrumental in bringing Luke's dream to life.

"Yes, they did," he agreed. "I remember when Slade first drew up the plans for it. I could envision just how it would look then. Slade and Blade did a great job."

Already Luke had a waiting list of eager students. And to top it off, the foal from Luke's stallion, Cisco, and Mac's buckskin mare, Princess, had been born a few weeks ago. Luke and Mac had been ecstatic. You would have thought they had given birth to their first child.

"Did I tell you how nice you look?" he asked, thinking *nice* was too mild a word to describe how sexy she looked.

"Yes, and you look nice, too."

"Thanks."

Kenna couldn't help but smile inside. She had just purchased the long, flowing, two-piece off-the-shoulder ensemble, with a neckline that accentuated her décolletage and a fitted bodice that showed off her small waist.

When she'd seen it, she thought the style was exquisite, despite the fact that the outfit had cost more than she'd intended to spend. But she had so desperately wanted to see Reese's reaction that it was well worth the price.

They were making small talk and they both knew it. Neither of them wanted to talk about what was really on their minds, which was the kiss that had somehow driven them apart.

"Ernest seems quite taken with you," said Reese, who quickly regretted the comment, since he was certain Kenna had heard the irritation in his voice.

"He's a nice guy."

"He likes women," he countered.

She angled her head and looked at him. "What man doesn't?"

"Curtis."

Kenna tried not to smile, but she couldn't suppress her laughter. This was the Reese she knew, the one who could make her laugh. Even when the subject wasn't supposed to be funny, he could find humor in it anyway.

"God, I needed to hear that again," he leaned in and whispered softly against her ear.

She smiled. "Hear what?"

"Your laugh."

It was then that she realized she hadn't laughed since that night he'd kissed her. Secretly, she smiled every time she thought about it. She practically glowed. But he hadn't known that.

"Trying to pretend nothing happened between us isn't working, Kenna. More than anything we need to talk about it."

She thought about arguing the point, but figured there was no use, especially when images of the kiss they'd shared continually looped in her head. "Why do we need to talk? Why can't we just move beyond what happened?"

"I honestly don't know."

She didn't know either. "Do you want to go outside and talk now?" she asked, deciding that they might as well get it over with.

He shook his head. "No, later. We can talk about it on our way back to the hotel."

They had opted to stay at a hotel in town instead of crowding Luke and Mac, like other guests attending the rodeo school opening. "All right."

It wasn't a conversation she was looking forward to.

"Mind if I cut in?"

Reese looked over his shoulder and smiled. It was Blade's brother-in-law, Angelo Di Meglio, an attorney from New York.

Despite Angelo's tall, dark and handsome good looks—he was a mixture of Italian and African-American—Reese didn't feel threatened by him so far as Kenna was concerned. Anyone could see Angelo Di Meglio was wearing his heart on his sleeve, and his heart belonged to Peyton Mahoney. Peyton had become close friends with Mac and Angelo's sister Sam in law school. The three women became law partners and had set up a firm in Oklahoma City. Sam moved to Houston after marrying Blade.

"No problem," Reese said to Angelo, stepping aside. He had every intention of reclaiming Kenna once she finished dancing with Angelo, in case Ernest got any ideas.

He walked over to the buffet table and smiled when he saw Peyton standing nearby talking to Christy. He wondered why Angelo was dancing with Kenna instead of with Peyton. He looked over his shoulder at Kenna and Angelo dancing, and saw that his eyes were glued to Peyton the entire time he was dancing with Kenna. Peyton, however, was oblivious to Angelo's attention.

A smile spread across Reese's lips. Although everyone else could see how Angelo felt about Peyton, it seemed she was still clueless. Hell, he had picked up on Angelo's romantic interest in Peyton at Luke and Mac's wedding more than a year ago. Reese wondered just how long Angelo was going to take before he let his feelings for Peyton be known.

Reese shrugged. He couldn't worry about Angelo and Peyton right now. He had his own issues with Kenna to deal with.

The woman got out of her car with a look of frustration. She couldn't believe she had a flat tire. Didn't she just buy new tires a few months ago?

She glanced at her watch and saw that she was already ten minutes late for her dinner meeting with a client. This was certainly not her night. She let out a sigh of relief when an SUV passed by but then slowed down and began to back up.

"Need help, miss?"

She knew she should be leery of strangers, but this time she would make an exception. Besides, it wasn't as if she was on a deserted street. Cars passed this way all the time. She looked at the man. "Yes, I got a flat."

"No problem. I can change it for you."

A smile touched her face as she watched the Good Samaritan park his SUV and get out. She noticed he was rather good-looking. "Hi," she said, smiling and extending her hand. "I'm Melanie."

He smiled back. "And I'm Eric. Let's see what you got," he said, bending down beside her tire. Moments later he stood up. "It's a slow leak, probably from running over a nail or something. You can get it repaired tomorrow. But what I need to do is change this tire. You do have a spare, don't you?"

She grinned. "Yes, it's in the trunk," she said, leading the way. "My husband always said he was going to show me how to change a tire, but so far he hasn't gotten around to it."

She opened the trunk.

"Boy, you've got a lot of space in here," he said.

"Yes. That's the main reason I bought this car. I'm a pharmaceutical rep and I usually have a lot of stuff to haul around," she said, leaning over to shift a few items around in the trunk to make it easier for him to get to the spare tire.

Those were the last words she said. The Samaritan hit her on the head with a wrench, knocking her out cold before shoving her into the trunk and quickly slamming down the hood before any cars passed by.

He smiled as the adrenaline surged through his veins. Tonight was going to be his night.

Chapter 13

Reese tossed his jacket across a chair once he settled into his hotel room. He and Kenna hadn't had a chance to talk like they'd planned, since his twenty-year-old cousin Victoria rode back to the hotel with them.

He glanced at his watch and saw it was almost two in the morning. When he and Kenna had left the party, there were still plenty of family members at Luke's place partying the night away. Even his parents had taken to the dance floor.

He unbuttoned his shirt, thinking how proud he was of his older brother. For a long time everyone assumed the rodeo circuit was going to be Luke's life, but now it was plain to see that Mac was. Luke had discovered he could have the best of both worlds—being married to Mac, operating the rodeo school and competing on the circuit. Luke was happy, and Reese was happy for him.

Now, Reese thought, if he could only find some of that happiness for himself. He plopped down in the chair and stretched his legs out. He thought about the question Mac had posed earlier that night. It definitely had made him think, and the answer he finally came up with hadn't really surprised him. He wasn't sure how Kenna was going to feel about it, but he no longer wanted her as his best friend. He definitely wanted more, especially after he'd reached the conclusion that his sudden attraction to Kenna hadn't been so sudden after all.

If he was honest with himself, he would have to admit that he'd always been conscious of her beauty. And the only reason he'd never acted on his attraction was because whenever he was free, she wasn't, and vice versa. Now, they were both unattached.

By nature he was pretty easygoing unless he was provoked. But seeing all those cowboys salivating over Kenna tonight had made him angry. He'd never been the jealous type where women were concerned, but he had been tonight—and at Alyson's party.

His phone rang and he wondered if it was Kenna. Their rooms were across the hall from each other, but she had seemed exhausted. And for that reason when he'd walked her to her room, he hadn't suggested that they talk.

"Hello?"

"You okay?"

Hearing Clayton's familiar voice, Reese glanced out the window at Oklahoma City's skyline. Down the street was where Madaris Construction was erecting the Mosley Building, and from the designs he'd seen, it was going to be a beautiful skyscraper—another landmark.

"Reese?"

A wry smile touched the corners of Reese's lips. "Yes, Clayton, I'm fine."

Reese remembered growing up that their older cousins—Justin, Dex and Clayton—had been their idols. Whenever the three brothers were home from college they would take their younger cousins to the movies, on cookouts or just to have fun on their uncle Jake's ranch. All the Madaris kids knew that if they ever needed to talk to one of them about anything, there was always an open door.

Of the three, Clayton was the most fun, since he was the most laid-back. He could relate to them despite being older. His philosophy was, there was nothing wrong with being naughty if you were nice every once in a while. Justin, who was the oldest of the three, always gave good advice. Dex was the serious one, and extremely loyal when it came to family.

At fourteen, Reese, Lee and Nolan saw their first *Playboy* centerfold browsing through some magazines they'd found in Clayton's apartment. Instead of getting angry, Clayton sat them down and gave them his version of the facts of life. Needless to say, Clayton Madaris's rendition had been far more interesting than the one their parents had told them. Of course all of them had known about the case of condoms Clayton kept in his closet. And they appreciated that he never kept an accurate count or else he would have noticed that they had swiped a few from time to time.

"Maybe I need to rephrase that question and ask is everything okay with you and Kenna?" Clayton said, breaking into Reese's thoughts. "Seems to me the two of you were avoiding each other most of the night."

"I'm not sure if everything is okay," he said truthfully. He paused again, unsure how to proceed. "I need to ask you a question, and your answer might help me figure something out."

"Okay, what do you want to know?" Clayton said.

"I've heard the story a number of times about how you and Syneda were nothing more than friends who decided to go on vacation together to Florida, right?"

"Yes, that's right. She was stressed at work, and since I had planned to go on vacation alone I figured I'd invite her to go along with me—enjoy the beach and loosen up a bit."

"So you're saying that before the trip you never noticed how attractive she was?" Reese asked.

He heard Clayton chuckle. "Hey, we're talking about Syneda. Of course I noticed how good she looked. I had eyes. I definitely wasn't blind. But I also knew she was off-limits."

"Why? Because she was your friend?"

"No, because she was Lorren's best friend. And at the time everyone knew my reputation. So the last thing Lorren would have wanted was for me to hook up with her best friend."

Lorren and Syneda had been best friends since childhood. And since Lorren was Justin's wife, she was family.

"But you got together anyway," Reese said.

"Yes. While we were on vacation together I began seeing Syneda in a whole new light. Funny what being under the same roof for a while will do. I became more aware of her than ever and felt an attraction that I couldn't ignore."

Reese nodded. "Did the two of you talk about it?"

Clayton chuckled. "Talk about it? There was nothing to talk about. Some things you don't waste time discussing. You act on it. Talking would have gotten us nowhere. Syneda would have tried to convince me that we would be ruining a perfectly good friendship if we got involved. I was determined to show her the benefits of a different kind of relationship."

Clayton paused. "Women are *show me* creatures, Reese. They prefer action to words. Talk is cheap. But to a woman, actions mean much more."

There was no sense in asking Clayton if he was sure of what he was talking about. "I don't know what's going on with you and Kenna," Clayton continued. "Although I think I have a pretty good idea. Now you realize that you just might want more than friendship out of your relationship, and you're not sure how it will affect the two of you."

"Yes, I've started seeing her in a whole new light as well. At first I felt guilty. And then I thought I would be crazy to risk losing her friendship."

"Hey, chill for a moment. There's nothing wrong with making the move from friends to lovers, Reese, trust me. But Kenna has to want to make the same move. Women can be difficult. They like to do things their way and in their own good time. Men have to be a step ahead, so you may have to use romantic persuasion to bring her around to your way of thinking."

Reese lifted a brow. *Romantic persuasion? Wasn't that just another term for seduction?* It had been years since he'd had to seduce a woman. Usually women would come on to him.

After Reese ended the call with Clayton he walked over to the window and looked out. Something was urging him to find out if the attraction between him and Kenna was one-sided. For some reason he didn't think so. In fact, every time he replayed their kiss in his mind and remembered the intensity of it, he was convinced that it wasn't. But he needed to know for certain. What if she had been fighting her attraction to him the same way he'd been fighting his desire for her all these years?

He was very well aware that finding out the truth was risky. What if she wasn't attracted to him and was repulsed by his advances? That would put an even bigger strain on their relationship, and possibly end it. He froze at the thought of losing the only woman who meant the world to him—the only woman who knew him better than he knew himself. Kenna was also the only woman he'd truly ever loved.

He leaned back against the windowsill as the alternative gripped him. He and Kenna had shared years of friendship, trust and respect. They knew how to laugh together, talk and even share their pain. He had been the one who'd held her when she'd learned of her grandmother's death. He was the one to sit beside her at the funeral, the one to stand beside her when the only family she had was lowered into the ground.

Likewise, she had been there waiting with his family at the

hospital after Clayton had been struck by a car. She had prayed with his family when Christy's husband, Alex, had been fighting for his life, and in happier times at many Madaris weddings.

He drew in a deep breath. Mac was right. He didn't want his best friend back. But there was something else she deserved, and that was to know there was a man who adored her in a way Terrence, Lamont or Curtis never had.

He felt a shudder that coursed through every muscle in his body. He would take things slow. He would be thorough. And LaKenna James wouldn't know what hit her until it was too late.

He smiled. He was going to enjoy using *romantic persuasion* to bring her around to his way of thinking. They had an early flight back to Houston, since Kenna had to start work on Monday morning.

It was time for her to realize that their kiss was just the beginning.

"So I would have wasted my time and yours trying to convince you that we would be ruining a perfectly good friendship?" Syneda said, leaning against the doorway of the bathroom in their hotel suite.

Clayton smiled as he turned toward his wife. His breath caught in his throat when he looked at her. She had some of the sexiest poses, especially standing there wearing a very short, seductive sheer negligee that sent heat sizzling through his veins. She gently rubbed her hand across her slightly protruding belly, evidence of *his* romantic persuasion.

"Oh, yes. I also can't forget how women can be difficult and like to do things their way and in their own good time," she added, "and that men have to be a step ahead and use romantic persuasion to sway a woman to your way of thinking."

He held out his arms. "Come here and let me kiss that pout off your lips."

She narrowed her gaze. "I'm not sure I want you to do that,

Madaris. You know how difficult we women can be, and how we enjoy doing things in our own good time."

"Is that a hint that I'll be suffering for a while?" he asked, his gaze roaming over her body before settling on her face, something that still took his breath away.

"What do you think?"

"I think I need to explain," he said, deciding it would be worth his while to get back in her good graces. "I was merely using us as an example—a very good one—to show how good friends can become lovers."

She crossed the room and stood in front of him. "And did you also tell him that friends make the best lovers?"

"We didn't get that far. Besides, there are some things Reese and Kenna will have to figure out on their own."

"That's true."

He reached out and grabbed her hand and pulled her into his arms. "How's my son doing?"

Syneda smiled. "He's misbehaving like his old man does every once in a while. It's after two in the morning and he hasn't settled down yet. Sound familiar?"

Clayton beamed proudly. "I can see he's going to be a party animal."

"Whatever." A slight frown settled on her face. "I just hope Reese realizes he cares for Kenna. Men can be so slow."

"I was never slow," Clayton responded.

Syneda smiled. "No, you were too fast for your own good. But I guess I shouldn't complain, should I?" she said, wrapping her arms around his neck. "Umm, how about a little of that romantic persuasion you seem to know so much about?"

He pulled her closer into his arms and smiled. "Ready when you are."

He let himself into his apartment, closed the door and locked it behind him. His face split into a huge grin. What a night. He threw the bag he was carrying on the table and a single shoe fell out. It was a nice one—a round-toe black pump with a three-inch heel. He was too tired to pick it up now and would wait until morning to add it to his collection.

He headed for the bathroom to take a shower and to administer first aid. She'd had the nerve to try and fight him once she came to. In a way, he liked that, and had even let her think that she was getting the best of him for a while. When he'd gotten tired of playing games, he'd taught her a lesson. She learned the hard way never to forget the proverbial parental warning: never talk to strangers.

Chapter 14

"Here, let me take care of that," Reese said, leaning over Kenna after she slid into the leather seat of his truck.

"There's no need, Reese, I can buckle my own seat belt." He either didn't hear her or was pretending he hadn't. Too late, the friction she felt whenever he was near coursed through her body in reaction to his masculine scent.

They had caught an early-morning flight out of Oklahoma City and now they were back in Houston and it wasn't eight o'clock yet. Reese had left his SUV at the airport, and it didn't take long to locate it in the parking lot.

She watched as he walked around the truck to get in on the other side, remembering how difficult it had been to sit beside him on the small plane. He hadn't had much to say, which had been fine with her. It had given her a chance to close her eyes and catch up on the sleep she hadn't gotten the night before.

After Reese had walked her to her hotel room, she had gotten ready for bed, but wasn't sure if he would eventually knock on her door to talk. He never showed up, and since he hadn't mentioned anything about it this morning, she could only assume he had changed his mind, which was fine with her.

"You want to stop for breakfast somewhere or do you want me to take you straight home?" he asked her, after getting inside the truck and fastening his seat belt.

She smiled thinking how easy it was for him to think of his home as hers. "No, I'm fine. It's still early. I can make breakfast when we get there."

"I'll help," he said, glancing over at her before putting the key in the ignition.

"Okay." *She'd said okay, but she wasn't really sure. With both of them in the kitchen, things could get overheated. Still, she was certain she would feel the heat more than he would.*

"Did you enjoy the party, Kenna?"

She glanced over at him. "Yes. That's one of the things I enjoy about your family. They love getting together and having a good time."

He chuckled. "Yes, the Madarises will find just about any reason to throw a party."

"This time, it was a special occasion. I think Luke opening up a rodeo school is wonderful. Is he seriously thinking about opening up one here in Houston in another year or two?"

"Yes, he's serious," Reese said, reaching to turn on the radio to get a traffic update. Even though it was a Sunday morning, there were sometimes traffic jams with people going to early-morning church service.

He was surfing the channels. "Wait! Hold it," Kenna said. "I want to listen to the news report."

"Again, we repeat," the reporter said, "the body of a twenty-eight-year-old Houston woman was found by joggers in a ditch off Long Weather Road this morning. The body has yet to be identified. However, according to police several items of clothing were missing, including one of her shoes..."

"Oh, no," Kenna said, groaning.

Reese glanced over at her with concern. "What's wrong?"

"I need to get a full news report. I hope it's just a coincidence that the murdered woman's shoe is missing."

"Why?"

"It might be the work of a serial murderer known as the 'Shoe Killer.' He rapes, tortures and kills his victims and then takes one of their shoes."

Reese frowned. "Why would he do that?"

"Probably some kind of souvenir. So far, he's killed more than a dozen women across the country, mostly in the Midwest. He killed six women in the Minneapolis area last year. I hope he hasn't resurfaced in Houston."

"Have there been any leads, any witnesses?"

"No, there haven't been any survivors."

It took a little longer than usual for them to get home, since Reese decided to stop at a roadside market and get some fresh fruit. The moment they walked through the door Kenna turned on the television.

"You want me to take this up to your room?" Reese asked, holding her carry-on bag that he had taken out of the trunk.

"Yes, please. And where is everyone? The place looked deserted when we pulled up."

"Most of the hands usually go to church on Sunday morning or visit with family and friends in town." He chuckled. "Some of the men stay out late on Saturday nights and sleep in on Sunday mornings to recover."

Reese came back downstairs moments after putting their bags in their rooms. "I'm going to check things out and then I'll be back to help you with breakfast."

"I'll probably be finished by then," she said as she began watering several plants in the living room. The plants had been given to her by coworkers and friends as going-away gifts. She intended to keep them alive and move them to her new place once it was completed.

She released a deep sigh when the door closed behind Reese. So much for thinking that things were back to normal between them. Although they weren't acting as skittish around each other as they had a few days ago, she was more aware of his presence than ever before.

He had knocked on her hotel room around five that morning and she had opened the door to find him standing there, sexier than any man had a right to look at that hour of morning. He was wearing a pair of jeans, a pullover shirt and aviator sunglasses, and was holding a cup of hot coffee in his hand.

He had handed her the cup of coffee before grabbing her overnight bag and then quickly ushered her down the hall to the elevator. By the time they'd made it to the ground floor, she had given him back the cup of coffee to drink. It was only then that she remembered what Alyson had said.

It was hard to believe she'd never paid much attention to how often they drank from the same cup of coffee or bottle of beer. And in all honesty, she wouldn't have noticed if Alyson hadn't pointed it out during her tirade. Now that she had, every time Kenna thought about it she felt an intense ache deep down.

The news report grabbed her attention and she turned up the volume on the flat-screen TV.

According to the reporter, the body had been positively identified as Melanie Tate, who had been killed just one month shy of her first wedding anniversary. It was heartbreaking to hear the details, she thought. *Such a senseless murder.*

Kenna turned off the television and made her way to the kitchen. When she'd worked for the Austin PD, she'd had a few friends in the homicide division. That's when she'd first heard about the "Shoe Killer" investigation, and knew that law enforcement didn't have any leads yet. A shudder ran through Kenna's body. She knew there was a distinct possibility that the

Houston PD might be dealing with a copycat, or it could be the real "Shoe Killer."

She had already put the frozen chicken in the microwave to thaw when the back door opened and Reese walked in. He smiled at her and she immediately felt her nipples harden. "Everything's okay?" she asked.

"Yes. Joe's here and so are a few other ranch hands. They were watching the news report about the woman who was murdered."

Kenna nodded. "My heart goes out to her family."

Suddenly she felt a pressing need to change the subject. "I thought we would have a light meal today. I'll make a salad and steam some veggies if you'll cook the chicken."

He nodded as he headed over to the sink to wash his hands. "How do you want it?"

She shrugged. "Any way you want."

His deep, dark, penetrating gaze lingered on her face for a while.

She noticed how his nostrils flared. It was too late when she realized what she'd said. She tried to ignore the fierce pounding of her heart, and tried convincing herself that she was just imagining things. Her fantasies were just running wild. But if that was the case, how could she explain the look in Reese's eyes that was holding her hostage and making the air around them sizzle with sexual tension? She nervously licked her lips with the tip of her tongue and watched his gaze track her every move.

He smiled. It was a smile that was so full of carnal desire it nearly took her breath away. It was then that she realized he had wiped his hands on the kitchen towel and was moving toward her. She bit her bottom lip when he stopped and stood in front of her. She swallowed and tried to ignore the pressure she felt building at the juncture of her thighs, making that part of her body feel sensitive and achy. "Reese?" she said quietly, searching his face and admiring the deep, rich, coppery skin. "Is anything wrong?"

His grin was quick. And it made her suddenly feel wet and hot.

"No, there's nothing wrong. But since I have the option of doing it any way I want, I think I want to do it this way. And this time I won't apologize."

He backed her against the kitchen counter, trapped her between his arms—which were on either side of her—and proceeded to meld her body to his masculine length. A shiver of awareness trailed over her skin, and before she could completely exhale, he sucked her breath right off her lips as he leaned in to kiss her.

Incredible, Reese thought. Capturing Kenna's tongue and mating with it so intensely, he felt his entire body become aroused like never before. This was what he wanted. This was what he needed, and this was definitely the way it should always be. Their first kiss had been good, but this one was even better.

The last time they'd kissed he'd only gotten a sample of her soft lips, a taste of her sweetness. Now he was practically drowning in the flavor of her, savoring her spiciness and eating away at her mouth with a hunger so desperate it erased any misgivings he had about taking their relationship to the next level. His tongue stroked every inch of her mouth so possessively that it had her moaning.

He liked the sound of it. He wanted more as he continued to claim and possess her mouth in a way that he'd never experienced with any other woman. The lower part of his body began to throb as he felt his desire rising. His lips made tortured demands that he intended for her to heed.

There was no hesitation on her part. She returned his kiss with equal fervor, but for all the wrong reasons Reese believed. He knew she thought he was just horny, willing to temporarily set aside their friendship to fulfill his needs. Boy, was she wrong, and he would enjoy proving to her just how wrong she was.

In the distance, he heard the faintest sound of vehicles approaching, as some of the men began returning to the ranch. It was time to take one final taste of her mouth for now, he thought, as he slowly broke off the kiss.

In a daze Kenna studied Reese's face, silently acknowledging what they'd just shared. They had kissed a second time and again he had been the one to initiate it. She decided to sort out her emotions later. But for now, all she wanted was to savor his kiss—so intense that it left a lingering sting on her lips.

He had said he wasn't going to apologize this time. And that meant there would be no regrets. He had wanted her—the bulge of his erection pressed against her had been evidence of that. But now as the gravity of the moment was setting in, she wondered what he was thinking.

She pulled in a sharp breath when he reached out to trace her jawline with his fingertip as his gaze held hers. She quickly concluded that he'd decided not to think about their dilemma—at least not now. A ragged moan escaped her lips when he slowly lowered his fingertip to trace a path down her neck toward to the center of her breasts. He moved his finger to the right, and rubbed it back and forth against her blouse.

She watched the movement of his hand before slowly returning her gaze to his face. "I thought we were talking about the chicken," she said throatily, her voice overwhelmed with arousal. She felt a tremor of desire ease up her spine as her gaze held his deep, dark penetrating eyes.

"What makes you think we weren't?"

As unexpectedly as his seduction had started, it ended when he released her and he walked over to the sink.

Chapter 15

Kenna had been quiet through most of their dinner, Reese noticed as he helped clear the table. If she was in shock from the kiss they'd shared earlier, she hadn't seen anything yet, he thought. He loved her and he intended to do whatever he had to do to put those words into action and show her just what she meant to him.

Admittedly, part of what he felt was physical—unadulterated sexual desire. After all he had a healthy libido and had gone without sex for months. But he was also in love with the woman he craved so desperately. When they shared a bed, it wouldn't be purely sexual. He would be sharing his body, his mind and his soul with the woman who had his heart.

He leaned against the counter and watched as she tried to avoid eye contact. He knew that she knew he was looking at her. Reining in his desire for her wasn't going to be easy, but he intended to try. "Dinner was good," he said, trying to break the ice.

She glanced over at him. "My part was easy." She gestured toward the leftover chicken on the stove. "You're the one who had the hard part. And the chicken was delicious, by the way."

"Thanks."

A few moments passed. "Reese?"

He looked at her intently. "Yes?"

He saw her swallow hard. "You don't have to help me clean up the kitchen. I can handle it alone."

He shrugged. "We've always cleaned up the kitchen together whenever we share a meal, Kenna. Why change now?" he asked innocently, as if he hadn't practically mauled her mouth a short while ago. The memory of it only heightened his awareness of how much he wanted her.

"I know, but..."

"But, what?"

She held his gaze for a second and then shook her head. "Nothing."

Oh, he would gladly show her what *nothing* meant. "Come on. Let's clean up the kitchen together."

"I do need to ask you something first," she said softly, looking everywhere but at him.

He leaned back against the counter. "You can ask me anything, Kenna. You know that."

She nodded then shifted her gaze to look him squarely in the eyes. "Why did you kiss me again?"

He focused on her mouth. "Because I didn't get enough of the taste of you the first time," he said, omitting the fact that it was even better than he remembered.

They stared at each other for the longest while. Neither said anything. He began to wonder just how long it would take before one of them broke the silence. "But you apologized for kissing me the first time."

He heard something akin to hurt in her voice, and it was at that moment he understood the reason for it. It wasn't about the kiss. She was hurt by his apology. He knew he had to backtrack and clear things up with her. "I wasn't apologizing for kissing you that day, Kenna," his voice deep with emotion. "I was apologizing because I enjoyed it too much, and if it had been left up to me things wouldn't have stopped at just a kiss."

He saw her blink in confusion and then he continued. "Look, I know you think you have this whole thing figured out, and in your mind the only reason that I'm coming on to you is because I'm hard up."

"Isn't it? Men have needs. And as far as I know, you haven't been sleeping with anyone since Alyson. You're not the type of man who would get involved with a woman just to satisfy his sexual needs," she said quietly.

He rubbed his hand across his face. Clayton was right when he said women could be difficult at times. "Yet knowing that about me you think I'd take advantage of you in that way?"

"Honestly, I don't know what to think anymore. So tell me, Reese, why would a man who wanted nothing more than to be my best friend before last week now want something else when nothing has changed between us?"

But everything had changed. He'd always been sexually aware of her, but had downplayed the attraction. Because they were both unattached now, he felt free to explore what else there could be. Evidently she hadn't figured that out yet, and there was no reason to spell it out for her. Actions spoke a hell of a lot louder than words when it came to winning a woman over, according to his cousin Clayton.

There was no reason to assume that just because he'd realized he was in love with her that the feeling was mutual. But that didn't mean that one day it wouldn't be. In fact, he planned on making sure that day came, and soon.

"A lot has changed, Kenna," he finally said. "We're living under the same roof now."

She rolled her eyes. "Your point?"

He slowly moved closer to her, trying to tamp down the rampant sexual urge stirring in him with every step. “The point, LaKenna James,” he said when he stopped directly in front of her, “is for whatever reason, there’s sexual chemistry between us that is now out in the open. You want me as much as I want you, and I intend to be honest about it and not try to hide from it. I know you better than any man on earth. I know you mentally and emotionally more than anything. I want to get to know you sexually.”

He saw fire leap into her eyes—raging fire, angry fire. “And what happens after I move into my own place? When I’m no longer living under your roof? Don’t you understand what we could stand to lose if we embark on a sexual relationship? There’s no way we’d be able to go back to being best friends after being lovers, Reese.”

A part of him wanted to tell her the truth—that he had no intention of them ever going back to the way it was. This was final. And he would make sure she felt the same way about him that he felt about her. “I don’t want to think about the future, Kenna. I just want what we have now.”

Okay, so he’d told a little white lie, but he knew Kenna. “Let’s table this discussion for now,” he suggested. “I’ll help you clean up the kitchen, then we can watch a movie and relax. You’re overthinking this,” he added.

“And you don’t think I should?” she snapped.

Suddenly, his need to make her understand some of what he was feeling became paramount. He moved closer to her, forcing her to retreat, pressing her back toward the counter. She was trapped. He was unnerving her, and in response to his closeness he heard her take in a sharp breath. Then he reached out and cupped her chin to tilt her head to meet his gaze. “What I suggest you spend your time thinking about is this.”

He lowered his mouth and seized her lips and tongue so passionately and so possessively that he felt it all the way to his groin. Pressing his lips against hers he proceeded to devour her, ravish her mouth and savor the tantalizing taste of her. He noticed that she had not pushed him away, but was kissing him back, displaying as much hunger as he was.

He sank his mouth deeper into hers, while pressing the thick ridge of his erection against her feminine mound. They were fully clothed, but it seemed their bodies refused to acknowledge anything separating them. The only problem he had with that was a burning desire to have nothing between them.

God, he loved the taste of her mouth, loved the way her tongue mated with his, the way her breasts were rubbing against his chest. And he loved the fact that she was just as ravenous as he was. His senses were spinning out of control, making him greedy and making feasting on her lips his immediate obsession.

When he heard the sound of Joe's voice as he approached the house, Reese tore his mouth from Kenna and released her. "Go on upstairs, take a long, leisurely bath and relax," he whispered softly. "You need to be well rested for your first day on the job tomorrow. I'll finish cleaning up the kitchen."

Silence hung in the air between them and he saw the uncertainty in her gaze. It had been hard sitting across from her at dinner. Desire had nearly consumed him, but he had fought to maintain control.

And he was fighting to maintain it now.

"You sure you don't mind?" she asked.

"I'm positive. Go on, I'll be fine."

She paused a few moments before moving around him, her tantalizing scent lingering in her wake. It was then that he drew in a deep breath, closed his eyes and leaned back against the kitchen counter as a rush of emotions flooded him. He knew that if he were to march upstairs and tell her how he truly felt, that he loved her not just as his best friend but as the woman he wanted to spend his life with, she wouldn't believe him. He hadn't given her a reason to do so yet.

For the first time in his life he was going to try his hand at winning a woman over, and he wasn't beyond pulling out all the stops to accomplish it.

In spite of having taken a long, leisurely bath like Reese suggested and getting into bed early with a good book, Kenna was still wide awake. It was midnight. She sat up in bed trying to vent her pent-up anxiety. She knew the reason she couldn't get to sleep: every time she closed her eyes, Reese's face appeared. Now, however, she was seeing him through different eyes.

She knew how it felt to be caught in his intense gaze and to feel his lips, knowing exactly how they tasted and just how they felt. But she didn't need to know any of those things to realize how much she loved him. Her feelings had been there for years, hidden. In the past, she'd never had a real reason to think about it. She just accepted it for what it was and knew eventually one day the right woman would come along and capture his heart. A part of her believed, and still did, that eventually she would meet a man who would marry her and give her the family she wanted.

Since she couldn't sleep, she decided to go downstairs and watch a movie. Even if she didn't stay awake through the entire movie, she would watch it long enough to fall asleep and wake up ready to start her new job.

Getting out of bed, she slipped into her robe and walked to the door and peeked out. It was dark and quiet. She glanced across the hall at Reese's room. She'd heard him come upstairs and go to his room hours ago, so more than likely he was asleep.

She closed the bedroom door behind her and tiptoed across the hall, trying not to make a sound. She quietly headed downstairs to the basement. She had been in Reese's home enough times to know her way around the basement in the dark. Her heart pounded with excitement in anticipation of watching her favorite movie. No matter how many times she saw it, she loved *Mr. and Mrs. Smith*.

The LED lighting along the floor of Reese's home theater guided her path. She turned on the light switch after crossing the room to where Reese kept his DVD library. She paused, sensing an unexpected surge of heat.

Reese knew the moment Kenna entered the room, even before she turned on the light. He wished she hadn't, because the LED lights embedded in the floor illuminated her short nightgown, making it obvious that she was wearing nothing underneath. And it was clear just what a voluptuous, curvy body she had.

He was sitting in one of the seats in the back of the home theater, so she didn't notice him. Desire was surging through every part of his body, and those erotic dreams that had awakened him were there in living color.

"I'm here, Kenna," he finally said. His voice sounded husky and deep, even to his own ears.

"Reese!" she said with a gasp, turning around and looking in the direction of his voice. "What are you doing up? I thought you were in bed."

"I couldn't sleep," he said, easing out of the leather seat and slowly walking toward her. "I take it you had the same problem."

Kenna swallowed as Reese moved toward the light. He was shirtless, and his jeans hung low on his hips. His wide shoulders and the well-defined muscles of his upper arms were proof he worked out regularly. She began to feel warm just looking at him. He was beautiful, muscular and built to perfection.

"Kenna?"

"Yes?" She averted her eyes from his body and looked at his face. She was embarrassed to realize he'd noticed her checking him out.

He smiled. "I said I take it you couldn't sleep either."

"No," she replied. "I couldn't sleep and thought I'd watch a movie."

He nodded slowly. "And I just finished watching one."

"Oh. Which one?"

"Mr. and Mrs. Smith."

She laughed softly. They had gone to see it together when the movie first hit theaters. He had enjoyed all the action, and she had appreciated the romance. "That's what I was going to watch, too."

"It's already loaded. Here's the remote."

"Thanks."

The moment their fingers touched she jerked away when she felt a surge of electricity. She inhaled a deep, uneven breath. "I guess you're on your way back to bed now, right?"

His eyes gazed down at hers. "Are you trying to get rid of me?"

"Of course not. In case you've forgotten, this is *your* house."

"I haven't forgotten, and if I remember correctly, this home theater was *your* idea."

She couldn't help but smile. She'd known he would appreciate a media room since he enjoyed watching movies as much she did. In college, they'd often gone to the movies together. "Are you complaining?"

"No, in fact this room has given me a lot of enjoyable hours, even when I'm not watching a movie. It's peaceful and quiet, and this is where I come when I need to think."

"And it seems I interrupted you. I'm sorry."

"Don't apologize. Besides, I was thinking about you."

She swallowed. "Were you?"

"Yes."

She wanted to ask him for details, but decided she was better off not knowing. "Then I'll leave you alone with your thoughts. Good night."

She turned to leave, and he reached out and grabbed her hand. The touch was electrifying. It sent sparks and a swell of warmth through her body. She tried to pull her hand away but Reese held tight. She glanced down at the hand holding hers and then looked into his face. It was filled with a heated emotion she'd never seen before. "Reese?"

"I just need to hold you for a minute, Kenna," he said in a voice laced with such raw need that she felt it in her own body.

She hesitated and then without saying a word she moved closer to him as he pulled her into his arms and held her tight. Laying her head on his chest she closed her eyes, thinking that if this was a dream she didn't want to wake up. How many times had she envisioned Reese holding her this way?

She breathed in his manly scent and felt the unevenness of his respiration. Slowly she became aware of the erection pressing against her, and she instinctively angled her body closer to him.

He rumbled a low groan in her ear and lowered his hands from her waist to settle them on her backside, pulling her even closer. It was as if he wanted her to feel the strength of his desire. And what she felt had nothing to do with friendship.

She couldn't ever recall responding to any man so quickly and easily. And knowing the man generating that reaction was Reese made the lower part of her body, which was tightly pressed against him, ignite in anticipation.

As her head nestled against his chest, she could feel his heart pound, and his pulse begin to race.

And talk about hard…

As if on cue, his erection began to throb against her body as he became more engorged. She heard him moan just as he cupped the back of her head and tilted her face to look up at him. And for a tense, sexually charged moment they simply stared at each other.

Kenna wasn't sure how long he planned to stand there looking at her, seducing her with his gaze while her heart beat wildly. His eyes shifted lower and became fixated on her mouth. She nervously licked her lips in response, which elicited a deep groan from his throat just seconds before he dipped his head down and kissed her.

Reese wasn't sure just what it was, but something in him snapped, and he was kissing Kenna as if his life depended on it. And she was returning the kiss in equal measure as his tongue probed her mouth from one end to the other, touching and tasting everything.

The greedy exchange incinerated any thoughts about taking things slow. He was hot and wanted to share his heat with her. He cupped her backside and slid her nightgown above her waist, so that the bulge of his erection would graze her skin. That still wasn't enough. He broke off the kiss and reached for the front of her gown. Reese knew that tearing Kenna's nightie was insanity, but at that moment he didn't care. He wanted them skin to skin. He wanted to feel the heat of her flesh against his. But more than anything, he wanted to know how it felt for his thickness to be inside her.

He heard her take in a sharp breath when he ripped the gown and tossed it to the floor. Before she could voice her displeasure, he cupped her bare breast in his hand, lowered his head and sucked a hardened nipple into his mouth.

"Reese!"

His lips moved from one torrid nipple to the other. He glanced up at her face and saw the fiery look in her eyes, which made his body throb even more, and reignited a passion to taste her all over.

He continued to pay homage to her breasts with his mouth, using his tongue to trace a pattern across her velvety skin, licking and pulling her nipples before trailing kisses along her throat and then using the tip of his tongue to retrace his movements in slow, downward, sensuous strokes.

"What are you doing to me, Reese?"

Her voice shuddered and responded in a way that revealed her desperate need for him. He heard it. He detected it in her breathing. He noticed it in her scent. "Umm, let's find out together," he said, breathing the words close to her ear. His hand began to roam over her body and slide between her legs, where he discovered she was primed and ready for him.

"Oh, Reese."

Now it was Kenna who found his lips, Kenna whose tongue became more adventurous and explored his mouth from one corner to the other. While she indulged his mouth, Reese's hands were between her legs—spreading her thighs and inserting his finger inside of her, making slow, circular motions deep in her wetness.

She broke off the kiss, threw her head back and quietly uttered his name deep in her throat. Her knees became weak as he swept her naked body into his arms.

Knowing there was no way he could make it upstairs to the bedroom, he placed her in one of the leather chairs and pushed the button to fully recline the seat. He took a step back as his eyes roamed over her naked body. She was gorgeous.

"I was afraid for you to see me naked," she whispered. Her words were so soft he barely heard them.

"Why? You're beautiful."

She shook her head. "There's so much more of me."

He came and knelt down beside her. *More to love,* he thought. "And I wouldn't have it any other way," he whispered.

He leaned forward to pick up where he'd left off—tasting her skin, drawing her nipple into his mouth and suckling it with a need that had his groin throbbing.

He kissed her again, all the while moving his hand over her curvy body. He palmed her thighs, stroked her stomach and drew circles around her feminine mound before running his fingers through the damp curls covering it.

She moaned into his mouth and he nearly exploded. He released her mouth so that his lips could slowly travel down her body. When he reached her waist, he placed kisses around her belly button.

He lifted his head and met her heated gaze. "I want to taste you," he said huskily, his hands planted between her legs.

And before she could say anything, as if he was half-crazy with lust, he dipped his head low, spreading her thighs even wider to receive his mouth. The touch of his tongue to her flesh had Kenna arching her back off the recliner. He thought he'd never tasted anything so delicious. His tongue delved deeper and with its own greedy rhythm he strummed and licked her into an orgasm.

He felt her body explode in his mouth, getting a taste of her. The sensation made her moan as she squirmed frantically from the sexual torture of his tongue, grabbing hold of his head to keep his mouth in place.

It was only when the last wave of ecstasy had passed that he removed his mouth from her, stood in front of her fully erect and took off his clothes. He slid his jeans down his legs and then rolled a condom over his engorged shaft. He glanced at Kenna. Her eyes were closed and her thighs were still spread. Her breasts were full and firm, with hardened nipples that were ready for his lips.

"You haven't gone to sleep on me, have you?" he asked softly.

He watched her eyes flicker open and saw the satisfied smile that touched her lips. "No, I haven't gone to sleep on you."

"Good, because I intend to keep you awake for a while," he said, straddling her body in the recliner. He lowered his body atop hers, then inhaled deeply when his shaft gently brushed against her satiny thigh. "I don't want you to think this is all we're going to do," he said in a throaty voice. "I just enjoy feeling my way around."

He continued to feel his way around her body, grazing his shaft against her bare thighs and using his fingers to massage her clitoris. She reached up to stroke his shoulders. He glanced down at their bodies and saw the head of his erection pointed just where it belonged, and held her gaze as he slid his shaft inside her, easing into her wet warmth and filling her completely. When her inner walls became tighter, he drew in a deep breath before sliding back out and then easing back in with a hard thrust.

He could feel her muscles clench him, tighten around him, and start milking him in a fevered way. And then he began moving, riding her, stroking her and mating with her. He could hear her moans with his every stroke and the sound urged him on, made him want her even more.

When she arched her back and tilted her hips to take him even deeper, he obliged by pumping her even harder, with concentrated strokes.

Then his body exploded, obliterating his thoughts and his doubts. He couldn't utter a word—nothing. Not his desire. Not his need. Not even his love. He knew she wasn't ready to hear him declare his love just yet, but she could feel this. She had to.

Moments later, when Kenna exploded in another orgasm, he was there, smothering her moans and groans with his lips. It was fitting that the best lovemaking of his life had been with Kenna, the only woman he'd ever loved. He felt a satisfaction he'd never experienced before flowing through his body. And it made him hard all over again.

As if on cue, Kenna's inner muscles clenched his shaft mercilessly, almost driving him over the edge again. He was ready for another round. Indeed, his body demanded it—just not here. He wanted her in his bed.

He looked up at her face and trailed a series of kisses along her neck and the underside of her ear before easing off her, immediately feeling the loss of their intimate connection.

She moaned in protest before he leaned over and swept her into his arms. He looked down into her glassy eyes. “Don’t worry. I don’t plan to be away for long.”

Chapter 16

"I don't know if I'll be ready for work in the morning," Kenna said, groaning as her body ached from an overdose of pure sexual ecstasy.

They were lying on their sides facing one another, their legs entwined, with Reese still embedded inside her. It was a good thing she was on the Pill, she thought, since every time he came, he would come hard. But instead of being satisfied, her vaginal muscles would contract, trying to pull even more out of him.

"I'll set the alarm," he said, as if that would make getting up any easier.

She lifted a brow. "It will take more than an alarm clock to get this body in gear in the morning, Reese," she said sleepily. "It wouldn't look good if I missed my first day of work, would it?"

"No, it wouldn't."

"I was afraid you would say that."

They hugged and then she tried pushing him away. "Stop that!"

He smiled innocently. "Stop what?"

"You're getting bigger and harder inside of me. Maybe staying connected this way isn't such a good idea after all."

"I've never gone to sleep with a woman this way," he whispered snuggling even closer to her. "But now I can't sleep unless I'm still inside of you."

She groaned again. Reese could turn her on just by what he said, and over the past few hours he'd said a lot. He could arouse her with his words. When they were making love, he would tell her just what he was doing to her, how he was doing it and the outcome he intended to achieve. In the end, she had writhed, whimpered and practically begged him for mercy. And he'd given her just what she wanted, thrusting into her, driving deeper into her and stroking her into orgasm after orgasm. Reese Madaris was definitely a bad boy.

He moved his thigh, shifting their bodies and making her groan again. He was huge and throbbing. She glanced over his shoulder at the clock. Was it really almost three in the morning? Wasn't she supposed to get up at six?

"Umm, what are you thinking about?"

She glanced back at him and saw he was watching her through glassy, lustful eyes. She drew in a deep breath. "I was wondering how your family and friends will feel once they know there's more between us than just friendship."

"In our defense, we didn't know." He paused for a moment. "Although I've always thought that you were hot."

Her sleepy eyes widened. "Really? You never told me."

He smiled. "I couldn't. You were always involved with someone else and I don't believe in trespassing on another man's territory. Besides, I tried not to think of my best friend as being hot."

"Oh. What happened this time? What was the difference?"

"I couldn't help myself."

Neither could she. But then her attraction grew out of love. His was merely a matter of satisfying his sexual needs, and in this case she was more than happy to oblige. What were best friends for?

She felt the throbbing from his erection increase and realized that he'd reached the same conclusion: that best friends made the best bed partners.

"You want to come again?"

He had the nerve to ask her that, while his finger traced slow circles around her hardened nipples. "Hmm, haven't I come enough already?"

"No." And then to show that he was serious he leaned in and began licking her nipples. He pulled back and smiled. "You're getting wet."

Drenched was more like it, she thought, and wondered how he could tell when she was always well lubricated around him. He shifted again and her breath caught when his embedded erection went deeper into her.

"What are we going to tell everyone?" she asked in order to get her mind off what he was doing to her.

"I doubt we'll have to tell them anything. They will figure it out eventually."

And then what? she thought. *Should I tell them this is a phase we're going through, an exploratory phase that doesn't really mean anything other than satisfying each other's sexual needs?*

"This time I want to watch you."

She was a little apprehensive at the prospect of that. "Why? Besides, I'm pretty sure you've already seen me tonight."

He chuckled. "I don't remember. This time I plan on giving you my full attention."

Any more of his attention would probably do her in, she thought. Before she could say anything the lower part of his anatomy began moving. He began thrusting into her, in and out, in slow, torturous, deliberate, concentrated strokes.

He held her gaze as if he wanted to see every facial expression, every breath, every moan she made when she climaxed. He leaned in slightly as if deciding to shift the tempo, adjust the rhythm. Yet all she could do was gaze at him with bedroom eyes that revealed an intense fervor and longing.

When she couldn't take it anymore, when the pleasure was too much, she felt him take control. She met his every thrust as her muscles greedily gripped him tightly. It was then that she felt his explosion, felt the essence of him saturate her womb. She began trembling as she watched him through lowered eyelids. He came and then came again, but he refused to close his eyes. He growled deep in his throat as he kept surging deeper inside her.

And then she came, more forcefully than ever before. She called out his name as back-to-back orgasms ripped through her. She clenched her teeth, refusing to cry out, but ultimately succumbed and let out a passionate, primal scream.

He quickly covered her mouth with his, drowning out her voice. When would enough be enough? *There had to be a limit to this,* she thought. *Hadn't there?*

She had her answer when Reese maneuvered his body to mount her. And they were on again, as they gave his mattress another workout. She couldn't help wondering what the morning would bring.

Reese reached out and turned off the alarm before looking over at Kenna. She hadn't moved. She'd only gotten a couple of hours sleep and he was feeling guilty. Guilty, but totally and completely satisfied.

Never had he enjoyed making love to a woman so much, and knowing that woman had been Kenna sent shudders through his body. It was then that he remembered he was still embedded in her. Like he'd told her, that was a first. With any other woman he would have rushed to the bathroom, disposed of the condom and then spent a few minutes of time alone before returning to the bed—that is, if he had a desire to return. Usually, he would get dressed and see her the next day. And on one of the rare occasions when he did sleep over, he would hold her in his arms during the night, but never entwined as their bodies were now. With Kenna, it felt so right.

The alarm went off again. He glanced at Kenna when he heard her whimper in protest just moments before she slowly opened her eyes. She blinked as if trying to figure out what they were doing in bed together.

"Tell me I have at least another five hours to sleep," she whispered.

"Wish I could."

Her eyes narrowed. "But I don't."

"I'd be lying if I did. I bet we could probably come up with a good excuse for why you can't come in today."

"Nobody misses their first day of a new job," she said groggily.

"Syneda did."

Kenna couldn't help but smile. Reese had told her the story about Clayton and Syneda having decided to practice law together once they were married. The first day Syneda was supposed to show up at Clayton's office, she didn't. Clayton didn't show up either. However, neither of them knew the family had planned a little celebration for her. But it didn't take long to figure out why they didn't come into the office. Go figure.

"Can I go back to sleep?"

"No. Get up and get dressed. I'll be nice and drive you in to work."

Her eyes widened. "But you work on the outskirts of the city."

"Not this week. I'll be on site near downtown. So we can ride in to work together. That way you'll get at least thirty minutes more sleep."

From the expression on her face you would have thought Reese had given her a million dollars. "It's the least I can do, since I'm responsible for your being sleep-deprived."

He grudgingly eased his manhood out of her. "That was nice." He felt the loss immediately. "I'll start your bath and make breakfast," he said, getting out of bed. His erection was still hard as stone.

"Thanks."

"You're welcome, and don't go back to sleep."

"I won't."

Before he could respond, her eyes were closed and she began breathing easily. He smiled. She had gone back to sleep. He thought about waking her up again, but decided to give her another fifteen minutes. He reset the alarm and left the room thinking that it was the least he could do for the woman who'd given him a night he would always remember.

Kenna turned off the alarm and drew in a quick breath. Why did her body feel so battered, so sore? She slowly opened her eyes and the memories came flooding back to her. Despite her discomfort, all she could do was moan in pleasure.

When had Reese become a sex fiend? Maybe he had always been like that. She looked at the headboard, surprised that it was still in one piece. She eased out of bed slowly, knowing her body wasn't ready for Reese's idea of a sexual marathon.

It took her a little longer to get moving, but finding out that Reese had run the bath water for her helped. She was almost finished with the curling iron when Reese walked into the bathroom fully dressed with a cup of coffee in his hand. He handed it to her. "Just the way you like."

She smiled at him before taking a sip. "Thanks."

Her gaze roamed over him. Jeans, a Western shirt, boots and

a great body—*oh my.* "Are you sure you want to drive me to work this morning?" she asked, giving the cup of coffee back to him.

He took a sip. "Positive. We're making good time. Breakfast is ready when you are."

"Thanks."

He turned to leave the bathroom, but then surprised her when he leaned over and kissed her. "I'm ready to go. I'll be downstairs waiting."

Once he closed the door behind him Kenna drew in a deep breath. She remembered something her grandmother had always said: *when something was too good to be true, it usually wasn't.* She was on cloud nine, but how long would it last? When would Reese wake up and decide that he wanted them to just be friends again? Could they even *be* friends again?

Less than thirty minutes later, she was downstairs. She was in a pretty good mood until she saw Reese and Joe in the kitchen with grim expressions on their faces. "What's wrong?"

"Since you'll be working for HPD, you'll probably be able to tell us what's going on," Reese said in disgust.

"What do you mean?"

Reese shoved his hands his jeans pockets. "This morning's news reported that another woman was raped, tortured and killed. And there was…"

"…a shoe missing," said Kenna, finishing the sentence.

Reese nodded. "Yes."

From what she'd remembered he usually went for days, sometimes weeks before killing again. Why had that changed? What could have possibly made him kill two days in a row?

"The HPD is dealing with a violent serial killer," Joe said angrily. "It looks like the police department is going to have its hands full. The police chief and the mayor are holding a press conference this morning at ten. This is going to be one hell of a first day of work for you Kenna," he said.

She smiled wryly. "I'll be fine. Unless there's a survivor in one of these attacks there won't be much I can do," she said.

"I don't like this," Reese said through clenched teeth. "I'd like to get my hands on the bastard."

"Wait in line," Joe chimed in. "The boys have already decided we got first dibs. His latest victim was only nineteen."

Kenna glanced at Reese. "I need to get to work."

"What about your breakfast?" he asked her. "You should eat something."

She looked at the table and saw that he had prepared an egg sandwich on toast—just the way she liked it—and had poured a glass of orange juice for her. "Thanks. I'll eat it on the way in."

Chapter 17

Kenna glanced around her new office. She loved it. Back in Austin, all she'd had was a large cubicle that she'd shared with three other people. The office her new boss showed her when she arrived at work had a huge window that faced south and provided a beautiful view of downtown Houston's skyline. In the distance, she could see the campus of the University of Houston.

Downtown Houston was busy. It wasn't yet lunchtime and already the streets were crowded with pedestrians.

Kenna had grown up in the small Arizona town of Leupp. When she'd attended Spelman, an all-girls college in Atlanta, she had been in for a rude awakening. All of a sudden she had to find her way around a big city. Reese had followed in the footsteps of his older cousin Dex and his brother Luke to Morehouse, an all-male school near Spelman. He had helped Kenna make the transition from a small town to the big city fairly easy. When Reese had decided to get his graduate degree at the University of Texas in Austin, Kenna turned down a chance to study art in Paris to follow him to Austin instead.

She figured that sooner or later he would figure out why she always seemed to follow him. But when he decided to move back home to Houston five years ago, she made up her mind that it was time for her to stay put. They often talked on the phone and she was satisfied with his occasional visits to Austin to see her. When the offer to take the job in Houston came, Reese had been the one to encourage her to take it, and she had.

Now they were together in the same city again, and after last night they were together in a way they'd never been before. She had slept with Reese. She shook her head, remembering that they really hadn't gotten much sleep. At least he hadn't apologized this morning or tried to pretend nothing had happened. In fact, she was convinced that if they'd had enough time, they would have made love again this morning. He'd certainly been ready.

During the drive into work he hadn't brought it up. Maybe it was because they were both preoccupied listening to the radio for information about the serial killer. Everything else took a back seat. He had complimented her on the outfit she'd chosen to wear for her first day on the job. When she'd seen him checking her out before they left the ranch, it had boosted her confidence.

When he'd dropped her off for work, he had kissed her—and it hadn't been a little peck on the cheek. He had slid his tongue between her lips and mated hungrily with hers as if he needed her taste to get him through the day. It had been some kiss, and her lips were still tender just thinking about it.

By the time she had filled out her personnel paperwork, toured HPD headquarters and familiarized herself with the police computer system, it was half past eleven.

"Welcome to HPD."

Kenna glanced up and saw three police officers standing in

the doorway of her office. The two men and one woman had friendly smiles. "Thanks."

"I'm Lynette Cummings," the woman officer said, extending her hand. "And this is my partner, soon-to-be detective Steven Byrd, and Officer Shaun Woodson." They exchanged handshakes.

"We wanted to welcome you sooner, but things have been a little crazy lately with the serial killer," Lynette said. "And to think I was complaining a few weeks ago that things were pretty boring around here. I never expected anything like this, especially in Houston."

Kenna nodded. "Any leads?"

"No. Whoever this guy is, he's careful not to leave as much as a fingernail. I'm told the crime lab combed every inch of the locations where the women were found, but didn't come across anything," Steven added in frustration.

"There was a news brief earlier today, and a hotline has been set up for tips—an abandoned vehicle, anyone acting strange, conversations they might have overheard—just about anything that might lead to a suspect," Officer Shaun Woodson added. "A two hundred-fifty thousand dollar reward has been set up, and for that kind of money people will turn in their own mother."

The police needed leads. And with the right incentive, the community would be more careful and would be more aware of people and their surroundings.

"We're headed to lunch. Do you want to join us?" Lynette asked. "You'll probably be working closely with police officers, and we thought we could introduce you around."

"Thanks. I'd like that. Let me grab my purse." Kenna knew she was the new kid on the block and appreciated the offer. She had worked in a precinct long enough to know that more often than not new employees had a hard time being accepted right away. She appreciated the officers including her in the mix on her first day.

They went to a nearby diner called Rowdy's that seemed to be a favorite HPD hangout, judging by the number of officers that were eating there. They introduced Kenna to Flo Walker, the owner of Rowdy's, and her staff. According to Shaun, Flo's personality depended on which day of the week it was. Wednesdays were not good days to cross her. If the waitress got your order wrong that day, it was better to just roll with the flow. Despite Flo's temperament, the woman served the best breakfast in downtown Houston, and the diner was usually standing room only for lunch, which is why they always arrived early to make sure they got a seat.

Over lunch Kenna soon discovered that the trio was a talkative bunch. Lynette was a twenty-seven-year-old divorcée with a little girl name Aleena. Steven was thirty-two, married and the father of two little boys; and thirty-one-year-old Shaun had been a police officer in another state until six months ago. He was single and obviously on the prowl. It didn't take long to figure that out once she noticed him checking her out every chance he got. He was a shameless flirt and there was nothing subtle about him.

They told her about the police athletic league that worked to get kids off the street and into sports and activities at the local community centers, and about the police officers' bowling league.

"So you really don't know how to bowl?" Shaun asked, smiling.

She had to admit he was a cutie, but not the rugged, sexy heartthrob that Reese was. She smiled. "No, I've never gone bowling before."

"Then I need to make sure I teach you," Shaun responded.

"Please take off your player game face, Shaun," Lynette said, shaking her head. "For all you know, Kenna might have a boyfriend."

Shaun looked at Kenna curiously. "Do you? Are you involved with someone?"

Kenna wasn't sure how to answer the question. Would Reese fall in the category of boyfriend? Was she seriously involved with him? In the past she'd never slept with anyone she wasn't seriously involved with. She always applied the 180-day rule. If she and a guy made it past six months, then she considered it somewhat serious. Only Terrence and Lamont had made the cut-off. Curtis had been a couple of weeks shy—thank goodness.

She looked up from her tea and discovered three pairs of eyes watching her, awaiting her response. She cleared her throat and gave the only answer she could. "No, I'm not seriously involved with anyone."

Inwardly she winced in light of her and Reese's lovemaking last night and well into the morning. If that wasn't seriously involved, then what was? She would leave it up to him to define their relationship, she thought. She wouldn't assume that their bond was more than it really was.

Reese had said that they were moving from best friends to lovers. But she wasn't sure how she felt about that, especially since it would be her heart that was on the line. Last night was last night, but she had no idea what to expect in the future. They were friends. But depending on who you asked, everyone had a different opinion about this friends-to-lovers thing. Some said it was better to leave well enough alone, and going from friends to lovers was the worst mistake anyone could make. Others believed that best friends made the best lovers. Reese had certainly proven that was true. Still, she wasn't quite sure. He'd seen her at her best and her worst. He knew all of her secrets and she felt more comfortable with him than with any other man on earth. And she loved him.

She drew in a deep breath. When Reese picked her up after work, she decided she would mention Shaun's question and see what he thought about her answer.

"Well, Shaun," Lynette said, "I guess that means you're still in the game. Had you struck out I would have encouraged you to turn your attention to that blond waitress over there. She's been watching you since Flo hired her a few months ago. I think she likes you."

Shaun glanced over at the woman in question and rolled his eyes. "Not my type."

"Funny, I thought all women were your type," Lynette said.

"What can I say? Women just like me," Shaun said, in a cocky way. "It's the uniform."

"Is that why you wear your uniform just about everywhere—even to church?" Steven said, laughing.

Shaun frowned. "You know why I wear my uniform to church—because I help direct traffic."

Lynette leaned back in her chair and rolled her eyes. "You direct the ladies more than traffic. I heard quite a few of them manage to get your number on Sunday morning."

Kenna watched in amusement as Shaun sat up straight. "Who told you that?"

"Does it matter?" Lynette countered. "You have no shame hitting on churchgoing sisters."

Shaun eased back in his chair as a smile spread across his lips. "No."

"I figured you didn't," Lynette said in a testy voice. Shaun apparently didn't pick up on her tone.

As Kenna bit into her sandwich, she recognized as an expert in trying to hide her feelings, that there was more happening between Lynette and Shaun than they let on. Although Lynette tried to hide it, Kenna believed if given the opportunity, Lynette wouldn't hesitate to get involved with Shaun herself.

"So how are things going, Reese?"

He glanced up from his menu to look at the two men—Trevor Grant and Trask Maxwell—who had stopped at his table. Both were close friends of his older cousins Justin, Dex and Clayton. And Trask was married to Reese's cousin Felicia. What's more,

Reese had taken Trevor's old job as foreman with Madaris Explorations after Trevor became CEO of his own company.

"Things are going fine," he said, smiling. "Have a seat and join me. What are the two of you doing in downtown Houston?" he asked. The men sat down.

"I was at the courthouse on business and ran into Trask coming out of the television station after his interview," said Trevor. A well-known former football player for several NFL teams, Trask was pretty popular in Houston, appearing on several sports talk shows and promoting his charity work.

"The interview was cancelled," Trask said, "preempted by the news conference with the mayor and police chief. I hope they catch this guy and get him off the streets fast. That's the last thing we need."

Reese nodded. "At least women are aware that there's a serial killer, and hopefully they're being cautious."

"Yes, but the police aren't moving fast enough," Trevor said angrily. "You heard what he did to his latest victims, especially that young girl who was found before dawn this morning."

"Maybe we should get Sir Drake involved," Trask said teasingly.

Getting Drake Warren involved in any case was serious, Reese thought. Sir Drake, as he was affectionately nicknamed, was an ex-Marine, ex-CIA agent and modern-day ass-kicker. He was a black Rambo if ever there was one. No one—not even a serial killer—would want to cross his path.

The waitress came back and dropped off two more menus. Reese studied the two men while they decided what to order. Both were now happily married, but Reese knew that neither of their wives had liked them very much in the beginning. It was just the opposite with him and Kenna. They'd always gotten along, and after last night he figured it would get even better in the days to come.

"So how are things with Kenna working out?" Trask asked,

as if he'd been reading Reese's mind. "This is her first day at her new job, right?"

Reese took a sip of his soda. "Yes, and we figured it would probably be hectic with everything that's going on. Since I'm working in town this week, we drove in together."

"Excuse me, I don't mean to interrupt," a woman said as she stood next to their table. "Aren't you Reese Madaris?"

A muscle twitched in Reese's jaw. "And if I am?"

The woman seemed taken aback at Reese's unexpectedly chilly response. She quickly regained her composure, and batted her long eyelashes at him. "If you are then I'd like to get to know you."

He stared at her. She was blatantly hitting on him in front of Trask and Trevor, and from the expressions on their faces they were finding the entire exchange rather amusing.

"Wrong place and wrong time, miss. Sorry," he said.

Her smile widened. "I'm not. Here's my number. Give me a call when it's the right place and the right time." She strolled away, swaying her hips in a way that had every man in the place staring in her wake. Reese shook his head and looked at Trevor and Trask to find them looking at him curiously. "What?" he asked.

Trevor chuckled. "Must be hard filling Blade's shoes."

Reese rolled his eyes. "It's not something I'm trying to do, trust me."

Trask lifted a brow. "You sure?"

Reese met his curious gaze. "Positive."

He scanned the area as adrenaline pumped through his veins. He hadn't meant to kill again so soon, but the girl last night was an invitation he couldn't resist. She had practically asked for it, walking home late at night by herself.

She'd refused his offer of a ride and then tried to get away from him. She had been fast, but he'd been faster. In the end, her mouth had gotten her into trouble. Even when he had managed to handcuff her, she had cursed him, telling him what her big brother would do to him when he got ahold of him. He had merely laughed and figured she would learn her lesson.

That was his goal, to teach them all a lesson and then punish them the way he'd been punished. That was all it took—one shoe. All he had to do was close his eyes and remember the pain one shoe could cause. He remembered how his mother would beat him with the heel of her shoe whenever her dates went sour—just one shoe.

He snapped his eyes open. He'd heard the news report. They were looking for him, hoping he'd slip up. He had no intention of doing that. But he had no intention of stopping his killing spree.

He liked this town and decided he would hang around awhile. He chuckled. Things were about to get even more interesting.

Chapter 18

"How was your first day?" Reese asked when Kenna got into his SUV.

After buckling her seat belt, she turned toward him and smiled. "Busy. My boss barely had time to show me around before he had to go downstairs for the news conference. Later he gave me a tour, introduced me to a lot of the people I'll be working with and I even tagged along to an interview of a purse-snatching victim. She was such a sweet old lady that she reminded me a lot of your great-grandmother."

Kenna chuckled. "He still managed to get her purse, even though she clobbered him a few times with her cane."

"Did she give a good description of the guy?" Reese asked.

She smiled. "Yes. And the detectives are pretty sure they know who he is. He's a habitual thief who preys on the elderly."

For a moment she didn't say anything. "I went to lunch today with three of the officers—Lynette, Steven and Shaun. They were a lot of fun. Shaun was a riot. He flirted with me through most of my meal. He even asked if I was seriously involved with someone."

Kenna studied Reese. She saw how his shoulder muscles tensed. He glanced over at her when the car stopped at a traffic light. "And what did you tell him?"

She decided to turn the question back on him. "What was I supposed to tell him?"

He held her gaze. "That yes, you *are* seriously involved with someone."

"Am I?" she asked in a low voice.

Instead of answering her, he pulled into the parking lot of a restaurant and turned off the engine. He unsnapped his seat belt and reached over and unbuckled hers. Without saying a word, he cupped her face, leaned closer and captured her mouth with his.

Reese had meant for it to be a gentle kiss, but the moment his tongue eased inside her mouth, his emotions kicked in and he couldn't stop his tongue from tangling with hers, stroking and sliding everywhere. For a moment he forgot they were sitting in the parking lot of Hunter's BBQ, one of his grandfather and grand-uncle's favorite eating places. The only thing he could think about was just how good she tasted.

He resented the car's confinement. He wished he could have waited until they'd gotten home to his ranch. But when she'd mentioned a guy had flirted with her and she wasn't quite sure of their status, he'd decided to take action then and there. She'd asked about the nature of their relationship, and instead of wasting words he'd decided to show her.

"What do you think now?" he said, breathing into her mouth as his lips finally pulled away from hers.

She drew in a ragged breath, and met his gaze. "Umm, point made. But I'd still like to hear you say it."

"You and I are in a serious relationship. Kenna," he whispered huskily. "You will always be my best friend, the one woman I can talk to, share things with. But I want more. We moved from friends to lovers last night. I guess I need to make sure that you're comfortable with that, so I'm asking now."

She couldn't help the smile that tugged at the corner of her lips. "Yes, that's what I want." She paused. "But until we're absolutely sure, I'd prefer that we keep this to ourselves for now."

He knew there was no need getting into an argument. Like Clayton said, women prefer that you show them rather than tell them. "If that's what you want, we'll take things one day at a time," he said in a throaty voice. Leaning closer to her, he used his tongue to trace a line around her lips. "Any more questions?"

She moaned deep in her throat. What Reese was doing to her with the tip of his tongue was pure torture. "Yes. How quickly can we get home?"

He chuckled. The sound was low and rich with sexiness that only added to her desire to get home. "Did you forget that we promised my grandparents while we were in Oklahoma that we would have dinner with them this evening?"

She sighed inwardly. She had forgotten. His grandparents had invited them for dinner at Luke's grand opening the past weekend. "Oops. I'd forgotten."

"We can always come up with an excuse and cancel," he suggested.

"No, we can't do that."

He chuckled again. "Yes, we can. I'd like nothing better than to stay at home and watch another movie with you."

"If I remember correctly, I never got to watch the movie last night."

"You've seen it plenty of times before," he said. "And about that guy who was flirting with you today. The next time he asks, tell him you're taken."

She was ecstatic inside, and didn't have a problem telling

Shaun she was in a relationship. Even if Reese hadn't clarified the nature of their relationship, Kenna had already decided that Shaun was off-limits. Maybe one day he would pick up on the fact that Lynette was attracted to him.

Gathered around the dining room, Reese saw three generations of Madarises. His grandfather, Lucas Madaris Sr., had married Carrie Emerson right out of college and they'd had one son, Luke Jr. Their son, Luke, had married Sarah Reese, and from their union they had four sons: Luke III, the eldest; Reese; Emerson and then Chancellor.

Reese and his brothers were close, engaging in the usual skirmishes that brothers went through. Reese loved his family and wouldn't hesitate to do anything for them. Likewise, he knew they would do anything for him.

Usually the family got together a few times a month at his grandparents' home for dinner. This was one of those times. As he glanced around, he immediately realized someone was missing.

"Where's Mama Laverne?" he asked his grandmother when they were all seated at the table. Kenna was seated on his right and his brother Chancellor was to his left. His parents were sitting across from him and Emerson was sitting next to his father. His grandparents sat at the head and front of the table.

Grandma Carrie looked over at him and smiled. "She's spending the next couple of weeks with Jake and Diamond."

"Oh."

"Missing the old girl?" Chance leaned over to whisper with a smirk. "Get with me later and I'll tell you about the rumors she's putting out about you and Kenna."

Reese rolled his eyes. As usual, Chance was the last one to hear the family gossip. Reese already knew his great-grandmother was speculating about him and Kenna yet again. But because Chance lived out in the boondocks, less than thirty minutes from

Whispering Pines, he rarely left his ranch—except when there was a free meal—and was often out of touch with his brothers.

Chance had joined the army right out of high school and had been a Ranger for ten years. Everyone thought he would be a career military man, but an injury in Iraq left him in a wheelchair. When he returned home, he'd been told there was a chance he would never walk again. But the army doctors hadn't discussed that prognosis with Mama Laverne. It wasn't that their great-grandmother had been a miracle worker. But she had refused to give up on her great-grandson and had refused to let him give up on himself. In less than a year, Chance was out of the wheelchair and riding horseback again. Now, along with the ten men who worked for him, Chance ran his two-hundred-acre ranch. And along with his uncle Jake, he raised some of the best cattle in Texas.

"I kept the television off most of the day. I just couldn't stand to hear about those two girls that were murdered," Carrie Madaris said sadly.

"It breaks my heart, too," Kenna said, shaking her head. "And there still aren't any leads."

"Well, I hope they catch this serial killer. Until they do, no woman will be safe in these parts," Reese's grandfather said. "I figure now is a good time to load my shotguns and keep them ready."

The men at the table exchanged glances. That was the last thing they wanted to hear. "I don't think that's necessary, Pop," Luke Jr. said. "Besides, Sarah and I are right up the road. We could get here in no time."

"That's if you two can wake up. You and Sarah can't even hear your phone ring when you're asleep. You two can sleep through just about anything."

Reese tried to hide his grin. He remembered how when they were in high school, Emerson had snuck a girl into his bedroom. Everyone knew what was going on except for their parents. There were times when his brother Luke would wait for their folks to fall asleep and sneak out at night. To this day, his parents never figured out why Blade had always wanted to spend the weekends with them.

Trying to avoid a heated argument about the wisdom of their grandfather carrying a loaded gun, Reese caught Emerson's eye and slowly nodded. "I'm sure when this serial killer is caught you'll prosecute him to the fullest extent of the law, Emerson."

Emerson, who was a prosecutor with the Houston district attorney's office, smiled slowly. "We might have to fight extradition to other states where he's also a suspect. But I'd love to be able to try him here."

Once the conversation was over, his mother asked Kenna how her first day of work with the HPD went. Reese ate quietly and listened. He glanced around the table and, as usual, everyone was fascinated by her conversation. It had always been that way with her, and his family had let him know how much they liked her from the start. He liked her, too, and initially he'd told them they were just friends. Some had bought into the explanation, and some did not. Eventually the truth would come out and he would be confronted with those I-told-you-so looks. He could handle it. He just hoped that Kenna could, too.

Apparently Kenna wasn't ready to let others in on their relationship just yet, since she wanted to be sure things between them would work out. That was fine with him, since he didn't intend on going anywhere. As far as he was concerned, they were in it for the long haul, and he intended to make sure she was, too.

Before dawn, Kenna awakened in much the same position as she had the previous morning—in Reese's bed. She smiled, thinking how nice dinner with the Madarises had been last night. She enjoyed being around Reese's family. Her smile eased into a full-fledged grin when she thought about what had happened once they'd gotten back home.

If there were any doubts in her mind that Reese wanted her, those doubts were dispelled last night. He hadn't just made love to her, he had literally cherished her body in a way that even now made her shiver just thinking about it.

In many ways, she was indebted to Reese for making her realize that making love wasn't overrated. She'd found something in his arms she hadn't found in Terrence or Lamont's. She had barely reached one orgasm with them, but with little effort Reese could bring her to a second, and even a third in the same lovemaking session. *Incredible.*

She glanced over at the alarm clock and saw that Reese had deliberately given her an extra half hour. There was no way she could go back to sleep now, so she decided to get up and do a little more work on her painting. Painting had always been her favorite pastime, but now it seemed that making love to Reese was getting top billing.

She eased out of Reese's arms and slid out of bed. Moments later, after slipping one of his huge T-shirts over her naked body, she tiptoed into the spare room she used as her artist's studio. The only light she needed was the moonlight coming in through the windows and the night-light shining from the hallway. She gathered her brushes and paints, and tried to capture the image in her mind.

She wondered if Reese had realized that she was painting a portrait of him sitting on a horse. She didn't need him to pose, since his likeness was so deeply rooted in her mind. The portrait captured the very first time she realized she'd fallen in love with him. That was the year her grandmother had died and she had no place to call home. Reese had invited her to spend the summer with him at his parents' home in Texas. It was that summer that she first saw Reese's skills as a horseman, watching in total fascination as he and his brothers easily handled the horses.

That was the same summer he and his brothers had taught her to ride.

The moment she'd fallen in love with him was the morning they had ridden out together. Trotted was more like it, since her horse had been so docile and moved rather slowly. Once they reached their destination—a lake on his parents' land that connected to his grandparents' land—she had turned to tell him just how beautiful the landscape was when she was awed by the sight of him on the horse next to her, wearing a Stetson and a beautiful smile on his lips.

In that instant, she'd known two things: that image would be etched in her memory forever, and that she had fallen in love with him. The hopelessness of the latter hit home when they'd returned to the ranch and were greeted by Sandra Adams, who'd been Reese's girlfriend at the time. She had looked beautiful, radiant and stunning in a way that Kenna knew she never could.

Kenna ended her reverie, and a half hour later she was satisfied with what she'd accomplished on canvas and began putting away her paintbrushes. Once she was finished, she stretched her limbs, walked over to the window and looked outside. It was pitch black, with a full moon shining bright overhead.

She was about to turn away from the window when movement below caught her eye. She pressed her face against the glass and peered out and saw one of Reese's men returning to the ranch. Her expression softened. Evidently, she and Reese weren't the only ones having late-night rendezvous.

She studied the man, and when the moonlight cast a glow on his face, she recognized the new guy. Evidently he was a fast worker, since he already had a girlfriend. She chuckled, thinking of Reese. Not only was he fast, but he was thorough.

She turned away from the window and decided that she would greet Reese with a steaming hot cup of coffee this morning.

Chapter 19

"Hey, Kenna, Steven is out today. Do you want to tag along with me for a while?"

Kenna glanced up and smiled at Lynette. "I'd love to."

She gathered up her purse and in no time she and Lynette were heading out the door toward the patrol car. It didn't seem like she'd been working at the station for two weeks, but she had. She had gotten to meet a lot of the detectives and had even interviewed a witness in an attempted burglary.

Lynette, Steven and Shaun had turned out to be her regular lunch buddies, and she found there was never a dull moment with them around. She really liked them, and had even met Lynette's four-year-old daughter, Aleena, when Lynette brought her into the office one day. Like her mother, the little girl had a head full of curly red hair and beautiful green eyes.

Kenna knew that Steven was happily married and a proud father. He was active in his sons' Little League games as well as involved in activities at his sons' school. According to Steven, his wife was a paralegal. They'd met in college and had gotten married five years ago.

Shaun, on the other hand, was a piece of work. He was a flirt, but Kenna wouldn't necessarily call him a ladies' man. For whatever reason, he wanted to give the appearance of being a womanizer, but for the life of her she couldn't figure out why. She was used to womanizers. Although Reese's now-happily-married cousin Blade could probably write a book on the subject. Blade's two close friends—Tanner Jamison and Wyatt Bannister—were even worse. Kenna wondered if perhaps Shaun was trying to come across as a Lothario for Lynette's sake. And if so, why?

Although Lynette never said much about her private life, Kenna knew that besides being a single mother she was also the oldest of eight—six girls and two boys—and her youngest sibling was still in middle school. She joked about the fact that her parents still had an active sex life.

Over the past few weeks, there hadn't been any more Shoe Killer slayings, but a lot of groups were organizing to teach women how to protect themselves. One group had met at Sisters, a local nightclub and restaurant in Houston that was popular with women. Drake Warren's wife, Tori, who was a former CIA agent and a friend of the Madaris family, provided free self-defense classes at a local high-school gymnasium to a huge turnout. No one was taking chances. Although it seemed the killer was lying low, to law enforcement that meant nothing.

"Where's Shaun today?" Kenna asked Lynette after getting into the patrol car.

"He's working undercover. The chief decided to put some officers on the street after dark as a precautionary measure, especially since there're no other major crimes. The men's body-building competition at the civic center is tonight and a lot of people are expected to attend. Next week I'll be going undercover at the Astros baseball game."

Kenna nodded. After stopping at a fast-food restaurant for coffee they idled in the parking lot.

"I hate to admit it, but I miss Shaun," Lynette said, taking a sip of her coffee.

Kenna chuckled softly. "I'm sure you do."

Lynette frowned as she glanced over at her. "What do you mean by that?"

Kenna was suddenly aware that Lynette was a little ticked off. Moments later she decided to be honest. "You like him, don't you?"

Lynette shrugged. "Of course I like him. I consider him a friend."

Kenna wondered if she'd overstepped her boundaries in light of Lynette's defensiveness. She didn't want Lynette to think she was getting into her business. "Sorry I said something."

"That's okay. But I'm curious as to what made you think such a thing."

Now it was Kenna's time to shrug. "Because I have a friend who I secretly cared for a whole lot more than I let on, and there's something about the way you act around Shaun that reminds me of how I used to act around my friend."

Lynette didn't say anything, and for a while Kenna thought it was best to just let it go, but something wouldn't let her. She glanced at Lynette. "Well?"

Lynette looked back at her. "Well, what?"

"Nothing."

Moments passed. "Okay, maybe," Lynette murmured. "Maybe I do like him a little."

Kenna couldn't help but smile as she met Lynette's gaze. "A little?"

Lynette grinned. "Okay, okay, I like him a whole lot. I hate that I'm so transparent."

"You're not. Like I said, I'm in the same boat, so I can pick up on it."

Lynette smiled. "So does your guy know how you feel?" she asked faintly.

Kenna shook her head. "If you're asking if Reese knows just how crazy I am about him, then the answer is no. But as best friends he knows I adore him and wouldn't trade him for all the tea in China."

"Reese?"

"Yes," Kenna said, smiling.

"Nice name."

"Nice guy" was Kenna's response before she took another sip of her coffee.

"And do you think the two of you will ever move from being friends to being lovers?"

Kenna chuckled. "We're working on it, testing the waters so to speak. I was reluctant at first, since I would be devastated if things didn't work out. It's not like things can go back to the way they used to be."

Lynette nodded as she gave her a sympathetic look. "Scary, isn't it?"

"Yes, very." It was quiet for a moment. "So, does Shaun have any idea how you feel?" Kenna asked.

"Heck, no! You've gotten to know Shaun. He's a ladies' man. He probably doesn't see me as his type. Hell, he's hit on just about every woman in Houston, except me."

"Probably because in his eyes you're special."

"Whatever."

Kenna smiled. She knew just how Lynette felt and just what she was thinking. She'd been there and done that. In a way, she was still there. She just hoped testing the waters wouldn't threaten her friendship with Reese.

"I hope things work out between you and your guy," Lynette said softly.

Kenna took a long sip of her coffee. "Me, too, and I hope things will eventually work out for you and Shaun as well."

At that moment the dispatcher broke in instructing officers to immediately head to an area on the outskirts of the city. A woman's body had been found, and from all indications it looked as if the Shoe Killer had struck again.

Reese's eyes narrowed on the road ahead. His jaw tightened and his stomach clenched. The radio station he'd been listening to had just interrupted its regular programming to announce that another woman's body had been found. The identification of the victim was being held back until the family had been notified. But from all accounts, it looked like the work of the Shoe Killer.

He drew in a deep breath when his cell phone went off. He clicked on the speakerphone on his dashboard. "Yes?"

"Reese, this is Joe. Kenna isn't home yet. You told me to expect her around four and she isn't here. I don't like it, especially since that serial killer is out there somewhere."

Reese didn't have to ask Joe why he was concerned. He knew. Everybody in Houston knew. There was a serial killer out there somewhere. Besides, he didn't have time to figure out why Kenna would be late getting to the ranch.

"Reese?"

"Did you try her cell phone?" he asked. When he'd been working on a project downtown last week, he had driven Kenna to work twice. But since then, he'd been on another side of town, miles away.

"Yes, I did that before calling you. She didn't answer."

He frowned. It wasn't like Kenna not to answer her cell phone. He glanced at his watch. It was close to six and it would be getting dark soon. The hairs on his nape stood up. Any other time he would have told Joe to chill and that Kenna was fine. She'd probably stopped somewhere and would be back at the ranch fairly soon. But not this time—not since the Shoe Killer.

"I'll call the police department and see if perhaps she was

detained. Maybe she's in a meeting or something. I'll call you back." He knew Joe cared about Kenna. All his men did. And the thought of not knowing her whereabouts right now rattled him.

He racked his brain trying to recall the names of the officers she'd mentioned. Maybe they knew where she was. He pulled into a gas station to dial directory assistance and was immediately put through to the HPD.

"Yes, I need to talk to LaKenna James. She's a sketch artist there," he said.

"Hold on," the officer said and clicked off the line. He came back moments later. "She already left." Before Reese could ask him anything else, the officer hung up.

Trying to quell his anxiety he called back. He remembered one of the officers Kenna usually had lunch with was a woman name Lynette, although he didn't know her last name. Hopefully the person who answered the phone would. He re-dialed the police department.

"Houston Police Department."

"I'd like to speak with Lynette," he said.

"I need a last name."

He gritted his teeth. "I don't know her last name, but this is important."

There was a pause. "Who's calling?"

It was on the tip of his tongue to snap back and say, *Who wants to know,* but he was at the mercy of the officer on the other end of the line. "Reese Madaris."

"Madaris?"

"Yes."

"Are you related to that Madaris? The one who's married to the actress Diamond Swain?"

Reese would have smiled if he hadn't been so agitated. "Yes, my uncle Jake is married to Diamond."

"Wow!"

Reese chuckled. Years ago his uncle Jake had married former movie star Diamond Swain. Since then, she had traded in the bright lights of Hollywood for being a stay-at-home mom and rancher's wife. Occasionally, she would appear in a movie, but she much preferred her solitude at the Whispering Pines ranch.

"I think you're probably looking for Lynette Cummings," the man said, interrupting his thoughts. "You're in luck. She's usually out on patrol, but she's back now. Hold on. When you see Diamond Swain again let her know that Devin Crawford loves her to death—in a respectful way of course."

Reese shook his head. "I'll tell her."

He waited to be transferred to Lynette's line. Reese glanced around. It was getting dark. Panic was beginning to seize him. What was taking so long for this Lynette person to come on line?

"This is Officer Lynette Cummings, may I help you?"

"Yes," he spoke up quickly. "I'm a friend of LaKenna James and I'm trying to reach her."

"Don't you have her cell number?"

Reese tried retaining his cool. He knew the question was to be expected. "Yes, I have her cell phone number but she isn't answering. She didn't mention that she had any plans or stops to make. And considering everything that's been happening around here, I'm a little worried."

There was a pause. "And what's your name?"

"Reese. Reese Madaris."

"Oh, yes," Lynette said, sounding thoughtful. "She's mentioned you before."

Thank God for that, Reese thought. "Did she say if she was going somewhere before heading home today?" he asked.

"Yes. She said she was going to stop by and check on her condo, to see how it was coming along. I think someone called her and said they needed her to check out something with the lighting she'd ordered."

Reese was already putting his truck in gear and backing out of the parking lot. "Thanks."

Kenna tried to keep panic from pushing her over the edge, but she was worried. How could she have been so stupid and not called Reese to let him know just where she would be? And now her cell phone battery was low, all the construction workers had left and her rental car wouldn't start.

Things wouldn't have been so bad if she hadn't been in the patrol car with Lynette when she'd gotten the call to go to the crime scene.

She drew in a deep breath and tried not to think about it, just like she tried not to think about the fact that it had gotten dark. She could start walking up the road, since there was an occupied subdivision a couple of miles away. But for some reason she felt it was safer to stay put. Hopefully, a security patrol would arrive sooner or later, if for no other reason than to check to make sure thieves didn't make off with any of the building equipment.

She nervously rubbed her arms. Reese was probably a little concerned by now, wondering where she was. She hadn't mentioned making any stops after work when they'd parted at breakfast this morning. But her builder had called and told her that he needed her to sign off on the lighting fixtures that had arrived that day. Excited, since the ones she'd chosen had been special-ordered, she had rushed over after work.

Nervousness thrummed through her and she began pacing. She stopped when the sound of her footsteps on the wooden planks was too loud. She thought about going outside and sitting in her car, but for some reason she felt safer on her condo site, under the roof and rafters, and the solid masonry walls. Windows had been installed and the plumbing was in, all except for the jetted-tub for the master bath that was still on order.

Now more than anything she regretted not taking Blade up on his offer to buy an already-built condo close to the Madaris Building. It was one of the Madaris Construction Company's business ventures, and she had fallen in love with the building when Blade and Slade had given her a tour.

The only drawback had been the condos were close—within minutes of the Madaris Office Park where Reese worked when he wasn't off-site. She figured it would seem suspicious if she moved too close to the Madaris family.

She turned slowly when she thought she heard a sound. Lord help her. Hopefully her mind was playing tricks on her and there was no one beyond the door. Fear squeezed her throat, making screaming all but impossible. How long she stood there frozen in one spot, she wasn't sure. She tried telling herself that she hadn't actually heard anything but…

Okay, Kenna. You didn't hear a car pull up, so there's no one out there, she tried convincing herself. *And if you did hear a noise it was probably some stray cat or dog. There were probably armadillos around since the housing complex was practically out in the middle of nowhere.*

She drew in a sharp breath when she heard a sound again. She was certain this time that she'd definitely heard something, and nearly jumped out of her skin when she heard what she knew for certain were footsteps.

She took a step back and cringed when she heard a board crack under her feet. The hairs on the back of her neck stood up when she heard the doorknob turning and immediately picked up a loose board and held it in her hand, ready to defend herself.

"Kenna?"

She let out a sigh of relief when she recognized the voice and fought the tears that threatened to blur her vision. "Reese!"

She shouldn't have been surprised that he was there, since he'd always looked out for her—had always come to her rescue. When he pushed open the door and walked into the room and shined the flashlight on her face, she dropped the board from her hand and rushed across the room to him. He caught her in his arms and held her tight, as if he would never let her go.

And then he kissed her.

The moment their lips touched Kenna felt safe and secure because of the way he was holding her, the way the heat emanated from his body to the pit of her stomach. When he latched on to her tongue and began devouring her like a starving man, she settled her body into his and began consuming him. Her thighs began quivering under the onslaught of his mouth. His hunger combined with hers stoked their passion. And then the thought that a serial killer was on the loose somewhere in the city and that she could have been in danger only made their union that much more fiery.

It was as if he needed to hold her, kiss her and thoroughly taste her in an effort to assure himself that she was all right, safe and sound and in one piece. And she needed to do the same. Their tongues continued to tangle, explore, stroke and mate, causing a heated sensation to overtake them.

He continued to kiss her fiercely. He kissed her hard and deep and devoured her like this would be the last time to do so. His hands roamed up and down her back as if to make doubly sure she was really there, and he could hear her moans from deep within her throat.

He pulled away slowly but not before taking a final lick across her lips, causing fire to shoot through her thighs and straight to the juncture between them. She shifted, felt his hard erection and intentionally moved again to cradle his hardness to her middle.

"Don't you ever scare me like that again, Kenna." And then after dragging in a deep breath he narrowed his gaze and in a voice that was gruff, tight and strained with emotions, he added, "And you better have a good reason for not calling me."

She felt him shudder and in response she quivered. Never had she felt so protected. It was hard to believe that just moments ago she'd been on the verge of hysteria, thinking she might be the Shoe Killer's next victim. Normally her mind didn't succumb to such panic attacks, but she had been there today when Lynette was called to the crime scene.

"Kenna?"

She met Reese's gaze and saw the concern in his eyes. "My cell phone battery died and my car wouldn't start."

She breathed in deeply. "I've never been so scared in my life. When it started getting dark all I could think about was that that crazy man was still out there and no telling where."

She drew in a deep breath and almost choked. "I was there today, Reese, with Lynette when the call came in about the woman they found earlier."

His eyebrows arched. "You were?"

"Yes, I heard the description over the radio."

She closed her eyes as if trying to forget, but her mind refused to let her. She opened her eyes, and met his intense gaze. "It was awful, Reese." Her voice broke, and when she was no longer capable of holding back the tears, he pulled her back into his arms.

"She was somebody's mother, Reese. Probably someone's wife," she said through her tears. "She belonged to someone and that—that crazy person took her away from them in such a brutal way. It's scary."

Reese rubbed Kenna's back as he continued to hold her, thinking that regardless of the fact that she worked for a law-enforcement agency, it had to have been a lot for her to endure. He'd heard some details in the news report as he raced over here. The victim's identity hadn't yet been released, but she was in her forties, and like the others had been raped, tortured and killed.

"Someone has to stop him, Reese. Tonight, stranded here, even I was scared."

He tightened his hold on her while thinking, yes, she was

right. Someone had to stop this killer. No woman was safe until they did.

"Come on, let's go. I want to get you home and take care of you," he said gently.

"What about my car? I think the battery died."

"We'll call the rental company in the morning to pick it up. You can drive mine to work until this weekend. Then we'll go buy you one."

She shook her head. "I don't want a car payment until after I move into my condo, Reese."

He rolled his eyes. "Fine, then I'll buy it and you can drive it."

She brushed off his words. "Don't be ridiculous, Reese. You—"

Reese leaned down and kissed her, deciding at the moment she was talking too much. He refused to let her be without reliable transportation again. He intended on calling the car rental company tomorrow and giving them a piece of his mind. How dare they give his woman a car that broke down?

His woman.

He smiled as he continued to kiss her. Yes, she was definitely his woman, and he intended to take whatever steps he needed to in order to keep her safe.

A pair of blue eyes, creased with concern, stared across the room at the four men who'd come highly recommend by a personal friend in Homeland Security. She knew *of* these men more than she knew them personally. Two were natives of Houston, and the other two had pretty much adopted the city as their home over the past five years.

All four were handsome men, and when they needed to be they were dangerous men. They had reputations for getting things done, at times in very unorthodox ways. What she liked about them was they knew how to cut through the red tape and get down to the real nitty-gritty, and at that moment that was exactly what she needed. That was what her city needed. And that's why she'd requested this private meeting with them at an undisclosed location, away from the prying eyes of the media, or anyone else who might want to interfere.

One of the men flashed a smile that didn't quite reach his eyes. "I take it there's a reason we were summoned here, Mayor?"

She carefully schooled her expression not to smile as she perched her hip on the corner of the desk. The way the question had been asked, one would have thought they were members of her own special task force, a group she could call upon at will to handle serious business. That was not the case, and they all knew it. The fact that she had called upon them at all was a mystery.

"Yes, Mr. Sinclair, there is a reason," she said, scanning their faces one at a time. "A mutual friend in Homeland Security identified the four of you as operatives who can help me. Help my city."

No one said anything for a while, not even to ask the identity of this so-called *mutual* friend.

"And what seems to be the problem?" said Ashton Sinclair.

"Houston is in crisis. We have a serial killer on the loose and I want him caught." There, she'd said it. She'd stated the problem and said exactly what she wanted from them. But she knew they wouldn't immediately respond. They needed more information—not that the media wasn't full of it, mind you. But they would want to know why she had called them in when the HPD was out in full force and the FBI had its own specialists that were assisting. She knew more was needed, and had known exactly who to call to arrange this private meeting.

"Yes, we're aware of the serial killer," said Alex Maxwell, one of the men invited to the meeting. The youngest of the four, Maxwell was a former FBI agent who had a private investigations firm and had solved a number of high-profile crimes.

"Then you know of his latest victim, the woman whose body

was discovered earlier today. I believe he's playing a game with us," the mayor said, trying to keep her anger at bay. "And it's a game that has cost several women their lives. He has to be stopped!"

"Then the best thing to do is to find out who he is and make him suffer the same way those women have. Cut off his hands, his feet..." said Drake Warren, one of the four men called by the mayor.

"There's no need to go into detail, Sir Drake," said Trevor Grant, staring at the man sitting next to him.

The mayor knew Grant, a former Marine, since he and Maxwell had been born and raised in Houston like her.

From what she'd heard, Drake Warren, who was known as Sir Drake, hailed from the mountains of Tennessee and still had a home there and one in Houston. He had become friends with Sinclair and Grant when the three had served together in the Marines' special-forces unit. Drake later became a CIA agent and had recently retired from the agency after getting married. Ironically, his wife had also been a Marine and a CIA agent.

Ashton Sinclair was the more relaxed of the four, and was part Cherokee and African-American. In the military his reputation as a tracker was known far and wide. He could track down anything and anyone, and was supposedly clairvoyant. His wife owned a Houston restaurant called Sisters that was a popular spot for single women.

The mayor knew she had called in the big guns. She needed them. Houston needed them.

"Will we be able to work the way we want to or will there be limitations?" Ashton Sinclair asked.

"No limitations. I just want him caught and put behind bars or in a coffin," she said without remorse. "But everything has to be by the book."

"Aw, shucks," Sir Drake said with a disappointed frown. "Does that mean I can't feed his body parts to the sharks?"

"Afraid not," the mayor said.

Drake shrugged his massive shoulders. She'd heard stories that Sir Drake did whatever the hell he wanted and most of the time it wasn't pretty. If given the chance, she was sure he'd make good on his promise to feed the sharks.

She drew in a deep breath. "The next time we meet, gentlemen, will be—"

"To let you know the killer has been caught," Alex Maxwell said, finishing the mayor's sentence. "Will we have access to all the evidence that's already been collected?" he asked.

She wasn't sure how she was going to arrange that, but she would. "Yes, you will have access to anything you need."

He nodded.

"If all goes well…and the four of you succeed, you will definitely be doing this city a great service," she said.

Trevor Grant smiled. "Then consider it done."

Chapter 20

"Are you sure that you're okay, Kenna?"

The husky tone of Reese's deep voice sent a surge of warmth rushing through her body. When he moved closer to her and wrapped his arms around her waist from behind, she instinctively settled back against him. She had been staring out of the living room window into the night. It was a beautiful night—peaceful and serene.

"Yes, I'm fine," she said, tilting her head back over her shoulder to look at him. Her blood stirred when her eyes traced the perfect angle of his chiseled jawline, the beauty of his coppery skin tone and the sexiness of his brown, bedroom eyes. And on top of all that, he smelled simply delicious.

They had said very little on the drive home from her condo, and she preferred it that way. She needed the time to calm her nerves. When they reached the ranch he literally picked her up in his arms and carried her inside.

"I was never in any real danger, Reese. I freaked out when

it got dark and got paranoid thinking about the possibility of becoming the serial killer's next victim. I just overreacted."

His arms tightened around her waist as he turned her to face him. "No you didn't. Your mind was dealing with reality. There is a killer out there, and you need to take every precaution."

He paused for a moment. "In fact, I just finished talking to Clayton, and he's calling a family meeting."

Kenna lifted her brow. "A family meeting?"

"Yes, with the Madaris women. Considering what's going on, he thinks we need to make sure that everyone's safe."

She nodded. That was only one of the things she liked about Reese's family. They were extremely close-knit and looked out for each other. The men were especially protective of the women they loved.

"I'm working in town again tomorrow, so we can ride in together and afterward we'll swing by Uncle Jonathan's. That's where everyone is meeting."

"You want me to go?"

Reese's brow arched as if her question was odd. "Yes, of course. Why wouldn't I? I think whatever is being said will be beneficial to you as well."

She chuckled softly. "Probably especially beneficial to me, since I acted like an idiot tonight. I know I have to take every precaution, but I don't want to start being afraid of my own shadow."

"And you won't. You should feel safe on the ranch. You've known most of the guys for a while, except for the new one, and Joe had him checked out real good before bringing him on. But I do want you to promise me that you won't go riding alone. Either wait for me, so we can ride together, or let Joe know so he'll send one of the men with you."

She didn't think his request was unreasonable. "All right."

"So, are you hungry? I've put dinner on the table."

She smiled up at him. "Thanks."

She'd expected him to pull his arms from around her waist, but he didn't. Instead he leaned in closer toward her mouth and she parted her lips for him. The moment his tongue mated with hers, a silky warmth and sultry pleasure seeped deep into her bones. His tongue roamed all over her mouth and seemed to grow thicker with every place it touched.

She felt his erection pressing hard against the juncture of her thighs, and placed her hands on his shoulders more for her sake than his. At any moment she felt her knees would weaken and eventually buckle.

"Lord, give me strength," she murmured when he finally released her mouth. She quickly concluded that Reese's tongue was dangerous. It was as if he'd tried absorbing her taste with it.

She suddenly arched her brow when she thought of something. "You never did say how you knew I was at the condo site."

He nuzzled her neck with his lips. "You never asked."

Her mouth curled into a smile. "Very well, now I'm asking."

Instead of answering, he kept right on doing what he had been doing, but now he'd taken the tip of his tongue and was licking the underside of her chin, leaving a hot, wet trail in its wake and sending jolts of electricity to her core.

She had never considered herself a sexually passionate woman until Reese. She could barely remember the last time she'd slept in her bed alone. It seemed the most natural thing for them to be together throughout the night, and she had gotten used to the hard, masculine body snuggled against hers. It was as if they'd made the transition from friends to lovers with ease.

"Umm, if you keep this up," she murmured when he started nibbling on her earlobe, "I might have to make you sleep alone in your own bed tonight."

He suddenly stopped and straightened and met her gaze. "Why?"

"...because we wouldn't be doing much sleeping tonight."

He grinned. The look on his lips was so sexy it sent a jolt of desire rushing through her. "But we don't do much sleeping most nights anyway," he countered.

"I know, but there's always a first time," she said softly.

"True. But not for us, and definitely not tonight. Come on and let's go eat, so we can make love on a full stomach."

Kenna glanced across the table at Reese and thought he certainly had a hearty appetite. She blushed when she remembered what he'd said about making love on a full stomach. Just the thought that he apparently enjoyed making love to her filled her with desire.

"Umm, what are you thinking about over there that has you smiling and blushing all over the place?"

"I just realize you haven't answered my question."

"And what question is that?"

"How did you know where to find me this evening?" she asked.

He took a sip of his tea and then leaned back in his chair. "What will I get if I tell you?"

She tilted her head back. "I can tell you what you won't be getting if you don't tell me."

His lips curved into a smile. "Sounds like blackmail to me."

"Call it whatever you like," she answered.

"Blackmail."

She laughed and it felt good. She needed that.

"You sound good," he said in a throaty whisper. "You smell good, too. And to answer your question, your coworker Lynette told me. But only after she was convinced I was okay and wasn't some stalker."

"Oh."

Without warning he reached across the table and took her hand in his. "Ready for dessert?"

She glanced around the kitchen. "I didn't know you prepared dessert."

"I didn't."

His gaze held hers as sexual awareness passed between them. The chemistry was so thick you could not only cut it with a knife, you could probably butter bread with it.

"What are you thinking?" she found herself asking him.

A seductive smile touched his lips. "I'm thinking of the best place to make love to you."

She swallowed deeply. "Oh, I see."

"No, I don't think you do. But if you close your eyes I'll paint a vivid picture for you. And you have to keep them closed until I tell you to open them."

Kenna tried to resist the urge to do what he'd asked but couldn't, so she slowly closed her eyes.

"Envision this," he said huskily and the deep sound of his voice seemed to travel across the room and touch her intimately. "The two of us on a tropical island after being shipwrecked. There's no one else on the island but us. Not another living soul. It's our island to do with as we please, and the only thing I want us to do for starters is get naked."

Typical man, she thought as she leaned back against her chair. Relaxed and feeling like she was on a tropical island with the sun overhead as a breeze floated through the air, she could almost feel the wind caressing her bare skin. And yes, she was naked, as naked as a jaybird, but then so was Reese.

"What's next?" she asked. Now that he'd gotten her into this little game of his, she found that she was rather enjoying it. She was convinced that if she wiggled her toes, she would feel sand beneath her feet.

"Shh," he whispered, as the sound came closer.

She heard the chair scraping across the floor at the same time she felt it being moved backward. Then she was scooped up into Reese's strong arms. "Keep your eyes closed," Reese instructed within inches of her lips.

Kenna smiled softly, thinking he was getting bossier. "Where are you taking me?"

"Not far."

She groaned. That wasn't saying a lot.

"Let's get back to your vision. We were on an island lounging under a huge palm tree," he whispered. "But there's too much sun for our naked bodies."

"Speak for yourself. I was enjoying it."

"But not as much as you're going to enjoy this."

"What?"

"Open your eyes."

She slowly opened her eyes and looked around. She blinked, not recognizing where she was at first. "Hey, wait a minute. Wasn't this a storage room—the one off the downstairs hallway?"

"Yes, and see what I've done with it."

Reese had installed a huge hot tub.

She grinned. "When did you do this?"

"Last month."

She scowled playfully. "And you didn't tell me. How could you? I've been here almost four weeks already."

"I wanted to surprise you. Besides, I've been waiting for a missing part to come in. They installed it today."

"So you haven't tried it out yet?" she said, kicking her sandals off.

"No, I thought we would try it out together."

Kenna shrieked with happiness and threw her arms around Reese before turning back to look at the huge hot tub. It took up nearly the entire room. "What made you decide to get a hot tub?"

"Umm, over the years I've heard just how much fun Uncle

Jake has in his. Clayton and Syneda installed one in their home last year, and rumor has it that's where she got pregnant," Reese leaned over and whispered.

Kenna chuckled. She already knew what he was thinking. He hadn't brought her in here to show her how the jets worked. "Do you mind if we try it out now?" she asked, wiggling out of her skirt.

"If you want to…"

Kenna chuckled and shook her head. *Like it's not what you really want to do right now,* she thought.

Her pulse raced just looking at the way Reese watched her, so she decided she might as well make it worth his while. She didn't have a body like Alyson Richards, but she was in pretty good shape. "Are you going to just stand there and watch me or do you plan to take off your clothes?"

The sexiest mouth she'd ever seen spread into a half mocking smile. "I plan to watch."

"Suit yourself," she said, tossing off her blouse, followed by her bra.

She couldn't take her eyes off of him, especially the way he was looking at her. He'd seen her body before, but it was as if he was still entranced by what he saw. She figured he liked her breasts since he would kiss them every chance he got and use his tongue to torture her nipples, which were getting hard the more he stared.

She drew in a deep breath. There was only one thing left covering her body, and she watched him lick his lips as she eased her fingers under the waistband of her panties, slowly sliding the scrap of silk down her thighs.

He groaned deep in his throat. She heard it and then she felt heat emanating from his body, making her striptease more daring and provocative. This was Reese. He was her best-friend-turned-lover and with him she could always be herself. At that moment she was standing in front of him without a stitch of clothing on. And he was definitely taking it all in. The way his gaze was roaming all over her body suggested he wasn't missing a thing.

"When you get bored watching, let me know," she said.

He chuckled as he kicked off his own shoes. "I could never get bored looking at you, sweetheart."

Reese meant every single word he'd said. He doubted Kenna knew just how beautiful she was. Whenever he buried his hard length between that pair of luscious thighs—heaven help him. He was a goner for sure. And on those nights that she rode him…

He pulled in a heated breath just thinking about it. "I hope the water is warm enough," he said, tossing off his shirt. "If it's not, I'm sure we'll heat it up pretty quickly."

"Probably."

As far as he was concerned there was no *probably* to it. He needed to make love to her. He needed to know that she was out of danger, because whether she knew it or not, she had been in danger tonight. Any woman on the streets of Houston was at risk. But he would never let anyone harm a single hair on her beautiful head.

"Now I see you're watching," he said, easing off his belt.

"Surely you didn't expect me not to."

He smiled as he worked his fingers under the waistband of his jeans after unzipping them. Then he slowly eased them down his thighs, over his huge erection that was straining for release. "You know when you asked me about dessert earlier?"

"Yes."

"Making love to you tonight will be all the sweets I need," he said huskily in a deep baritone as he reached out and pulled her toward him.

She rubbed her finger tip across his jawline. "Thanks for coming to my rescue tonight," she said softly.

"You've already thanked me more times tonight than you need to. I will always protect you, Kenna. You know that." *And although you have absolutely no idea, I will always love you. But I intend to show you and eventually you will.*

"Yes, I know."

Although they hadn't discussed it, Reese knew she assumed that they had reached some sort of understanding about their relationship. She thought they would do this *lovers thing* for a while and then go back to being friends again. He intended to show her they could be best friends *and* lovers, and that they would never be one or the other.

He started backing her up toward the hot tub while slowly running his hands over her waist. "Did you notice that table over there?"

She glanced behind her. She hadn't. It was a massage table.

"Today left you tense. I want to massage your body first." He scooped her into his arms, took her over to the table and placed her on her stomach.

After rubbing warm massage oil into his hands, he went to work, kneading the tension out of her shoulders while thinking her skin was so beautiful and soft. He enjoyed rubbing his hands over her, and of their own volition they would slide below her waist, stroking the firm cheeks of her bottom. It was the very curviest backside he'd ever seen, he thought. He leaned forward and placed a kiss in the center of her back and heard her breathe in a ragged breath.

"You take such good care of me," he heard her murmur softly.

He smiled, thinking she hadn't seen anything yet. After massaging her legs all the way down to the calves he worked his way up her body again, and the way she moaned only hardened his erection.

"Let me turn you over, baby," he said, easing her onto her back.

She stared up at him, met his gaze and felt his heat. If only she knew just how hot he was for her she wouldn't be looking at him that way, he thought, squirting more of the massage oil into his palms.

He started with her breasts and saw how they responded to his touch. How her nipples swelled under the palms of his hand. Unable to resist, he leaned down and sucked a hardened tip into his mouth and began laving it with his tongue.

"Reese…"

She'd said his name softly, but before it was all over he intended for her to scream it. Moving his hand, he inserted it between her thighs and began parting them, inhaling her seductive scent and gazing at the most intimate part of her body. He remembered the first time he had feasted on her and his taste buds hadn't been the same since. She tasted sweet and he would always yearn for her essence. *Like now.*

She watched as he began trailing kisses from her breasts down to her stomach and then began licking his way in between her legs. The moment his tongue touched her feminine mound and began circling her clitoris with the tip of his tongue before dipping it deep inside of her, she swallowed a moan deep in her throat.

"Oh, Reese…"

The sound of that was a little better, he thought, as he began feasting on her just as he'd been imagining all day long. His lips locked on her core as he began alternately sucking gently and stroking her.

She squirmed from the foreplay of his mouth, and he knew that the exact moment she lifted her hips off the table was his cue to delve deeper. And he did so with a ravenous hunger. He didn't intend to let up until he heard what he wanted to hear.

"Reese!"

When she screamed his name he was glad he'd remembered to close the door, or his men might think they were in some sort of danger. The only danger either of them risked was too much lovemaking. He doubted that he would ever get enough of her.

He tasted her orgasm as her thighs trembled under his lips. It was only then that he released her—but not for long. He eased on top of the table with her, and spread her luscious thighs wider.

She was watching him through a haze, with eyes that still shimmered from her climax. He lifted her hips up in his hands. "Don't get too comfortable, baby," he said softly as the head of his erection eased into her, stretching her as it kept moving, sliding deeper into her as her muscles clenched him all the way.

He threw his head back when he felt he was inside her to the hilt. Her inner walls milked him hard as he began moving, thrusting back and forth inside of her, going in and out, right to left, left to right. He was pounding hard, yet in his mind not hard enough. They would be in one hell of a fix if the table broke under their weight. But dammit, he was determined to have her like this. Chalk it up as just one of his many fantasies, since he had plenty where Kenna was concerned and was making up new ones every day.

The table rocked, and a time or two he thought it might have rolled, but it held firm and did what they needed it to do. It withstood the endless pounding, thrusting and stroking, and when she screamed his name again, the sound triggered an explosion that he felt all the way to his toes.

He growled out her name as he felt himself come…and come…and come. Making love to her was off the charts. It was never like this with any other woman—only with her. Pleasure surged through him, touching every part of his body, and he leaned down and kissed her, tasted the sweetness from her lips. He knew at that moment that she would never move into the condo she was building, because he intended to keep her here with him always.

He slowly pulled out of her and got off the table. Once his legs were steady enough for him to stand on, he gathered her into his arms and carried her to the hot tub. He gently eased them down into the warm water. He couldn't remember a time that he'd enjoyed a woman more. But Kenna wasn't just any woman. She was the one woman he wanted to spend his life with, and each and every day he intended to make sure she knew it. Hopefully his "show me" approach would convey the emotions he had yet to put into words.

Chapter 21

Lynette leaned across the table as her lips curved in a half-mocking smile. "Must be nice."

"What?" Kenna asked, looking up from her menu. She had agreed to join Lynette for lunch at Rowdy's. Because of everything that had happened yesterday, Steven and Shaun had the night shift for the rest of the week.

"To have a sex-all-night glow on your face that lasts through lunch," Lynette said, smiling.

Sheer willpower was keeping the heated blush off of Kenna's face. "You're imagining things," she admonished

"I don't think so. Besides, if the blush didn't give you away, that passion mark you tried covering up with makeup did. Admit you've been caught."

Kenna was saved from admitting anything when one of the waitresses came to take their order. Lynette shook her head when the blond-haired woman walked off. "I bet she was just itching to ask where Shaun was today."

Kenna glanced over at the waitress, who had gone back behind the counter. "You think?"

"Hell, I don't know and I shouldn't even care," Lynette moaned.

"But you do."

Lynette nodded and chuckled. "Yeah, you're right, I do care. But I don't think she's his type. She doesn't have enough curves."

To be honest, Kenna didn't think the waitress was all that attractive anyway and wasn't much competition, at least not in the way Alyson was. She still couldn't understand why Reese wasn't taken with Alyson, when it had been apparent at the party that most men were. Instead, Alyson had tried encouraging them to take an interest in her.

"So what's the latest on the woman who was found yesterday?"

Lynette lifted a brow. "You haven't heard?"

Kenna looked confused. "No. What?"

"The details were released to the press a short while ago. It was bad enough she'd been raped, but it seems she was thrown into a pit with rattlesnakes while she was still alive. She had bite marks all over her body. There was enough venom in her body to take down an elephant. The bastard probably sat there and watched her die."

Kenna shivered at the thought of someone dying so horribly. It seemed the killer was becoming more and more vicious. He probably stayed awake at night trying to come up with new ways to torture his next victim.

"People are beginning to panic. They are arming themselves for protection. We've hired more people just to keep up with all the calls we're getting and to work the tip line. According to CNN he's killed sixteen women now. But he usually has at least six kills before moving on to another place," Lynette said.

The thought that the serial killings would continue angered Kenna.

"I'm glad Reese got to you yesterday," Lynette said interrupting Kenna's thoughts. "I'm not saying you were in any danger out there by yourself, but right now I wouldn't take chances. Even when I'm working undercover next week, the captain has assigned a partner to act as my boyfriend."

Kenna lifted a brow. "Who? Shaun?"

"No. Some rookie who joined the force a few months ago. That means I'm going to have to look out for his back as well as mine."

"Well, well, if it isn't LaKenna James."

Kenna glanced up and wished she hadn't. It was Alyson, and she was with, of all people, Wendell Thomas. She plastered a smile on her face. "Alyson. Wendell. Yes, and how are the two of you doing?"

"Fine. We were downtown strolling around and thought we would drop in here, although now I wished we hadn't. It's not what I thought," Alyson said, putting her hand in the crook of Wendell's arm to make sure Kenna got the picture.

Kenna introduced them to Lynette. But when she introduced him as Wendell Thomas, he immediately corrected her. "I'm *Doctor* Wendell Thomas," he said. "I'm one of the head neurologists at Park Plaza Hospital."

Kenna hid her smile. If he was trying to impress Lynette he was wasting his time. In fact, Kenna had to fight back her laughter when Lynette batted her eyelashes and said, "Evidently there's a reason for you wanting me to know, but last time I checked my nervous system was working just fine."

The smile on Wendell's face turned into a frown. "Well, I'll leave you ladies to your meal." He then quickly ushered Alyson toward the exit.

"Was it something I said?" Lynette shrugged with an innocent look on her face.

Kenna couldn't hold back as she and Lynette burst out laughing at the same time.

"Who are they?" Lynette asked, shaking her head. "I've never met two more self-centered people in my life."

"Alyson is Reese's ex-girlfriend and Dr. Wendell Thomas is the guy she was all but throwing in my face," Kenna said. "Now it looks like she has him all to herself."

Lynette chuckled. "Yes, it looks that way." She checked her watch. "It's taking forever for them to bring our food. But today is Wednesday, Flo's bad day, and I for one don't intend to get on her bad side."

Kenna grinned. "Is she that mean?"

"I bet you won't ask me that a month from now," Lynette said, taking a sip of her soda. "Are you sure it's okay for me to bring Aleena out to the ranch Saturday? She loves horses, and to think I actually know someone who owns one."

"It's not me who owns the horses. It's Reese, and he has several. I know he wouldn't mind."

"You sure?"

"I'm positive," Kenna said, smiling.

"He sure sounds like a nice guy."

"He is, and you deserve a nice guy, too." Kenna paused a moment. "I'm the last person to give advice about affairs of the heart, but if you're so sure Shaun won't ever come around, then…"

Lynette drew in a deep breath. "I know. I know. My mom and my sisters think I need my head examined, and they're probably right." She paused a moment. "Not sure if you've heard, but there's a rumor floating around the station that Shaun is being hit with a paternity suit. One of the dispatchers is claiming she's pregnant by him. The last thing I need is to get involved with all that drama. I'm a hard-working woman who has a lot to offer, and I shouldn't settle for a man who might end up causing me nothing but heartache."

Kenna didn't say anything and was glad when the waitress finally brought their food. Although Reese was a good man, she couldn't help but wonder if he could end up causing her nothing but heartache.

"Hey, what's this I hear about Kenna being missing the other night?" Dex Madaris asked as he slid onto the bench next to Reese. They were working on a site downtown, getting the area prepped for what would be a major department store.

It was lunchtime, and the workers had scattered to eat. Reese, who wasn't hungry, had brought a copy of *The Wall Street Journal* to read.

"I can just guess who told you," Reese said, shaking his head. News traveled fast in his family by way of Mama Laverne. "Kenna wasn't exactly missing. Her car wouldn't start once she got to where they're building her condo, and her cell phone battery died. Luckily, she'd told one of her coworkers she was planning to stop by the site after work."

He frowned. "By the time I got there it was dark and she was a nervous wreck."

Dex nodded. "I can imagine with a killer on the loose."

"I hope they arrest him, and soon, or you're going to have people taking the law into their own hands and shooting anything that moves. Hell, Granddaddy Luke is talking about loading up his shotgun."

Dex chuckled. "Yeah, I heard about that. We might want to send Jake to talk to him. All Milton will do is help him load it."

Jake was the youngest of Reese's grandfather's brothers and Milton was the oldest; the difference in their ages was nearly twenty years. From what Reese had heard, Milton, who was Blade, Slade, Quantum and Jantzen's grandfather, had been hot-headed back in the day. Jake, the youngest of the seven Madaris brothers, had always kept a level head.

"Are you bringing Kenna to the meeting at Mom's tonight?" Dex asked.

"Yes, this thing is serious. Deadly serious," Reese replied. "There's never been a serial killer in Houston before, and I can't believe the police still don't have any leads."

"Yeah, well, I hear the killer has covered his tracks. I would just love to get my hands on him," Dex said angrily. "Even though most of the murders have happened at night, I don't plan on taking any chances where Caitlin and the girls are concerned. Caitlin and I are practically joined at the hip, and the girls are never out of our sight. But I've warned them about being careful during the daytime as well. Still, I'd loved to get my hands on him and give him a taste of his own medicine."

"I think you'll have to stand in line," Reese said.

That evening, his attention shifted from the magazine he was reading to the flat-screen television. He shook his head at the news report.

"This is the fourth woman that has been murdered in Houston within the past two weeks, and each was killed in a very violent way. They were all raped and then brutally tortured before being murdered. All the victim's bodies were found with only one shoe. So far, the police and the FBI don't have any real leads in finding a suspect in the Shoe Killer murders.

He smiled.

"Women are being warned to take every precaution. Houston police have increased their patrols around universities and shopping malls and they are encouraging businesses to install surveillance cameras in their parking lots to protect their employees, especially those who work at night. This is Cherie Saunders reporting for Channel 2 News."

He picked up the remote, turned off the television and continued reading his magazine.

* * *

Trevor looked over at Alex. "What have you been able to gather up so far?" he asked.

The four of them had met after their meeting with the mayor to determine the best way to proceed. They'd decided that it was best to involve as few people as possible—even their wives, although there would probably be hell to pay. But they eventually decided that it would be impossible to keep a secret from them, so they'd agreed to tell them tonight.

Since Alex's wife, Christy, was attending a meeting at her mother's house, they had decided to hold their meeting in the basement of his home. The place was set up with so much technical equipment and computers it looked like a NASA command center. Alex was able to pull in data from just about anywhere and had access to the FBI and Homeland Security intelligence.

Alex leaned back in his chair. "First, we are looking for a guy responsible for sixteen murders. His DNA is a positive match for all the women, but his DNA is not in any state or federal database. He's good at covering his tracks. But I think, as anxious as everyone is to get him off the streets, there are too many things that have been overlooked."

Ashton lifted a brow. "Such as?"

"There was a certain type of chewing gum wrapper found at a number of the crime scenes, but so far no one has determined what kind it is."

"That would matter?" Drake asked.

"Maybe, maybe not. Could be the clue we need. We can't leave any stone unturned. Here're the things that we do know. Number one, we are definitely looking for a man. The semen found on all the victims is from the same person. Number two, he takes the shoe of his victims as a souvenir, a trophy. And three, he kills just six women in each locale."

"That means he plans to kill two more women here in Houston before moving on," Trevor said.

"Yes," said Alex.

"What about the fact the majority of the women were handcuffed and stuffed in the trunk of a car? Are the handcuffs used by law enforcement?" Ashton asked.

"No," Alex replied. "Although they're just as effective, they're the kind you can pick up at any arts and crafts store." He shook his head, smiling. "They tried looking into bulk purchases of the handcuffs and found that they were a hot item for couples who're into bondage."

"Is there anything else about the information you've uncovered? I understand his first six victims were around Miami, and the next six were in Minneapolis," Sir Drake said.

"So far, all the women are professional women in some way, with nice jobs—not a prostitute among them. In fact, it seems he deliberately stays away from the seamier side."

Ashton nodded. "That is interesting. Apparently he's angry about something—maybe a wife or girlfriend. He's holding a grudge."

"Possibly," Alex said. "I also find it interesting that he seems to stay on top of what the police are doing. Like he might possibly have an inside connection."

"Or one of those police scanners," Trevor interjected.

"Precisely. They aren't hard to come by. I have one here myself," Alex said. "There're several places where they sell them in town. I'll run an inventory check to see if one has been recently purchased that raises a red flag."

"You mentioned the other killings were in Miami and Minneapolis," Trevor said thoughtfully. "Now he's here in Houston. Is that something significant we need to be concerned about?"

"Only if we can figure out a pattern that will tell us where he's going when he leaves Houston," Alex said softly. "But then I don't intend for him to leave here."

"At least not alive," Sir Drake said, standing. He was getting impatient. Everyone knew he was a man of few words but plenty of action. "Okay, where do we start? I'd like to get a move on before Ashton begins tracking him down. He'll take away all the fun."

"Then I guess the best way is to set up a trap," Ashton said, grinning.

"A trap?" Alex said, lifting a brow, hoping Ashton wasn't suggesting that one of them disguise themselves as a woman and hit the streets of Houston.

"Umm, trap. Did anyone call my name?" said a feminine voice behind them. They all turned around, surprised when Drake's wife, Tori, walked into the room.

Chapter 22

Kenna looked around the expansive, beautifully decorated great room. She had been to Reese's aunt's home once before. It was the same house his cousins Justin, Dex and Clayton were raised in. It had been a home filled with plenty of love, just like the house she'd grown up in as a child with her grandmother after her parents had died. Her grandfather had passed away before she was born, so she never got to know him. But Kenna figured that had he lived, he would have been much like Reese's grandfather—a crabby old man, who would do anything to protect his family. But then all the men in the Madaris family were that way. That was why it had been the men in the family who'd called the meeting and made sure that none of their wives had come alone.

"I think we all know why this meeting was called," Clayton Madaris said. "There's a serial killer in the Houston area, and until he is apprehended we want to make sure our families are safe."

The first thought that ran through Kenna's mind was that

technically she wasn't a part of the family. But evidently the Madarises felt that as Reese's friend she should be included. Reese hadn't given it much thought when he'd picked her up from work to drive her there.

Several of his aunts had prepared dinner for everyone, and the children had been ushered upstairs to the game room while the grown-ups held their meeting downstairs in the massive family room. According to Reese, the great room had been an addition to the house when his uncle Jonathan and aunt Marilyn needed a place for their growing number of grandchildren.

"Everyone should be paired up," Clayton said, interrupting her thoughts. "None of you ladies should be going anywhere alone, not even to get the mail out of your mailbox."

Dan Green smiled at his wife, Tracie. "I guess that means I'll be tagging along while you go shopping, sweetheart."

Kenna held back her laughter. Traci looked horrified at the thought. "But—but…I thought all the murders were committed at night," Traci stuttered.

"So far," Clayton said to his sister, trying to hide his smile. "But you never know when his pattern may change, so going shopping with your wife is a good idea, Dan," he said to his brother-in-law.

"What about those of us who have business trips and don't want to leave our wives and families alone?" asked Clayton's other brother-in-law, Raymond, who was married to Clayton's other sister, Kattie.

"Then she can stay with us until you return," Clayton said. "I take that back. She can come here and stay with the folks until you get back." The room burst into laughter. Reese leaned over to Kenna and said, "Kattie has a tendency to redecorate other people's homes, even when they don't ask her to."

Kenna looked over at Kattie, who smiled sweetly and shrugged. "I get bored easily."

"What about my shotgun?" Luke Madaris Sr. said loudly.

"Keep it handy, just in case," Milton Madaris suggested.

All eyes turned to Jake Madaris. "Nothing wrong with keeping it handy, Lucas, but it's not a good idea to load it right now," said Jake.

Lucas Sr. looked disappointed. "Not even one bullet?"

Jake hid a smile. "Not even one bullet."

"And if you're worried about your and Carrie's safety," Jake's wife, Diamond, said, "the two of you can certainly move in with us for a while. We have plenty of room."

Lucas's face broke into a huge grin. For any man to be under the same roof as the former Hollywood starlet was a dream come true, even if she was his sister-in-law. "Why, thank you, Diamond. I might…I mean Carrie and I might take you up on your offer."

"So does everyone understand?" Clayton asked. "We're in this together and are committed to protecting each other."

He turned his gaze toward Reese and Kenna. "Reese, what about Kenna? She works downtown, and we all heard what happened this week with her car breaking down. Can we be certain nothing like that will happen again?"

Kenna was surprised by the question and was just about to reassure everyone she was fine when Reese interrupted. "She won't be in any danger again. Until she has reliable transportation, I'll be taking her to work and picking her up in the evenings."

"Really, Reese, you don't have to do that."

"Yes, I do, sweetheart." Then he surprised her by leaning over and kissing her on the lips.

She swallowed, almost afraid to look around as the entire room got quiet. She saw every single person staring at them. Some looked surprised, but most didn't. It was Reese's mother who cleared her throat and asked softly. "Kenna? Reese? Is there something we need to know?"

"No," Kenna said quickly

"Yes," Reese said just as quickly.

Clayton chuckled, clearly amused. "Well, when the two of you decide what the answer is, please let all of us know."

A deep scowl appeared on Sir Drake's face. "What are you doing here, Tori?"

"I should be asking you the same thing." She glanced around. "Evening, gentlemen. Did you think you could keep me out of your little party?"

Ashton shook his head and chuckled. "We're curious as to how you knew we were meeting."

"Drake talks in his sleep," she said.

"I do not! So how did you know?" Sir Drake asked.

She smiled. "I overheard you on the phone with Ashton when you thought I was putting the baby down for her nap."

Drake lifted a brow. "In other words, you eavesdropped."

She waved off his words. "I never eavesdrop."

The three other men in the room simply stared at her. She smiled. "Okay, maybe I do sometimes. But still, you should have told me what's going on. I'll forgive you, Alex, for not knowing better. But these other three *do* know better."

Alex felt relieved that he was being given a reprieve. He'd seen Tori in action when she'd brought down a man twice her size. He thought the same thing now that he did then—that he wouldn't want to run into the former Marine and CIA agent, who was an expert in martial arts, in a dark alley. "I planned on telling you tonight," Sir Drake said.

"You should have told me *last* night," she countered. She then turned on Trevor and Ashton. "And when Corinthians and Nettie find out what the two of you are up to," she said, referring to their wives, "I hope they make you sleep on the couch for a year."

"Oh, you're mean," Ashton said, frowning.

"A regular drill sergeant," Trevor added with a scowl.

"You get what you deserve," she said. "So now, what were

you saying, Ashton? You mentioned something about setting a trap."

"You *won't* be involved, Tori!" Sir Drake stormed. "This killer is crazy."

She smiled. "All the more reason for him to finally meet a woman who can kick his ass. I'd like to see how he likes being the one thrown into a pit with rattlesnakes."

Alex cleared his throat. "The mayor wants everything legal."

"And I'll keep things legal. I won't intentionally harm a single hair on his head," she said, smiling sweetly.

Every man in the room gave her a skeptical look.

"Okay, I lied," she admitted, grinning. "But he deserves everything he has coming to him. And if he gets a few bones broken, his face smashed in and his eyeballs ripped from their sockets before the cops arrest him, so be it."

A smile curved Ashton's lips. "You've been hanging around Sir Drake too long."

Drake slowly crossed the room to his wife. "You were supposed to be at that meeting tonight with the other women," he said, his voice low, husky and surprisingly tender.

"I'm supposed to be here watching your back," she countered in a voice just as tender.

He reached out and caressed her cheek. "If anything were to happen to you…"

"It won't. You'll have my back," she said, entwining her fingers with his. She glanced behind him at the others. "All of you will. You all know me. I can hold my own."

The room got quiet and everyone looked at Drake. It would have to be his decision. After all, she was *his* wife. Moments passed as Drake stared at Tori. Then he reached out and wrapped his arms around her waist and held her against him. "If he harms you in any way, I'll kill him," Drake growled against her lips.

Tori chuckled. "If he harms me in any way I'll kill him myself."

Sir Drake couldn't help but smile at that.

"Is she in or not, Drake? The two of you are getting too mushy over there to suit me," Trevor said.

With his arms still draped around his wife, Drake nodded and said, "Yes, she's in."

Reese followed an angry Kenna through the front door. She had refused to say a single word to him all the way home. "I really don't know why you're upset."

She swung around to face him with fire in her eyes. "You kissed me—in front of your family."

He frowned. "It was just a kiss, Kenna. A small one."

"Yes, but friends don't exchange kisses on the lips like that," she said, tossing her purse on the table.

"I still don't see anything wrong with what I did."

She rolled her eyes. "Now you've got them all thinking that we're more than friends."

He threw up his hands in frustration. "First of all, most of them thought that anyway, and secondly," he said, following right on her heels into the kitchen, "we *are* more than friends."

"We're not!" she denied, swinging around so fast they almost bumped into each other. "We're only testing the waters to make sure things work out between us, which I figure they won't because I'm not the type of woman you're interested in. So no one was supposed to know we were lovers, Reese."

He opened his mouth to say something, but before he could Kenna continued her spiel. "Now, thanks to your kiss, your whole family knows, and I can only imagine what they think of me. They probably think I moved to Houston just to start something and that I'm some kind of stalker. They probably think that Alyson suits you a lot better than I do."

Reese didn't say anything for a moment as he tried to control his anger. Then he spoke in a low, tense tone. "If for one minute you assume my family thinks Alyson would be better for me than you are then you really don't know them at all. And if you assume I think something like that, too, then you don't know *me* either."

Evidently she saw the ferocious expression on his face and chose to keep quiet. As far as he was concerned that was a good move on her part, because he was past angry. He was in full-fledged rage, and he'd never been this mad at Kenna before. Not even close.

"You are one piece of work, lady," he said, feeling steam coming from his ears. "You can't see what's right in front of your eyes. I've tried showing you and you still can't see it. You are not only the friend I've come to know and trust, but I've fallen in love with you, Kenna. I was trying to put my words into action by showing you instead of just telling you how much I love you. And if you can't handle it, then I don't know what to say."

Heaving a sigh of frustration, he then turned and stormed out of the kitchen.

Kenna stood rooted in place, shocked. Did Reese just say he loved her? She shook her head, thinking she had a few screws loose, but then she knew she hadn't heard wrong. He *had* said he loved her. Yes, he'd actually said it, and he'd said it like he really meant it. And he was mad, literally pissed, that she didn't believe, couldn't believe that he wanted her and not Alyson.

Happiness suffused her heart and filled her with a warmth she'd never felt before. The incredibly sexy Reese Madaris loved her! She closed her eyes and breathed his name on a sigh. She quickly opened her eyes when she realized that at the moment, the incredibly sexy Reese Madaris was pretty angry at her for not believing he loved her.

On shaky legs she hurriedly followed him. When she reached

the living room she heard a noise upstairs and slowly walked up the staircase. Reese loved her, and she intended to show him just how much she loved him as well.

Chapter 23

Kenna didn't believe him, Reese thought, stripping off his shirt, sending buttons flying in the process. He was royally pissed. What was it with her thinking Alyson was supposed to be the one woman he wanted? She should have known from that night at the party that Alyson was so far out the picture that it wasn't funny. And the other day she had mentioned seeing Alyson and *Dr.* Wendell Thomas together. Had she expected to get some kind of rise out of him? Some sign that he was jealous? Clayton had been right when he'd warned him that women were complicated.

He went to the window and gazed out into the darkness. But he didn't need the daylight to see all of his land, all seventy-something acres. It was a drop in the bucket compared to what his uncle Jake and his brother Chance owned, but it was his. And more than anything he wanted to share it with Kenna.

Not only did he want to share his land, but he wanted them to have babies together, beautiful babies, as many as she wanted. He envisioned her standing at an easel painting, while several little ones were at her feet. That was an image he'd carried around with him for some time but was too afraid to ever see it for what it was or what it might mean. He didn't want to be just a godfather to her children, he wanted to father them. He wanted to plant the seed in her body that would procreate their family.

He heard the soft knock on his bedroom door. "Come in," he said without turning around. He didn't have to, since he could see her reflection in the window.

She was nervous. He could tell by the way she rubbed her hands together. She probably didn't know that he was very much aware that she was checking him out, taking note of the fact that he didn't have his shirt on.

Her eyes were taking him in, and in her reflection he saw the heated look in her gaze. His heartbeat raced as his chest tightened. He loved her so damn much, and before she left this room tonight, he would show her *and* tell her.

It was at that moment, after he'd made up his mind about how he would handle LaKenna James, that he turned around and said, "Is there something you want?"

Kenna gritted her teeth, forcing back what she really wanted to say, which was something like, *Oh yeah, I want to take those jeans off your body and then push you back on that bed and ride you in a way that I've never ridden Rollins.* When she walked into his room she hadn't expected to find him half naked, displaying a strong, muscular back and the thick cords of his broad shoulders. And she couldn't overlook how his jeans clung perfectly to his backside. She unconsciously licked her lips.

"Kenna?"

She blinked. She hated that her mind wandered. "I want to talk…to make sure I heard you correctly downstairs when you said…"

Kenna swallowed, unable to get the words out because she

couldn't comprehend having a man say he loved her and truly meaning it. Terrence had said it like it was nothing, but that hadn't stopped him from finding his way into another woman's bed. Lamont had claimed he loved her in one breath, while voicing his distrust of her and Reese's relationship with the next. Now she had serious doubts that either of them had loved her at all. She realized they had been saying what they thought she wanted to hear, but it definitely wasn't in their hearts. She didn't want to think about Curtis and how deceitful he'd been. He had claimed he loved her, too, but in the end she'd discovered he'd only wanted her to help him keep his secret.

"When I said what, Kenna?"

She unconsciously licked her lips again when Reese interrupted her thoughts. "When you said what you did in the kitchen."

Reese met her gaze and held it. He slowly began walking over to her. At first he decided to make it hard for her and make her come to him. But then he decided he would save her the trip. The sooner they cleared things up between them, the sooner they could spend the rest of the night in each other's arms. But that was only if she loved him. That was something that was still up in the air. Something he didn't have a clue about.

"What did I say in the kitchen, Kenna? You tell me," he said softly, forcing her to say the words aloud. "And if for some reason you can't repeat it because you don't feel the same way, then I understand and I accept that for now. But only for now, because I'm going to make you love me," he said with conviction.

He saw her eyes become moist before a single tear slid down her cheek. "But you don't have to do that, because I already love you, Reese. I've always loved you. You've been there for me. You've been my strength when I didn't have any. You were someone I could talk to about anything. You were my best friend, and that was what frightened me. I didn't know how you felt and I was afraid that if you found out how I felt, then you wouldn't want me as a friend any longer."

She swiped her tears away. “Everything was fine as long as you had a girlfriend and I had a boyfriend. But when that changed, my attention focused on you, and my attraction to you became too intense. I was afraid that you would find out the truth.”

He tried to follow what she was saying and suddenly a lightbulb went on his head. “Is that why you kept pushing Alyson in my face? You thought our friendship would be safe if I was with someone?”

“Yes. I thought it would be safe if you had a girlfriend and I had a boyfriend.”

Reese slowly nodded. “Okay, now I’m following you, although I don’t agree with it. So tell me why you thought we were just testing the waters? Why would you think after all we shared we could go back to being just friends?”

Kenna looked down at the floor, knowing she had to be honest and speak directly from her heart. She slowly raised her head to meet his gaze. “I was too afraid to think otherwise, too frightened to hope that you could possibly find something in me that you couldn’t in Alyson. She’s beautiful and refined and most of the time she looks like a model. She has a prestigious job and—”

“She’s as phony as a three-dollar bill. I can see right through her.”

“But the two of you dated for almost a year,” Kenna implored.

“Because she was convenient and fun, and because at the time you were dating Curtis.”

He chuckled. “My family had the right idea all along, which is why most of them weren’t surprised tonight by that kiss. I kept telling them we were just friends and none of them believed it. Oh, they pretended to, because they knew that’s what I wanted them to believe. But none of them really did.”

Kenna lifted a dark brow. “Are you saying that they’ve…”

“Been waiting for both of us to come to our senses and

realize what they already knew. There has always been more than friendship between us. I love you, Kenna, and you are—and forever will be—the only woman that I want."

"Oh, Reese." She moved closer as he pulled her into his arms, surrounding her with his embrace. He'd held her before. But she knew this time was different. Not only was this where she wanted to be, but this was where he wanted her to be.

And then he eased back and she caught a glimpse of the smoldering look in his eyes before he lowered his head to kiss her. She thought like she always did that there was nothing quite like a Reese Madaris kiss. As if on cue, her nipples hardened against his naked chest and the lower part of her body cradled his huge erection. A firestorm of desire swept through her on a wave that made her shiver all over. A warm and tingling sensation stirred in her stomach and had her heart pounding like crazy. Suddenly she was being swept off her feet into Reese's strong arms and she knew he was carrying her over to his bed.

And there he placed her, in the center of the bed, before taking a step back to relieve himself of his jeans and briefs. She watched, fascinated, enthralled as he stripped for her, revealing the sexiest body any man could possess. She couldn't help trembling in appreciation and anticipation.

And when he stood before her completely naked, her gaze roamed the full length of him. But time and time again her gaze returned to where his manhood stood proudly erect, jutting from a thatch of dark, curly hair.

"Like what you see, LaKenna James?"

"Yes, definitely, but I can't ask you the same thing because I still have my clothes on."

He chuckled. "Not for long."

He moved toward the bed, and when he reached for her she came to him and slid her arms around his neck. This time it was she who went for his mouth, needing the taste of him. Their tongues mated, tangled and twisted as she felt passion oozing from every pore.

He broke off the kiss and reached out and tilted her chin upward so their eyes could meet. “I love you,” he whispered.

His words sent everything within her spiraling and she fought back her tears when she whispered back, “And I love you, too.”

The corners of her lips curved into a smile, and then he began undressing her, chuckling in his throat and murmuring out loud that she had too many clothes on. By the time he had removed the last stitch of clothing from her body she intended to make the time he’d spent undressing her well worth it.

Chapter 24

"Thanks, Reese, for allowing my daughter to come see your horses," Lynette said as she walked beside him and Kenna as they headed toward the barn.

Reese smiled. "No problem. The two of you are welcome at Tall Oaks Ranch any time. "

He glanced over at Kenna and gave her a loving glance as he remembered what had taken place since they had professed their love for each other three nights ago. They had done a lot of talking and had reached the conclusion that they'd wasted a lot of years by keeping their true feelings hidden and that wouldn't ever happen again. They were now doing more than testing the waters. They were committed to building a solid relationship based on love. It was the kind of relationship they should have had years ago, but they accepted the fact that everything happened in due time and now was their time to be together.

He smiled as he observed Lynette's daughter as she skipped and hopped ahead of them, excited by the prospect of seeing his horses. In that instant he could imagine his own little girl, one who would have her mother's looks, but especially her smile. And the only woman he would want to be the mother of his children was Kenna.

"Is there anything I can help you with, Mr. Madaris?"

Reese glanced up and saw Clark Lovell. According to Joe, Lovell was a hard worker who stayed to himself. Although he periodically slept in the bunkhouse with the men, he kept a place somewhere in town.

"Yes, Lovell, this is Lynette Cummings and her daughter, Aleena. They're here as our guests for the day. Aleena is fascinated by horses, so I thought we'd show her some."

Lovell extended his hand to Lynette. "Nice to meet you, Ms, Cummings."

"It's a pleasure to meet you as well," Lynette said, accepting the man's handshake.

Lovell glanced down at Aleena and smiled. "She's a pretty little girl."

"Thanks, and she's dying to see the horses," Lynette said smiling.

"Would it be okay if I let her ride one of the ponies while I hold the reins and walk her around a couple of times?" Lovell asked.

Lynette's face showed concern. "Will it be safe?"

Lovell nodded and smiled. "Yes, I'll make sure that it is."

"All right then."

Reese and Kenna hung back and leaned against the post of the corral while Lovell led Lynette and Aleena to where one of the ponies was grazing. They watched how Lovell introduced the little girl to the pony and how she jumped up and down, obviously excited.

"Lovell surprises me," Reese said softly. "He seems comfortable with kids. Not everyone has the kind of patience with a child that he's showing Aleena."

Kenna studied the man and had to agree. She glanced over at Lynette, and from the look on her friend's face Kenna could see that Lynette was just as fascinated with Clark Lovell as Aleena was with the pony.

"Don't forget we're having dinner at my grandparents' place tomorrow," Reese reminded her.

She returned his smile and automatically felt an intimate connection, even though they weren't touching. There was a strong sexual chemistry between them, and just being close to him had her pulse beating rapidly.

"I know," she said softly. "And I hope you know they're going to expect us to give them an answer to your mother's question from the other night."

Reese chuckled. "Yes, that's a sure bet. Are you ready to satisfy their curiosity?"

"Yes."

His smile widened. "Good."

Just then Reese's cell phone went off. "Excuse me a minute. This is the call I've been expecting from Dex."

"All right." She watched as Reese walked back toward the house before she turned around to observe Clark Lovell placing Aleena on the pony's back to let her ride.

After satisfying herself that her little girl wouldn't fall off the pony and that Lovell had everything under control, Lynette strolled over to where Kenna stood.

"Aleena is having the time of her life," Lynette said, smiling.

Kenna chuckled. "Yes, I can see she is. And Lovell is good with her."

"He most certainly is, *and* he's extremely handsome," Lynette whispered.

Kenna laughed. "I see you noticed."

"Hey, you'd have to be blind not to. *Good-God-almighty,* look how he's wearing those jeans. The one thing he's not wearing is a wedding ring. Is he married? "

"I don't think so." Then Kenna remembered the night she saw him returning to the bunkhouse late. "But he might have a girlfriend, I'm not sure."

"Well, what are you sure about? What do you know about him?"

At that moment Kenna realized just how little she did know about Clark. "He's only worked here a month and he stays to himself. I've only had a brief conversation with him myself."

Lynette shook her head and smiled ruefully. "Then you're no help. I think I'll mosey back over there just to make sure he notices me like I'm noticing him."

Kenna lifted a brow. "And what about Shaun?"

"He's had his chance," Lynette said dryly. "Besides, sometimes reality hits you in the face and makes you realize when you've been wasting your time."

Kenna simply nodded and watched as Lynette returned to where Lovell was still walking Aleena around the corral on the pony. She stood there and stared, taking it all in, while Lynette did a little flirting. It was hard to tell from where Kenna was standing if Lovell was being receptive or not.

"Alex called after I finished talking to Dex. He's dropping by sometime tomorrow to pick up that book you had for Christy," Reese said, returning.

"All right."

He followed the direction of her gaze. "How are things going? Looks like Aleena is enjoying herself"

A smile touched Kenna's lips. She was tempted to say Aleena's mother was enjoying herself as well. "Things are going well, and yes, I think Aleena is having a good time."

"So what's this I hear about you and Kenna finally realizing that the two of you are more than friends?" Alex said as he slid into the chair in Reese's office.

Reese leaned back in his desk chair across from Alex, thinking news sure traveled fast. Christy certainly hadn't wasted time giving her husband the scoop. Any other time he would have denied everything, but the truth of the matter was that Alex was right. He and Kenna were more than friends. "Yes, you heard right."

Alex chuckled. "About time. I figured it out a while ago. When you've been in denial yourself, you tend to recognize it in others."

Everyone knew Christy had had a crush on Alex as a kid, but most people assumed she'd grow out of it. The family had been surprised to discover that wasn't the case. But Reese knew no one had been more surprised than Alex.

Unless they ran into each other at the Madaris Building, Reese and Alex rarely saw each other these days, so they spent the next few minutes catching up on their favorite sports teams.

The conversation was interrupted when Reese received a call from one of his men, whose wife was pregnant, announcing that he was the proud father of a baby boy. When Reese hung up the phone he noticed Alex was staring out the window.

"Who's that guy out here in the red shirt?" Alex asked. "I don't think I've ever seen him before."

Reese walked across the room to join Alex at the window and looked out. "That's Clark Lovell. I hired him about a month ago."

Alex nodded as he continued to stare at the man. "Is he from around here?"

"No, he's from somewhere up north. Boston, I think. He's a loner with no family. He came highly recommended from the last ranch he worked. He's good with horses."

Alex nodded again. "He lives here on the ranch?"

"Sometimes. But he also has a place in town and stays there most of the time." Reese studied Alex's features. "Why do you want to know about Lovell?"

Alex shrugged. "His face looks familiar. He reminds me of someone."

Alex felt his phone vibrate, letting him know he'd received a text message. Moments later he smiled after reading the text from his wife. "Christy needs me to make another stop before I get home. Since she can't go out by herself, she has me running all her errands."

Alex grinned. "But then there are benefits to keeping your woman locked behind closed doors. You might want to keep that in mind."

As Alex drove away from Tall Oaks, he had a nagging suspicion that he'd seen Clark Lovell somewhere before—either personally or on a case. But what case? Had the man been involved in something illegal? Did he remember him from a police lineup? Knowing he wouldn't be satisfied until he had some answers, he punched in a single number on the keypad on his dashboard.

"Yes, sweetheart. Did you forget what I asked you to bring home?" a sexy voice inquired.

He chuckled. "No, but I would like you to do me a favor after you've put A.C. down for her nap." A.C. was the nickname for their two-year-old daughter, Alexandria Christina.

"What's the favor?"

"I need you to put your investigative skills to work and come up with anything on a Clark Lovell. He's a new hire at Tall Oaks and there's something about him that's familiar."

"Familiar in what way?"

"His face. Although from what I remember, his hair might have been a darker shade of blond, even a light brown. I'm not sure."

"I'll see what I can come up with."

Before they'd married, Christy had been an investigative reporter and one of her assignments, which nearly ended her life, was an award-winning exposé. "Thanks, sweetheart."

He settled back in his seat, satisfied that he would soon have some answers.

* * *

He looked at himself in the mirror. It was time. He needed to kill like he needed to breathe. And he knew just what part of Houston he would hit this time. He knew he had the police scrambling and wondering what his next move would be. Too bad they didn't know, but he knew what their next move would be. Good for him, but tragic for them. He smiled as he headed out the door.

"I think Alex had the right idea," Reese said in a raspy voice as he stepped into the room that Kenna had been using as her art studio. He closed the door behind him and locked it.

Kenna glanced over at him and smiled. "The right idea about what?"

"Keeping your woman locked behind closed doors."

Kenna warmed with pleasure at the thought that he considered her *his woman.* And then there was the way he looked at her. It made her stomach quiver so much that she wondered how two people could generate so much heat.

She looked away from him and turned her attention back to the canvas. "Thanks for letting Aleena ride your pony. She and Lynette had a wonderful time."

"You don't have to thank me. It was wonderful having them. They can come back anytime."

"They'll like that, especially since I think Lynette has her eye on Clark."

Reese chuckled. "Does she?"

"Yes, and I have to admit that before she left she had managed to warm him up a bit. I saw him smile a few times."

"Did you?"

"Yes, I would have invited her and Aleena to dinner one evening next week, but starting tonight Lynette is going undercover for a week."

Reese raised a brow. "Who keeps Aleena when she's working undercover?"

"Her parents or one of her sisters. They're close like your family." She thought for a minute about just how close his family was. The meeting this week was just one example of how the Madaris family looked out for one another.

"So what are you painting?" he asked. Before she could respond, Reese walked around the easel to see for himself. She watched as a huge smile curved his sexy lips. "Hey, that's me."

She laughed. "Yes, it's you."

He studied the painting, taking in every detail and then giving her a sidelong glance. "You were able to paint a portrait without me posing?"

"Yes."

"How?" he asked, turning to her.

She glanced up at him. "From memory."

He glanced back at the canvas and then at her and held her gaze. She knew what was going through his mind. She had painted him from memory. She had captured every detail and nuance, leaving nothing out. There was the deep set of his eyebrows, his sculpted cheekbones and chiseled jawline, the dark brown shade of his bedroom eyes and the rich copper tone of his skin. She had drawn the perfect bow shape of his lips, in all their decadent splendor.

For her to do that meant he was etched in her memory in a way that Reese would never have thought possible. And from the look on his face, she could tell he was touched.

"You actually painted this from memory?" he asked in a low, husky tone.

"Yes."

He didn't say anything for a moment. "What possessed you to do that?"

She leaned close to him and snuggled against his body, needing to feel his warmth and the love he'd professed to her.

"I was going to put it in my new condo on my bedroom wall, so that you would be in my room every night."

It might have been what she said rather than the way she said it, or it could have been a combination of both. Whatever the reason, Reese pulled her closer into his arms and kissed her. He was kissing her in such a way that he left an indelible impression on her lips. It left no doubt in her mind just how he felt.

She'd always known he wasn't a man given to casual affairs, and most of the women he'd dated had been long-term relationships. But she doubted that any of them had ever been kissed this way by Reese Madaris. It was as if he had claimed her as his and his alone.

He slowly pulled his mouth away and then proceeded to use the tip of his tongue to trace the upper ridge of her lip and then sweep the outline of her mouth, licking, nibbling and doing naughty things to her. Heat was flooding every part of her body, and if she hadn't been leaning against him for support, she was certain she would have melted right to the floor.

"I never knew you cared that much," he whispered against her moistened lips. "I never suspected that you loved me."

"Typical," she teased in an attempt to make light of what he'd said when she knew deep down just how serious he was. "But how could you not have known—even though I tried hard to keep it from you. Didn't you suspect something when I turned down that scholarship to go to Paris?"

He pulled back, his brow furrowed and his brown eyes speculative when he realized what she had sacrificed. He remembered when she'd passed on the chance to study art in Paris. Instead, she had opted to remain in Austin while he was in grad school and use her gift by going to work for the police department as a sketch artist. "Are you saying you didn't go to Paris because of me?"

She eyed him warily, not certain if she'd revealed too much.

He had a right to know just how deeply she loved him and always had.

"Yes, there was no way I could have left you, Reese. I would have been miserable, heartbroken."

She exhaled a long breath. "And that's why I took the job in Austin, so I could be near you."

"Is that the reason you took the job here in Houston?" he asked, not breaking eye contact with her.

She shook her head. "No. To tell the truth, that's the main reason I didn't want to take it. I felt I had to face the fact that one day you would marry someone, and as much as another woman might say our 'best friend' relationship was fine with her, I couldn't allow myself to get too close. I thought that eventually you would realize that I wanted more than friendship and begin backing away."

"So you thought the best move was to put distance between us, right?"

She smiled, deciding maybe he wasn't all that slow after all. "Yes, that's right."

At that moment Reese didn't know what to say. But he did know he could never love her any more than he did at that very moment. For all those years she had loved him and he hadn't had a clue. He could only think of all those wasted years he'd spent with other women when he could have been with her. And all those times she'd spent with men like Terrence, Lamont, Curtis when it could have been...*should* have been him.

He should have been the one who showed her how a real man treated a woman. He should have been the one courting her, the man who would never have let her walk to her front door alone after a date. She deserved all those things and much more. And more than anything, she deserved to know just how much she was loved, just like she'd shown him how much she loved him with her selflessness.

"Do you know what I plan on doing?" he asked her softly, leaning closer to place a kiss on her temple.

"No, what are you planning to do?" she asked, smiling.

He tilted her chin up so their eyes connected. "Starting now, this hour, this minute, this very second, I plan to show you each and every day of your life just how much you are loved, admired, respected, honored and cherished. And then when you think you can't possibly get any more love from a man I'm going to prove you wrong."

He stood there, watching her, studying her features, seeing how her eyes lit up as the full impact of what he'd said took hold. There was something so spine-tinglingly sexy about that moment, seeing her standing there in her bare feet and wearing one of his old T-shirts that fit her voluptuous body perfectly. Just looking at her made his entire stomach flutter in a way it had never done before.

"And how do you plan to do that?" she asked softly, as curiosity shone in her gaze.

"I won't reveal my secrets, but it will be the Madaris way." And then to show her what he meant, he leaned down and slanted his mouth across hers.

Kenna heard herself moan when Reese deepened the kiss, and she stretched her limbs to tiptoe as her body reacted instinctively to his. She felt his hands trailing down her thighs, touching her bare flesh. The feel of his fingers was warm, and the slow seductive way they moved across her skin was stirring intense pleasure within her. When he slid his hands higher to make their way under her T-shirt she knew it was only a matter of time before he realized she wasn't wearing any panties.

Heat burned through her the moment the discovery was made, and when he touched her intimately, her thighs automatically widened to allow him all the access he wanted. With quick and sure fingers he moved beyond her womanly folds to insert one finger inside her.

His touch always had the power to send her over the edge, but for some reason she felt tonight he intended to toy with her, drive her crazy with desire, turn her body into a sexual frenzy before satisfying the need he was slowly stoking within her. He didn't prove her wrong when his gifted hands continued their torment, using the rhythm of his fingers to stroke and spin her out of control. "Reese…"

"Yes, baby," he whispered softly against her ear while slowly walking her backward until she felt her back pressed against a solid wall. Her breath caught with the intense look of heat in his eyes when he pulled his hands free from her.

"You have no idea how much I want you or how much I love you, Kenna," he murmured before nibbling hungrily at her mouth.

Then she felt herself being raised off her feet and she instinctively wrapped her legs around his waist. She moaned when she felt her feminine mound rub against the hard erection tucked behind his jeans.

"You want it?" he whispered against her moist lips.

"Yes," she whispered back without any hesitancy. "I want it."

He leveled his gaze at hers. "Are you sure?"

Oh, no. He's going to torture me. How could he be so cruel at a time like this? "Yes, I'm sure," she uttered in agony.

"Do you want it enough to marry me?"

She blinked and searched his face, not believing what he'd asked her.

"I know, it's a hell of a way to propose, but I figured now is as good a time as any. So will you marry me, Kenna, and take me out of my misery just as I'll be taking you out of yours?"

Her joy was overwhelming. "Ask me again later," Kenna said as she reached down and unzipped his pants. Probing him with her free hand, she worked her way past his briefs to take the fullness of his thick shaft into her hand. It felt hot, it was big and it was what she wanted. Pure, unadulterated desire ripped into her as she rubbed the massive head of his manhood with her fingers, awed by the smooth surface and the masculine scent that she inhaled through her nostrils.

But that wasn't enough. She adjusted her body slightly to lead him to her. The feel of him sliding through her hot wetness had every part of her throbbing and was sending sensations rippling through her all the way down to the soles of her feet. He used his knee to nudge her thighs apart even more to make the journey inside of her that much more titillating. He was hot, hard and huge, and as he made his way beyond her feminine folds her inner muscles began clenching him, milking him and priming him for what was to come.

And then he was there, inside of her to the hilt, tightening his hands on her backside, pulling his manhood out and then surging deeply back inside of her. He began moving, rocking his body against hers as he thrust in and out, pounding into her body hard, driving her delirious with sexual hunger.

"Now is later. Will you marry me?" he asked between thrusts while leaning close to her lips. "Will you take my name? Have my babies? Will you let me show you what love is all about?"

He didn't give her a chance to respond when he inserted his tongue into her mouth, taking hold of hers and kissing her deeply while he continued to grind into her, making her moan.

"That doesn't sound like a yes to me," he said, after breaking off the kiss and using his tongue to lick around her lips, nipping at the corners. He continued to thrust inside of her and she thought she would go out of her mind. Then he tilted her body and thrust deep into her at an angle that she'd never felt before. She let out a screeching "oooh."

"That still doesn't sound like a yes," he persisted. His voice was too deep and heavy with raw sexual need for her to be unaffected.

Then he reached down and touched her throbbing clitoris,

sending waves of heat to the juncture where their bodies were joined. Instinctively, she parted her thighs for him to go deeper still. She could feel him all the way to her core as they mated in a torrid, undulating, pounding rhythm.

"Come on, baby," he urged against her wet lips. "Say yes for me."

As if her body was heeding his command, it began shuddering, triggering an explosion that made her scream and scream loudly. "Yes! Yes! Ohhh, yes!"

"Now that's what I wanted to hear," he whispered, letting out a deep groan and climaxing with her in an orgasm that seemed to make the entire house shake. They were drenched in a tidal wave of pleasure that threatened to take them under, submerge them and drown them completely in their sexual juices. Their bodies continued to mate hungrily until there was nothing left to give.

Reese stayed inside of her, refusing to disengage as he drew in a sharp breath before licking the sweat off her forehead. She breathed in deeply, taking in his masculine scent through her nostrils. She met his gaze. "That was some proposal," she said, barely able to get the words out.

He smiled cockily and responded, "And that was one hell of a yes."

Chapter 25

Half an hour later, Reese was in his huge bed, holding Kenna protectively in his arms while she slept. He leaned over and pressed a kiss to her cheek while thinking, *I am officially an engaged man.* At his folks' dinner tomorrow evening he and Kenna would not only answer his mother's question, but they would have an even bigger surprise for everyone.

Reese paused, thinking maybe it wouldn't be such a surprise after all. Maybe it was the announcement his family had been expecting to hear. He smiled, realizing his family had been on to them long before they were even aware of their own feelings.

He had definitely been a bit slow. And to think Kenna had given up a chance to study art in Paris because she hadn't wanted to leave him. He hadn't had a clue. Nor had he ever suspected her reason for moving to Austin when he was in grad school. He had wanted her near him and had never questioned what he'd considered merely a stroke of good luck.

She was a gifted artist, and now that he knew the truth, he

would encourage her to pursue her talent. The first thing he intended to do after they married was to lease one of the spaces in the Madaris Building for her art gallery. He could see her work being displayed there for everyone to see what a gifted artist she was. And he would also get Blade and Slade to build her a studio somewhere on Tall Oaks, so she could paint to her heart's content.

He knew if he remained in bed with her much longer he would be tempted to wake her up and make love to her again. He eased from her side to sit on the edge of the bed. He was surprised when he heard the sound of a car outside. Seemed like one of his ranch hands had a late-night date planned. He glanced at the clock. It was past midnight, definitely a late night.

He moved toward the window in time to see Clark Lovell's truck heading down the road. He was surprised to see the man had come out of his shell as much as he had with Lynette and her little girl. He'd actually seemed to enjoy having them around.

"Reese?"

He turned around at the sound of Kenna's voice. He walked over to the bed and eased back beside her. "Yes?"

"I had this wonderful dream," she said softly, reaching out and taking the tip of her finger to run across the dark shadow covering his jaw.

"What was your dream about, sweetheart?"

A smile tugged at her lips. "This extremely handsome, sexy man asked me to marry him while we were in the middle of making love."

He chuckled. "Did you stop long enough to at least say yes?"

"I said yes, but we didn't stop. It was too good."

"How good?"

"This good."

She pushed him back on the bed and eased on top to straddle him, determined to show him just how good it was.

* * *

"Hey, sugar, you having car trouble?"

Tori lifted her head from under the hood of her car and gave the man approaching her a long, measured look. So far he was the third man to stop to help a damsel in distress. And so far all the others accepted her, "No, thank you, my friend is on the way." But from the swagger of this one, she had a feeling that wouldn't be the case.

He had an intense look on his face, and the tilt of his cowboy hat shielded his eyes in a way that kept his face hidden. What really raised her suspicion was when a car pulled up behind him and another man slowly got out.

She drew in a deep breath. A part of her didn't think either man was the Shoe Killer but two cowboys who'd come across a single woman at night stranded on a rarely traveled road. And from the look in the second man's eyes as he got out of his car, they intended to have a little fun. If either thought they were doing so at her expense, they were wrong and might end up dead wrong if Drake had anything to do with it.

"Drake, let me handle this," she said, barely moving her lips, into the hidden microphone in her bra. She fought to keep from smiling at the sound of his grunt.

"No, I don't need any help. I've already called someone," she said, speaking loudly when both men approached her.

"Well, sugar, you didn't have to call anyone."

"Yes, I did."

At that moment a car driven by a woman went by, slowing down after a quick glance at Tori, but kept on moving, even picking up speed. *Typical, decided to mind her own business,* Tori thought to herself. She couldn't blame the woman too much, especially in light of all that was going on in the city.

"Aren't you a pretty thing," the second man said.

"She sure is," the first agreed. "We want to have some fun."

Tori rolled her eyes. "Look guys, be nice and move on. I'm not in the mood."

"Boy, you're kind of feisty, aren't you? What if we told you that we don't want to move on and that we *are* in the mood?"

"Then I would tell you that kind of thinking could get you both killed. My husband is a very jealous man," she warned.

"Then he should have been smart enough not to let such a luscious-looking woman like yourself break down on the side of the road. You do know there's a killer on the loose don't you?" the second man said, grinning like it was a joke or something.

She tilted her head to size them up. "Are you making some kind of confession?"

"No, but we've been known to seize a few opportunities if given the chance."

"Seize a few opportunities like what?"

"Like this."

She saw them coming and was prepared when both men tried to jump her at the same time. She went karate-crazy on them, and before they could blink she had knocked their legs out from under them. They found themselves flat on their backsides on the ground. And from the look on their shocked faces, they were pissed.

But then so was Tori.

When the first man made a move to get up, Tori put her hands on her hips. "I would stay down if I were you. In case neither of you noticed, your forehead has an infrared beam on it. And that jealous husband of mine has you in the scope of his high-powered rifle and is set to blow both of your brains out."

The two men quickly looked at each other and saw the red dot on their foreheads shift from one man to the other. They looked terrified. "Hell, lady, call him off. We were only joking."

She smiled sweetly. "It's going to be hard to convince him of that, especially when there's no telling what the two of you would have done had I not been able to defend myself."

"Like I said, we were only joking," the second man said angrily, making an attempt to stand, but when a shot rang out that barely missed his ear, he quickly dropped back down to the ground.

"Lady, can we go?" the first man asked in a cowardly tone.

Tori glared at them. "I guess, but the next time you stop to help a woman, make sure your intentions are honorable," she said, although she doubted these two knew what being honorable meant.

"And because my husband is known to hold a grudge, I would suggest you look over your shoulders after tonight. No telling when he might show up, and trust me, he *will* show up again. He's not through with the two of you yet."

The men swallowed, looked at each other and then practically crawled back to their cars. But not before Drake shot holes in both of their hats. They took off like the devil himself was behind them.

Tori shook her head frowning. "You just had to show off didn't you, Drake?"

She heard his husky chuckle. "Yes. And what you told them was right. I'm not through with them yet. Go ahead and let's call it a night. We'll do it again tomorrow night."

Tori nodded as she got into her car. She had a feeling that the killer was out there tonight somewhere, and he was on the hunt.

Alex looked up when Christy placed the file on his desk. He smiled, thinking he'd married a beautiful woman. "What did you find out?"

She shrugged. "There're a lot of Clark Lovells out there, but none fit the description of the man you described and none from Boston."

Alex leaned back in his chair. "I've been racking my brain trying to remember where I know him from."

"But you're sure you know him from somewhere?" she asked circling his desk and sitting down on his lap.

He quickly wrapped his arms around her. "Yes and that's what bothers me."

He paused. "So does the information I've gathered about those murders in Minnesota and Miami that I'm going over with everyone tomorrow night. I might have found a connection. Also, I will have narrowed down that list of people in the Houston area who purchased police scanners recently by then."

She nodded. "I know where Sir Drake and Tori are tonight, but what about Trevor and Ashton?" Christy asked, snuggling closer into her husband's arms.

Alex smiled. "Both Trevor and Ashton are on patrol tonight." He chuckled. "In other words, they're hunting the hunter."

He entered the house and slammed the door closed. Tonight had been a bust, and he wasn't happy about it. There seemed to be police everywhere. He'd run into several roadblocks, and officers had checked his driver's license. It was a good thing he had several IDs, just in case they were keeping a record of everyone they stopped.

He sat down at the table to think about tonight. He refused to let a few police officers derail his plans. He would try his luck again tomorrow.

Chapter 26

By the time Reese arrived at his grandparents' home, he had decided how he would announce his engagement to everyone. Looking at the number of cars parked in the driveway, it appeared his grandparents had invited more than the usual number of guests.

After opening the car door for Kenna, he took her hand in his as they strolled up the walkway. Two of the parked cars he recognized belonged to his cousins Corbin and Lee. It wasn't unusual for the two to drop by his grandparents' home on Sundays, especially when everyone knew how Grandma Carrie loved to cook, and how good she was at it.

But then most of the women in the Madaris family knew their way around the kitchen—the men as well, thanks to Mama Laverne's mandatory cooking classes. He'd been forced to take her cooking class. And although he had resented it at the time, he appreciated it later. He wasn't the casserole chef that Luke was, but he could hold his own. Kenna always complimented him on the meals he made for her.

He glanced over at her. As usual she looked beautiful, and he'd made sure she had gotten a good night's sleep. He was glad of that.

"You okay?" he asked her softly.

She glanced up at him and smiled. "Yes. What about you?"

He chuckled. "I couldn't be better."

Even though they slept late, they'd dressed quickly and still made it to church before the preacher's sermon. After church they returned home and took a nap before getting dressed to come to his grandparents. He felt good. No—he felt great. At the moment, he couldn't be better.

Without warning he stopped walking and pulled Kenna into his arms. He kissed the surprised look off her face and deepened the kiss when he heard her soft moan of acceptance and surrender. He hadn't realized until now how much he enjoyed kissing, but that was only because it was Kenna.

He heard several family members clearing their throats, and for a while he ignored them. But when it seemed they wouldn't stop, he gave up. He released Kenna's mouth as he held her around the waist and glanced toward his grandmother's doorway where Corbin, Lee and Nolan stood. From the looks on their faces, they seemed rather amused.

"Aunt Carrie said not to give her neighbors something to talk about by kissing Kenna in the front yard, Reese," Lee said, grinning. "I've heard of kissing cousins but never kissing friends—must be a new thing."

Reese glanced down and saw the blush that appeared on Kenna's face and thought it was priceless. "Don't mind them," he whispered. "They're just jealous. Come on. Let's tell everyone our good news."

It was only when everyone was seated at the dinner table a half hour later that Reese, with Kenna sitting by his side, got everyone's attention by tapping his glass with his knife. Everyone got quiet and looked at him expectantly.

He smiled at the people gathered around the table who meant everything to him—his family. "I just want to say that a few days ago, when we met at Uncle Jonathan and Aunt Marilyn's home, my mother asked me a question that I did not answer." He smiled in his mother's direction. "Do you want to ask me the question again, Mom?"

Kenna sat next to Reese and tried to steady her heartbeat. They had talked about it earlier, and knew they wanted his parents, grandparents and brothers to know first. But it seemed fitting that his cousins, who were more like brothers, should hear the news as well.

"Yes, Reese," his mother said, smiling as she glanced from Reese to Kenna. "Something you did that night made us think that perhaps there was more going on between the two of you than friendship. Is there?"

Reese reached out and captured Kenna's hand in his. A smile touched his lips when he gazed over at Kenna before turning to his mother. "Yes, Mom, Kenna and I love each other. I've asked her to marry me and she's accepted."

Pandemonium broke out at the table and it was hard for Reese to decipher who was the happiest—his parents, grandparents, brothers or cousins. They all adored Kenna.

"About time," his grandfather roared after his father brought the table back to order. But that was only after everyone had given the couple congratulatory hugs.

"Mama said the two of you were more than friends and were just pulling our legs," his grandfather continued, beaming proudly.

Reese shook his head. "In all honesty, Grandpa, we were only friends. Things changed once we began living under the same roof."

"You came to your senses." His father laughed. "Just like Luke did with Mac."

"And we can't forget Clayton and Syneda," his grandmother chimed in.

"Yes, Madaris men might be slow at times, but in the end they prove just how smart they are," his mother added.

Reese lifted Kenna's hands to his lips, agreeing that his mother just might have something there.

Alex looked across the room at the four people assembled in his office and shook his head. Tori had been the bait, but other than the two cowboys who Drake had scared out of their wits, their trap had yielded nothing. It was the same with Trevor and Ashton.

"I can't believe the number of women out at night alone," Trevor said, shaking his head. "You wouldn't know that a serial killer was on the loose in the Houston area. We did surveillance at the mall last night and you wouldn't believe how many women were out shopping alone."

"More than one woman tried coming on to me as I walked around the Galleria. For all they knew, I could have been the serial killer," Ashton said in disgust.

"You know why," Tori said. "They don't think it will happen to them. They just can't fathom being a victim."

Ashton started pacing. "He's going to strike again. I can feel it." He turned to Alex. "What have you come up with since we last met?"

"It seems what we have is a killer who's as careful as he is methodical. He never leaves any forensic evidence and it seems he never kills his victims in the same place that they've been abducted. He takes them somewhere else, kills them and then dumps their bodies."

Ashton nodded. "That would account for why there's so

little evidence left behind, since he moves his victims from the abduction site."

Alex nodded. "I had a chance to speak with Professor Lawrence, a renowned criminology expert who has profiled serial killers. He's been studying the Shoe Killer and thinks the reason he targets women and takes their shoe may have something to do with his childhood experiences. The shoe is a symbol of some kind. He was probably abused as a child. And chances are he never got over it."

Sir Drake lifted a brow. "He has a vendetta against a damn shoe?"

"Yes, and that includes the woman wearing it."

No one said anything for a moment. "I still can't understand why he hasn't attracted any attention," said Trevor. "How is he able to just blend in?"

Alex leaned forward in his chair. "I don't think it's a matter of blending in. I think women probably feel comfortable around him, they feel they can trust him."

"Even after all the media coverage?" Drake said.

"Yes. You heard what Ashton said. Even with a serial killer out there, women were still coming on to him at the mall," Alex said.

"But Ashton is the exception," Tori said, grinning. "He's attractive, so women will take their chances."

She paused a moment. "I agree with Alex," she said. "Whoever this guy is, he's a person who presents himself as nonthreatening, someone a woman feels she can let her guard down with and trust. Ted Bundy lured women because of his smile and his easy manner. It wouldn't surprise me if this guy has some kind of professional job like a lawyer, a doctor, a college professor, or he might even be a wealthy businessman. It's a sad commentary, but some women don't take precautions when it's an attractive, seemingly well-mannered guy."

"I hear what you're saying, Tori," Trevor interjected. "But

I think he may have some sort of military training or is very athletic. You can't convince me that none of these women fought back."

Everyone got quiet again. "I'm having the gum wrappers analyzed," said Alex. "I couldn't believe the authorities in Miami and Minneapolis didn't take a closer look at that evidence. Plus, there was some sort of chalky substance on the clothing of several of the murder victims that I'm having analyzed as well."

Tori arched her brow. "And why wasn't it analyzed before?"

Alex shrugged. "It was, but was later dismissed as nothing important to the case. I'm having it examined again." He paused. "Also, I have recently discovered something else that's interesting."

"What?" Trevor asked, lifting his head.

"There's a man working for Reese who was hired just about a month ago."

Trevor's gaze sharpened. "Reese?"

"Yes. I saw him at Reese's ranch yesterday. There's something about him that's familiar. I've seen him before. I'm certain of it, but I can't recall where."

"Did you check him out?" asked Sir Drake, his curiosity piqued.

"Christy is handling it. So far we can't find anything on him. Good or bad," Alex said.

"Christy's good," Tori said thoughtfully. "If there's anything out there, she'll find it."

"And I have," Christy said, walking into the room looking rather smug. "I think all of you need to read this report."

Lynette sat at the restaurant with her partner, who'd been working undercover with her for a week. He was new to the department, a rookie by the name of Gus Ingram. They had gone to an Astros game, and after driving around posing as a couple and checking out several places, they'd decided to grab something to eat. Things were pretty quiet, other than a few people hanging around after the Astros win. No one was in a hurry to go home.

"I'm going to step outside a minute to call my mother to check on my little girl," Lynette said, grabbing her cell phone out of her purse. "I'll be back by the time our order is ready."

"Okay."

She smiled. Gus was okay was far as rookies were concerned, but she would have preferred a partner with more experience. Lynette stood not too far out of Gus's sight. She was near the restaurant entrance away from the door. She had just ended the call and was about to head back inside when someone tapped her on the shoulder. She turned around and for a brief moment recognized the face. Suddenly she felt a hand covering her mouth. The last thing she remembered was a hard blow to the back of her head.

Chapter 27

"You look happy, sweetheart," Reese said, opening the door to let Kenna inside once they'd returned home from the family dinner.

She gazed up at him. "I am. And it's all your fault. I think your mother is happy, too. She kept telling me over and over how much she wanted to help me plan the wedding. It means a lot to me, since I don't have any family."

Reese locked the door and then crossed the room, pulling Kenna into his arms. "But you do. You've always had me, and you had my family even when we were just friends."

Kenna nodded. A part of her had always known that.

"And speaking of weddings, don't you think we need to plan one before my family takes over and plans it for us? I seem to recall that you mentioned you didn't want a huge wedding and that you'd much prefer a small one."

She chuckled. "Yes, but is that possible with your family?"

"It's possible if that's what we want."

At that moment Kenna was overflowing with love for Reese. He was close to his family, but he was willing to do whatever made her happy. But nothing could make her happier than being his wife, so she wanted a huge wedding so that everyone could be there to share in their joy. She was about to tell him that when his cell phone rang.

"Umm, I wonder who's calling," Reese said, fishing his cell phone out of his back pocket. He smiled. "It's Clayton."

"Yes, Clayton, what's going on?"

"The womenfolk got cabin fever, so we thought we would take them to Sisters, if you and Kenna want to join us."

It would be a good time for them to announce their engagement to the rest of the Madaris family and friends.

"I'll check with Kenna, but that sounds like a plan."

Lynette slowly came to and winced at the pain from the whack on her head. It was dark and she was lying in a cramped space. It was then that she realized where she was and what was going on.

Oh, my God! I'm inside the trunk of a moving car.

She closed her eyes, remembering bits and pieces of what had happened. She'd stepped outside the restaurant to make a call to her mother to check on Aleena, and she'd been hit on the head. But how could that be? She'd felt a tap on her shoulder and turned around as recognition slowly dawned.

She drew in a deep breath and coughed when she inhaled the exhaust fumes from the car. She wiggled her hands free, grateful that the man hadn't taken the time to securely bind her wrists. The trunk wasn't very big, but she was able to shift her body around. Recalling her police academy training, she began feeling around for anything she could use to escape.

It didn't matter that the car was in motion. She didn't plan to be inside the trunk when her abductor reached his destination. She knew that if she didn't escape, she would likely be killed.

Her heart began beating faster and she tried not to think about the situation she was in. She knew the identity of the Shoe Killer and he was planning to make her his next victim. She would never see her little girl again, her mother, her family, her...

She shifted her body again, refusing to think of what could happen. He had everyone fooled and he certainly wasn't who he appeared to be. It was up to her to escape. She was good at reading people, but this time she hadn't picked up on anything.

She refused to give up and used her fingers to locate the latch to release the trunk. She felt something, like a small flashlight. Gripping it tightly with her hands, she removed the panel covering the taillight and with all the force she could muster, she began smashing it out. It was then that she saw the cable that connected the latch to open the trunk. She pulled the cable, and the trunk latch clicked. She hoped and prayed that the killer was unaware that she'd succeeded in unlocking the trunk. She opened it slightly.

The vehicle was moving fast, and she knew she was taking a big chance. But she also knew if she remained in the trunk she was in greater danger. She would wait a few minutes to see if he slowed down just a bit, and then she'd take her chances. The opportunity came a few seconds later. She drew in a deep breath, said a quick prayer and jumped out of the trunk, tumbling into the darkness and onto the street, hitting the pavement hard. She saw a car's blinding headlights coming straight toward her and caught her breath. The driver slammed on the brakes within a foot of her. He jumped from the car. "Hey lady, are you okay? What happened?"

Lynnette felt a sharp pain in her head, looked up into the man's shocked face and whispered, "The Shoe Killer." She then succumbed to total blackness.

Alex leaned back in his chair. "It appears that Clark Lovell isn't who he claims to be, and he's on the list of people who have purchased police scanners in the last month." He paused. "But I don't want to jump to any conclusions just yet."

Sir Drake's gaze narrowed. "Why, Alex?"

"Besides," Trevor added, "Lovell works for Reese, and that's too close to home to suit me. Reese is family."

Alex didn't say anything for a moment. Truthfully, he was the only one in the room related to Reese, since he was married to Christy, but he understood how the others felt. Because of their close relationships to the Madarises, they all felt as if they were part of the family.

"Remember what happened with Sam when we thought we knew who was trying to kill her," Alex said. "As you all know, it turned out to be someone we didn't suspect. Clark Lovell is a person of interest right now, but there's still something about him that I find oddly familiar, and I intend to find out what that is."

Alex's phone rang just then. "It's my contact at the Bureau," he said as he saw the caller ID.

The call lasted a few minutes. "Those wrappers were from a special kind of chewing gum that's not sold in stores. It can only be ordered online from overseas." He chuckled. "It includes an ingredient that supposedly guarantees to whiten your teeth every time you chew it."

Ashton rolled his eyes. "Whatever."

Alex chuckled again. "I'm going to see if the product has been shipped our way recently, and I also think we should let Reese know what's—"

At that moment another phone line rang in Alex's office. It was the direct link to his contact at HPD. "Excuse me, I need to get this."

He smiled. "Yes, Jonesy?"

Seconds later the smile was wiped from Alex's face and he sat straight up in his chair. "Damn! When did that happen?"

He drew in a deep breath and raked a hand down his face

in disgust and anger. "Okay, keep me informed. She might be the only eyewitness who can provide a description of the Shoe Killer."

After he hung up the phone he was met with four pair of eyes staring at him. "That was my contact from HPD. The Shoe Killer tried to capture another victim—number five. Unfortunately for him, she was an undercover cop. He put her in his trunk but she was able to escape. The car was moving, so she took a pretty nasty fall and was rushed to the hospital. Right now she's in a coma, but they're hoping when she comes to, she'll be able to help identify this guy."

He was furious—enraged, incensed. How had this happened? When he arrived at his destination, he'd discovered the woman had somehow escaped from the trunk of his car. He couldn't believe it. He should have taken the time to handcuff her like he'd done the others. But he'd taken a chance, grabbing her outside a busy restaurant and had wanted to get away as quickly as possible. Especially after he realized who she was, and he knew that she had recognized him. He had seen the look in her eyes before he'd knocked her out.

He began pacing. What if she talked? Even now she could have already revealed his identity to the police. He had to come up with a plan, and it had to be a good one.

He walked over to the television and turned it on. Surely the media was broadcasting some news about it. For all he knew his face could be flashed all over the television right now. He turned up the volume to listen to the reporter.

"We've received word that the Shoe Killer has struck again, but this time his victim, an undercover cop, managed to escape by jumping from the trunk of a moving vehicle speeding down the freeway. She was rushed to the hospital, and we're told her injuries are serious and that she's in a coma. The police are

hoping she comes out of it and gives them a description of her assailant."

He switched off the television, deciding now was not the time to lose his cool. She couldn't identify him in her present condition, but he had to do whatever he could to make sure she didn't come out of her coma. With that in mind, he walked out the door.

"Surprise!"

Reese's mouth twitched. He should have known there was more to Clayton's call than he'd let on when he had invited him and Kenna to join everyone at Sisters. He glanced around at the smiling faces as he pulled Kenna closer to his side. "Okay, how did all of you find out so soon?"

Syneda beamed at him. "Mama Laverne called me, and that's all it took."

Reese was convinced that the women in his family had an intelligence network that kept them up-to-date about all the family's top secrets. "But how did she know so quickly, when she's still out at Whispering Pines?"

"I'm sure Aunt Carrie called before you two went home," Clayton said, laughing. "And once the women found out, they convinced us that we needed to bring them here to celebrate. They were desperate for any excuse to get out of the house."

Syneda went over and gave Kenna a big hug. "You're going to have to give us the scoop," she said. "How did he propose? When and where?"

A deep blush covered Kenna's features and she quickly glanced over at Reese, who gave her an innocent look. She looked back at Syneda, and with a straight face said, "He proposed last night. Actually, he had my back against the wall and I couldn't help but say yes."

Reese laughed out loud as Kenna glared at him, mostly

because the two of them knew just how close to the truth her answer really was.

"And before you ask, Syneda, we're going ring shopping this week," Reese said, pulling Kenna into his arms and placing a kiss on her lips.

"It's about time the two of you figured out you were more than friends," Blade said, grinning. "I tried to tell you."

Just then Kenna's phone went off with a ring tone that indicated it was a call from HPD. "Excuse me, my boss is calling," she said, quickly retrieving the phone from her purse.

"LaKenna James."

"Ms. James, this is Lieutenant Boggs," the deep voice said.

"Yes, Lieutenant?"

"We need you over at Park Plaza Hospital as soon as you can get there."

Kenna frowned. "Why? What's going on?"

"The Shoe Killer struck again tonight. Luckily she was one of our own who was working undercover. She was able to escape from the trunk of a moving vehicle, but unfortunately she was severely injured and is in a coma. We're hoping she pulls through and can give you a description of her assailant."

The hairs on the back of her neck stood on end as panic swept through her. "The officer who was working undercover," she asked softly. "Who is she?" Kenna's throat tightened, dreading the response she had a feeling was coming.

"Officer Lynette Cummings."

Kenna gasped sharply. "Oh my God!"

Reese had been watching her the entire time, and immediately knew something was wrong. "Sweetheart, what is it?" he said as he drew her closer to him.

She stared at him for a moment. "It's Lynette. The Shoe Killer grabbed her when she was working undercover tonight. He put her in the trunk of his car, but she managed to escape while the car was moving. She was injured and is in a coma at Park General."

She fought back her tears. "They want me to go to the hospital immediately. They're hoping Lynette will be able to give me a description of her assailant when she comes to."

Everyone listened as Kenna described what had unfolded in the past few hours. Reese took Kenna's hand in his. "Come on, baby. I'll drive you there."

Alex stared at his computer screen. It had taken him several attempts to hack into the FBI's confidential files—with some inside help, of course—to obtain the information he needed. It explained a lot about Clark Lovell.

A blast of cold air seemed to come into the room and literally chill him to the bone. His eyes narrowed and his jaw tightened with each line he read. Another emotion—cold-blooded anger—tore into him as he tried to tamp it down.

He looked up at the light rap on his office door. Everyone had left an hour ago, after agreeing to keep tabs on the hospitalized woman who would have been the Shoe Killer's next victim. He had checked earlier and her condition was still the same.

Christy came into the room and glanced over at his computer. "Still reading?" she asked.

He rubbed a hand down his face. "Yes, and I think it's something you should read as well. Come and sit here," he said, standing to give her his chair.

She slid into the chair, leaned forward and began reading the information on the computer monitor while Alex crossed the room to pour another cup of coffee. The clock seemed to tick louder as he sipped his coffee and stared at the beautifully framed photographs that hung on his wall. One was of him and Christy on their wedding day. One was one of those glamour shots of Christy she'd had taken just before she'd gotten pregnant, and the other one was of her when she was pregnant. The rest were of their beautiful little girl, from the time she had come into the world and he'd held her for the first time, to the most recent one of her at her birthday party a few months ago. He drew in a deep breath. He loved his wife and daughter more than life itself.

"The mystery has been solved. Now you know who he is."

Alex turned at the sound of Christy's voice and met her intense expression. He slowly nodded. "Yes, now I know who he is."

He pulled into the hospital parking lot and decided to just sit there a minute after turning off his engine. He knew he would be taking a chance, but luckily for him there weren't as many police officers around as he'd expected. They were probably all out looking for the killer, not knowing he was right under their very noses.

He chuckled. He was going to enjoy reading how things went down in the newspapers the next morning. Everyone would wonder just how he was able to pull it off.

Adrenaline flowed through his veins like wildfire. He licked his lips. The taste of a kill was in the air and he intended to make it happen—tonight.

Chapter 28

Reese and Kenna arrived at the hospital and immediately caught the elevator to the eighth floor, the intensive care unit. An older couple, who Kenna assumed were Lynette's parents, were talking to a group of doctors, as several police officers wandered around in the waiting room. Kenna recognized Steven. He stood when he saw her enter.

She quickly introduced Reese to Steven. "How's she doing?"

Steven shook his head. "She took a hard hit to the head when the assailant knocked her out, and then hit her head again after jumping out of the moving car. Another car came within two feet of running her over. Luckily, the driver was alert and slammed on his brakes in the nick of time."

Kenna shuddered as the image of what could have happened flashed through her head. She was grateful when Reese wrapped his strong arms around her shoulders.

Shaun stepped off the elevator and quickly walked over to them. "I just got word, man. How is she?"

Steven then relayed the same information to Shaun he'd given Kenna moments before.

"Shaun, I'd like you to meet my fiancé, Reese Madaris."

Shaun's face showed surprise as he extended his hand to Reese and glanced over at her. "Fiancé? But just a few weeks ago you said you weren't seriously involved with anyone."

Kenna lifted a brow, thinking he actually sounded like he was disappointed. Evidently he was used to getting any woman he wanted. Now really wasn't the time to tell him how wrong he was. "Reese has the power to change a woman's mind on just about anything," she said, smiling up at Reese.

She glanced over at Steven. "Any news on the assailant, and are you sure it was the Shoe Killer? He took a big risk abducting her in a busy area."

Steven was about to answer when Shaun interrupted. "Look, you guys. I have a date tonight that I don't want to miss. Call me if Lynette's condition changes."

"Sure," Steven said as if he was used to Shaun's behavior. Kenna had only been around him a few weeks, but she'd had no idea he was so self-centered. He had just gotten to the hospital, and he was already leaving.

They watched Shaun get on the elevator. "No, no news on her assailant, but everyone believes it's the same guy," said Steven. "He did the same thing he did to the others by putting her in a trunk. I don't want to think about where he was taking her or what he planned to do once he got there," he continued in an infuriated voice.

"If he's smart he'll be miles away from here. I'm sure by now he knows he abducted a police officer. Hopefully when Lynette comes around she'll be able to give you a good description of the guy so we can arrest him."

Kenna nodded and drew in a deep breath. "I hope so, too."

Reese lovingly touched her arm. "I'm going down to the café on the ground floor to get a cup of coffee. You want some, baby?"

"Yes, thanks, and you know how I like it."

Reese smiled before walking off and Steven watched the exchanged. "He seems like a nice guy."

Kenna smiled up at Steven. "He is. He's the best."

Reese had made it to the ground floor when his cell phone rang. He checked and saw it was Alex. "Yes, Alex?"

"I'm out here at your place. Where are you?"

Reese wondered why Alex would be visiting him at this time of night. It was close to eleven. "I'm at the hospital."

"The hospital? Is anything wrong?"

"I guess you can say that." He told Alex about Lynette, as least as much as he knew.

"Yes, I heard the news report. I didn't know she was a friend of Kenna's."

"Yes, she was one of the first people to befriend Kenna when she started working for HPD. They're hoping if Lynette comes around, she'll be able to give Kenna a description of her assailant, so there's no telling how much longer we'll be here. I'm not leaving until Kenna does."

Reese paused. "And what's going on with you? Why are you at my place this time of night?"

"I wanted to talk to you about something and to talk to Clark Lovell, but he's not here and Joe said he hasn't been back all evening. Any idea where he is?"

Reese rubbed his chin. "No, he's probably at his place in town, but I have no idea where that is. What's going on, Alex? This is the second time you've inquired about Lovell."

Reese heard the hesitancy in Alex's voice before he said, "I'd rather we talk in person, Reese. I'm on my way to where you are."

* * *

"You don't have to hang around here, Reese. Honestly, I'll be fine," Kenna said a short while later when Reese returned with her coffee.

"Doesn't matter. I'm staying. When you leave here, we leave together."

Kenna shook her head. She had just explained to Reese that her boss had requested that she stay at the hospital with her sketch pad just in case Lynette came out of her coma sometime during the night. If Lynette said anything, it would be worth it. Kenna had no problem making herself comfortable next to Lynette's bed, but Reese refused to leave her alone and go home.

"You're wasting your time, Kenna, if you think you can convince me to leave," he said. "This whole thing with Lynette has freaked me out. Before, they were women I didn't know, but now the bastard has hurt someone I do know," he said.

"Besides, I'm meeting with Alex in a few. He's on his way here now," Reese said, interrupting her thoughts.

"Alex?"

"Yes, for some reason he wants to meet with me tonight. It's something about Clark Lovell."

Kenna nodded, wondering what it could possibly be about. "Well, I'll be by Lynette's bedside most of the night. They've stationed an officer right outside the door in case someone tries slipping in."

Reese brushed a strand of hair from her face. "I know you won't be able to use your cell phone up here, so I'll check back with you in an hour or so to see if you want a coffee refill."

She smiled, appreciating his care and concern. She reached up and placed a kiss on his cheek. "You are a jewel, Reese Madaris, and I plan on keeping you around."

"There's no doubt in my mind I'm keeping you, so get to work," he said, smiling. "I'll be right downstairs if you need me."

"All right." She placed another kiss on his lips before turning to walk in the opposite direction. She stopped long enough to speak to the police officer posted outside Lynette's room. She smiled at Reese before opening Lynette's hospital room door and going inside.

Alex was about to get out of his car when his cell phone rang. It was Christy. "Yes, baby, what's up?"

"That information you were waiting on came through regarding anyone in Houston who purchased that special type of gum. The list is pretty long, so it's not as unusual as we might have thought."

He nodded. "Okay, so everyone wants whiter teeth," he muttered. "How about taking those names and running a check against their employment history to see if any of them just moved to the area? It shouldn't take long to get the list. You should have it in your hands in less than an hour," he said.

"All right. Did you see Lovell?"

"No, he's at his place in town, wherever that is. I'm at the hospital getting ready to talk to Reese."

"Reese? What's Reese doing at the hospital?"

Alex took the next few minutes to tell Christy what Reese had told him. "How awful. At least she managed to escape before heavens knows what could have happened to her. The news broadcast said that the woman was an undercover cop, but I didn't know she was someone Kenna knew personally," Christy said.

"I can see them wanting to keep Kenna around just in case she comes to. She's probably the only woman who can positively identify the killer now."

Alex nodded as he glanced out of his windshield as his mind shifted from what Christy was saying to the figure that was getting out of a parked vehicle and hurriedly walking toward the hospital entrance.

"Christy, I have to go. Call me back as soon as you get that information."

Sir Drake glanced at the two men waiting to take their turn at pool. He studied one in particular. "Any reason you're so restless tonight, Ash?"

Ashton's hand tightened on the bottle of his beer. There was no reason for him to be anxious, but Drake was right, he was. He had talked to his wife, Nettie, a few moments earlier and knew she had left Sisters and had gotten their triplet sons ready for bed and had planned to retire herself. She was having their daughter in six months and according to her, their little girl was just as active during this pregnancy as her brothers had been. That meant they would definitely have their hands full when she arrived the first of the year.

"Not sure, Drake, but it has something to do with that damn killer. I can feel him."

Trevor glanced over at Ashton. "You can feel him."

"Yes."

Both Trevor and Drake gave Ashton their complete attention. "Why are you feeling him, Ashton? Is someone we know threatened?" Drake said slowly.

Ashton drew in a deep breath. "Not sure." He pushed the mass of hair that fell to his shoulders aside to rub the back of his neck. "And because I'm not sure, that's what worries me."

He asked both men a question. "If you were in the killer's shoes, knowing the person you tried to snatch was a cop and that every police officer in this city was gunning for you, what would you do?"

"If he's smart he would lay low for a while and then when the coast is clear, haul ass as far away from Houston as he can,"

Sir Drake said first. Drake paused. "But then we aren't dealing with a smart killer, are we?"

Ashton shook his head. "No, but we're dealing with a devious one."

"He believes every victim counts for something and that it's his God-given right to take that person's life in whatever way he sees fit," Trevor said in a voice that was beginning to sound just as uneasy as Ashton's.

Ashton put down his beer bottle with a loud thump. "And he's a bastard who's never had any victims survive," he said with concern.

"Especially someone who could finger him," Sir Drake added, putting down the cue stick.

"I think we need to go to the hospital. Most of the cops are out looking for the killer, and that makes the victim an open target," Trevor said as they headed out the door.

"We'll call Alex after we get there and check things out," Ashton threw over his shoulder.

Chapter 29

Clark Lovell turned around slowly to confront the person he knew had been following him. His stance was just as deadly as that of the man standing a few feet in front of him. "Is there a reason you're following me?" he asked with a steely voice.

"I know who you are," Alex said.

Lovell's features didn't change. "I don't have a clue as to what you're talking about, stranger."

Alex made sure he kept his hands out to his side to show Lovell he wasn't a threat. "I'm no stranger, really. Think back almost fifteen years ago. It was a chance meeting, but one that had a profound effect on me, and the first case I'd ever worked for the Bureau."

The man's features changed to a deep frown. "I still don't have a clue as to what you're talking about."

"I think you do. In fact, I *know* you do. You've tried changing your appearance, but it wouldn't take much for someone who was as impressed with you as I was during that time to remember."

Lovell sized Alex up as the intensity in his gaze deepened. "Who the hell are you?"

A tentative smile touched Alex features. "I'm Alex Maxwell. I was an FBI agent at the time—fifteen years ago. I wanted to be you when I grew up. You hadn't been an agent for long, but already you were a legend. And it—"

"And it cost me everything!" Lovell said through clenched teeth.

Alex knew what he meant. He had read the report tonight. "I'm sorry. I recently found out that the group you had taken down retaliated by killing your wife and newborn daughter."

Alex drew in a deep breath, thinking of his wife and daughter. He couldn't imagine something like that happening. He wouldn't know how he'd go on after such a tragedy. Lovell, whose real name was Brent Dawkins, had resigned from the Bureau, never to be heard of again.

"Okay, so now you know," Lovell said. "I died the day I lost my family. Leave me in peace. I'm no longer that person."

"You sure?"

At that moment the entrance door to the hospital swung open and Reese walked out. "I came out to get some fresh air," he said.

Reese knew why Alex was there, but he turned a curious look at his employee. "Lovell, what are you doing here?"

Lovell looked at Alex. "Reese is my in-law, and to be quite honest, Lovell, I'm wondering the same thing. What are you doing here?" Alex asked.

The man slowly walked down the hall past several police officers still lounging around. Other than glancing at him and nodding, they didn't take his presence as of any significance. He smiled. If they only knew.

He continued walking down the hall. He knew exactly what

room she was in. Unfortunately, she wouldn't be wearing any shoes for him to take something to remember her by.

He rounded the corner and slowed his pace when he saw a police officer stationed directly outside the hospital room door. He shifted directions and went down another hall. He'd assumed once he cleared the officers lounging in the waiting area he would have had clear passage, but he now saw that wasn't the case. He had to alter his plans. Then he smiled when he thought of something.

Clark looked from Reese to Alex. "Since this is a free country, I don't have to answer that," said Clark.

"You do if you want to live," a deadly voice said from behind. Alex glanced beyond Clark to see Sir Drake seemingly materialize out of nowhere. Not surprisingly, Trevor and Ashton also appeared. Alex shook his head. Sometimes he wondered about those three.

"It's okay, Drake. He's not a threat," Alex said, not taking his gaze away from Lovell.

"So you say," Trevor said gruffly.

Alex chuckled, still holding Lovell's gaze. "So I know."

Reese released a frustrated sigh. "Will someone please tell me what the hell is going on?"

"Nothing is going on," Lovell said in a quiet, yet steely tone. "This guy's got me confused with someone. A mistake I will accept."

Alex chuckled. "Any other time I would accept your right to privacy, Dawkins, but not this time. The stakes are too high. Too many women have been killed. You've been keeping up with what's been going on in town. I have proof you purchased a police scanner, which means it's still in your blood, regardless of what happened."

Alex paused. "So we can do things one of two ways. "You can meet with the five of us and—"

"The six of us," an irritated feminine voice said from behind Trevor, Drake and Ashton. None of the three turned, since they knew who the voice belonged to, and recognized the fact that they were in hot water.

Alex tried to keep the smile off his face when he said, "Okay, with the six of us, or I can request that one of those police officers that keep looking over here take you down to headquarters for questioning. Tonight they're not trusting anyone."

Lovell lifted his chin and his fiery gaze all but threw sparks at Alex. "Fine," he snapped. We will talk."

Then without saying anything else, Lovell turned and continued toward the hospital's entrance and the others followed.

Kenna found herself dozing and forced herself to wake up, stay alert. She glanced over at the bed where Lynette was resting silently. The doctor who had come in earlier had said she was doing well and breathing on her own, and that although she was still in a comatose state, he expected her to come out of it at some point.

That was what Kenna had needed to hear, and that piece of information had been the only thing that had finally sent Lynette's parents home. They knew that more than anything Lynette would want them to take care of Aleena and assure the little girl that her mother was fine.

Kenna checked her watch. It was close to two in the morning and Reese was still at the hospital, refusing to leave until she did. He could be such a stubborn man at times, but she smiled, thinking that was one of the reasons she loved him so much. He was loyal to those he cared about, and she knew without a doubt he cared about her.

He had asked her to marry him and she had accepted. Even now, whenever she thought about it she would get goose bumps all over her body, would want to pinch herself to make sure she wasn't dreaming.

Needing to stretch the kinks out of her body, she placed her sketch pad aside and stood. Earlier a nurse had come in and said things would be rather slow for the rest of the night and asked if she wanted a cot to be brought in. At the time she had declined, but now she wasn't sure that had been a good idea.

Moving over to the window she gazed out. It was pitch black outside. Earlier the parking lot had been swarming with reporters and police officers. Now there were only a few of each.

Wanting to switch her thoughts to pleasant things again, she recalled last night and how she had spent it in Reese arms, and how she had a feeling that once they were together again, he would make up for tonight, when they were apart.

She slowly turned around when she heard the sound of the hospital room door opening. She pasted a smile on her face when she recognized the person. "Wendell, you're making rounds pretty late, aren't you?"

He stopped short and she could tell he was surprised to see her there, standing over in the corner of the room beside the window. And then, as if he'd regained his composure, he stiffened and then said in an all-business and strictly professional tone, "I'm Dr. Thomas."

The five men and one woman decided to gather in the prayer room that was located next door to the hospital chapel. They felt it would provide the privacy they needed.

Sir Drake sat next to his wife and in a low growl asked, "Where're my children?"

Tori smiled sweetly at him then answered smartly, "Not home with their father, that's for sure."

His frown deepened. "Tori..." He said her name in that warning tone that let her know not to push him too far.

"I let Trudy know I was going out." Trudy was their sixty-something live-in nanny, and like them she had been a CIA agent in her former life. There was no doubt in either of their minds that their three offspring were in safe hands. Trudy was known to kill first and ask questions later.

"Now will someone tell me what's going on?" Reese asked again, clearly annoyed and impatient.

"I will, but first, like you, Reese, I want to know why Lovell is here," Alex said, giving the man a long, measured look.

It seemed everyone in the room did. Lovell kept his guard up, but then he finally met the gaze of the man who'd not only hired him but had treated him with dignity and respect since he'd come to work for the Tall Oaks ranch. He drew in a deep breath and said, "I heard about Ms. Cummings and what happened to her over the police scanner."

Alex nodded. "And what's it to you?" he asked curiously. "Do you know her personally?"

Lovell studied a painting on the wall for a long moment and then he looked back at Alex. "I met her yesterday." He paused a moment and then said, "She and her little girl made an impression on me."

"And where did this meeting take place?" Trevor wanted to know.

"Out at my ranch," Reese spoke up, and said. "Lynette Cummings is a friend of Kenna's and we invited her and her little girl, Aleena, to come to the ranch. Aleena is fascinated with horses and Lovell took the time to give the little girl pony rides."

"Oh, I see," Alex said, really seeing the whole picture, although he knew the others didn't. Lynette Cummings and her little girl had probably touched a spot within Lovell that he'd thought had been destroyed when he'd lost the family he loved.

"My patience is wearing thin, Alex," Reese warned.

Anyone knowing Reese knew that he could appear calm and composed on the outside but was not one to cross. "Introductions are in order, then."

He looked at Lovell and held the man's gaze. "I think you

need to be up front with everyone now because there might be a couple of people here that have gotten it into their minds you might be the Shoe Killer. It would be in your best interest to convince them that you're not."

Alex wasn't one of them that believed it, but felt it was up to Lovell to convince everyone otherwise. "You already know Reese. Well, these others—Trevor, Ashton, Drake and Tori, like you are former Marines, Special Forces, and the meaner of the four, Drake, along with his beautiful wife, Tori, were also CIA agents."

Alex didn't miss the look of admiration in Lovell's eyes. "Everyone, I want to introduce you to a man who has gone down in history as breaking up more crime rings as an FBI agent than anyone. Clark Lovell, by the way, isn't his real name. It will be up to him if he wants to share it with you," Alex said

Now it was admiration that shone in the others' eyes. "So, are you here working undercover?" a more relaxed Reese asked.

Lovell shook his head. "No, I resigned as an agent with the Bureau a little more than five years ago."

"Why did you leave?" Ashton asked.

The room got quiet, and Lovell's gaze concentrated on the picture hanging on the wall. "The brother of one of the men I sent to prison, the head of a drug cartel, ordered a hit on me and my family."

He didn't say anything again for a minute and then said. "I was supposed to be in the car with my wife and newborn baby girl that day on our way to my parents' place for Thanksgiving dinner, and I got an important call about my next assignment and told them to go ahead."

His voice got choked when he said, "I didn't know they had set the car to blow the moment someone turned the ignition."

"Oh my God!" Tori exclaimed, and turned and smothered her face in Drake's chest.

Lovell turned to look at Ashton. "I decided after that my life wasn't worth living, so I left the Bureau and since then just been moving from place to place."

The room got quiet again, and then Drake asked in a voice filled with rage, "But you did get the bastards responsible, right?"

Lovell shifted his gaze from Ashton to Drake. "Every last one of them."

A slow smile eased onto Sir Drake's lips. "Good."

Alex was about to say something when his cell phone went off. It was Christy. "Excuse me, I need to get this," he said quickly and excused himself from the room a minute to go out in the hallway.

"Christy? What's up?"

"I ran that report like you asked, and you're going to find all this rather interesting."

He frowned. "What?"

"There were ten people living in Houston who chew that brand of gum and have worked with their employer for less than a year. I then narrowed the list further to see where they'd lived before moving here. Three were from the Midwest. I then concentrated on those three to see where they lived before the Midwest. One actually lived in Miami a year before."

All sorts of red flags suddenly went up in Alex's head. "I do find that interesting. Anything else?"

"Yes, the one I've singled out used to be in the military. He worked as a military police officer for a while and was honorably discharged ten years ago. But it gets even more interesting."

"In what way?"

"He's a doctor who works right there at Park Plaza."

"Damn."

"I'm texting you his home address now."

Alex drew in a deep breath. "Thanks, baby. I owe you. Go to bed and get some rest."

A few moments later Alex quickly entered the room to rejoin

the others. “Sorry to interrupt this party, but we’re going to have to finish our chat later. Thanks to Christy we now have a prime person of interest. I got an address, and we need to pay him a visit tonight along with the police with a search warrant.”

“What makes him a prime suspect?” Trevor asked, already on his feet.

“He hit all the points we’d established in our earlier meetings. He was once military police, which can explain his proficiency in using handcuffs and being so attentive to detail as to not leave behind a single clue. And we can link him to the gum wrappers, and he lived and worked in both Miami and the Midwest before moving to Houston. A doctor by the name of Wendell Thomas.”

“Wendell Thomas?” Reese said, totally shocked.

Alex glanced over at Reese. “Yes, you know him?”

“He was invited to that party Alyson hosted for Kenna at her place a few weeks back. I didn’t care for him at the time, since he was coming on to Kenna.”

“Well, like I said, I have a strong suspicion he might be our Shoe Killer, and we need to find him now,” Alex replied.

“No need to leave the hospital,” Reese said. “While I was downstairs in the lobby waiting for you to arrive, Alex, I saw Dr. Thomas arrive. He didn’t see me but I saw him, and he caught the physician elevator.”

“Damn, we need to make it up to Ms. Cummings’s room,” Ashton said in a voice filled with panic, moving toward the door. “I have a feeling he’s here to finish up what he intended to do earlier, since he leaves no survivors.”

“Hell!” Reese said as cold fear seized his heart, causing him to rush out of the room ahead of everyone.

“Kenna’s in that room!” he hollered back over his shoulder. “She’s up there with Lynette!”

Chapter 30

Kenna forced a smile and shook her head, thinking for a moment she'd completely forgotten Wendell's egotistical nature. "Sorry, I stand corrected, *Dr.* Thomas."

"And you are forgiven, Ms. James," he said, crossing the room to Lynette's bed to review her chart.

"I'm surprised to see you here," he said, without looking up.

Kenna chuckled. "I'm surprised to see you here as well. The last doctor who came in over an hour ago said no one would be returning until morning and that she would be resting most of the night."

He then looked up and glanced over at her, and Kenna didn't know if she was imagining things or not, but his eyes looked as if their depths were simmering in rage. She shrugged and figured he must have had a bad day.

"As an esteemed physician at this facility, I can come and go as I please."

"I'm sure you can," she said, deciding she hadn't liked the sting of his words and was liking him even less.

"So, has she come out of it to tell you anything? I assume that's why you're here, to get a description of her attacker."

She hugged her arms around her. For some reason the room felt extremely cold all of a sudden. "No, she's been resting peacefully like the last doctor said she would."

"That's good, and I intend to make sure she continues to rest peacefully."

It wasn't what he said but how he said it that made the hairs on Kenna's nape rise for some reason. And then as she watched him, he pulled a needle and syringe out of his jacket. She found it odd he was the one administering the medication when the nurse had mentioned earlier Lynette wouldn't be receiving any additional dosage of anything until morning. However, the last thing she would do is question that he knew what he was doing.

"Now that that's taken care of," he said, smiling over at her with a look on his face that sent chills up her spine. "Now I can concentrate on you."

"Excuse me, come again?"

He chuckled as he reached into his jacket and pulled out something else. This time she blinked, not believing what she was seeing. He was holding a gun and it was aimed straight at her.

Reese raced to the elevator with Alex right on his heels. Ashton, Lovell and Trevor had taken the stairwell and Tori and Sir Drake were in the physician elevator. Alex was on the phone alerting the police.

"He's stupid to think he can get away with anything," Reese said, thinking the elevator wasn't moving fast enough.

Alex placed the phone in his pocket. "Look, Reese, I'm aware of how well you can handle a gun, but I much prefer for you to stay out of harm's way and let us handle this—"

"Like hell, Alex. I can't do that. That's my woman whose life might be in danger. I might not have the same expertise with firearms the rest of you have, but there's no way I'm not going to try and protect what's mine. And what happened to all those cops that were supposed to be surrounding this place?"

Alex drew in a deep breath. "Someone deliberately sent a false alarm saying the killer was spotted across town that sent everyone scrambling in the wrong direction. We don't have to wonder who's responsible for that."

The elevator finally came to a stop and the two men rushed off.

Kenna backed up. "If this is some joke, Dr. Thomas, then—"

"No joke, Kenna. She's number five and you'll be number six, and don't you dare consider screaming or I'll put a bullet in you here and now. I'd rather not make the mess, but I will if I have to. Besides, there's no one around to assist you. I've taken care of them already. Even that guard who was stationed outside your door."

"But—but you're a doctor. Why would you want—"

"To kill?" He chuckled again. "A long story, and I'll make sure I'll tell it to you later. Everyone hears it before they die, and then they understand."

He looked down at Lynette. "I've made her the exception. She's dying and hasn't heard it. Her loss. But then it's mine, too, because she's not wearing any shoes. She was nothing but a lot of trouble."

"Do you honestly think you're going to get away with this? Reese is downstairs. He'll think something when I don't call him in a minute to let him know how I'm doing."

"Then you better hope he doesn't, or I'll be forced to kill him as well. Come on, we're wasting time. The doctors have a special elevator we use, and we're going to take it so no one will notice us leaving."

Kenna knew she had to do something. If he thought Lynette had been trouble, then he hadn't seen anything yet. He had injected something into Lynette's IV. She had to do something before it could seep into her veins.

"Fine, let's go then," she said, walking toward him.

She saw his smile that made her skin crawl, and then when she reached the side of the bed she deliberately kicked the IV pole, which sent everything to the floor.

"Why, you bitch!" He grabbed at her, and before she could get away he grabbed her arm. "You want to save her from dying, then you will die with her, here and now."

The hospital room burst open and men with guns burst in. Kenna's gaze went immediately to Reese. Even he had a gun. And why was Clark Lovell there with a gun, too?

"Let her go, Thomas!" Alex ordered.

"No, I won't," he said, holding up a needle and syringe and placing it mere inches from Kenna's neck.

"At least that woman will die slowly, but all I need to do is puncture Kenna's skin and she'll be dead within seconds with this stuff. Is that what all of you want? What about you, Madaris?" Thomas snarled. "Is that the way you want your supposedly *best friend* to die?"

When no one said anything, but continued to stare at him while holding their guns on him, he smiled. "I thought you would see it my way, since I have nothing to lose by killing her now. My life is ruined now, thanks to that bitch lying there."

"Let her go, Thomas!" Alex shouted again.

"It's Dr. Thomas to you, and I want all of you to back off. Now."

"Let her go, Thomas," Reese said. "Take me, instead."

Thomas looked amused. "Why the hell would I want to take you instead of her?"

"Because if you harm her in any way, you're a dead man," Reese said in a lethal tone.

"And she will be a dead woman, just like the others. Now I plan on leaving here peacefully with her as my ticket. So I want all of you out my way."

The way Reese was looking at her alerted Kenna that something was about to go down. And when he called out and said, "Okay, Dr. Thomas, if that's the way you want to tango, then—"

Tango.

With that single word that Kenna knew was her cue, in perfect precision she snapped her head around away from the needle. That unexpected move was all that was needed, and several shots rang out by the time Kenna had dipped her body almost to the floor.

"Kenna!" She felt herself being pulled into strong arms. Arms belonging to the man she loved.

"Quick, Reese," Kenna cried out. "He put something in Lynette's IV. I kicked it over but I'm not sure I was quick enough." At that moment a slew of police officers stormed into the room. Steven was among them.

"Lynette's okay," Reese whispered against her lips. "When we all had our guns drawn, we were also shielding Tori while she disconnected all of Lynette's tubes."

She nodded as she buried her face in Reese's chest. She needed to be held by him, inhale his scent and hear the sound of his heart close to her ear. She then pulled back when a question flared in her mind. "Where did you get your gun?"

"It belonged to the officer that had been stationed by your door. Luckily, Thomas didn't want to waste any of the poison to kill them, so he knocked both the officer and the male nurse out cold."

Medical personnel were there to take care of Lynette, and Kenna watched her friend being wheeled to another hospital room. She didn't look over in Thomas's direction. She already knew his condition. He probably hadn't survived the first bullet.

She felt herself being lifted into Reese's arms and carried from the room, but not before he leaned down and gave her a kiss she definitely needed. From the way he was kissing her it seemed they both needed it.

"Will you let her come up for air, Reese?"

He released her mouth and she glanced over and saw Tori standing there, smiling.

"I guess I will for a minute or two," Reese said, chuckling softly.

And it was only for a minute or two. He walked out of the room, out of everyone's way, and took her into the waiting room, where he sat down with her in his lap. He then kissed her again, and her insides clenched with all the love she felt coming from his kiss.

He finally released her mouth and said in a quiet tone, "I've never been so frightened in my life. When I saw him holding that needle so close to your neck, knowing what a sicko he was and that he wouldn't hesitate to make good on his threat, I thought I would die. Had anything happened to you..."

"Nothing happened. Thanks to you, I picked up on the cue you sent me. Tango."

He smiled. "I took a chance. I wasn't sure you would pick up on it. All of us were waiting for the perfect opportunity to bring him down, all we needed was a little more space between that needle and you."

Kenna nodded. "And what is Clark Lovell doing here?"

Reese then told her about Clark's involvement and what the man had lost, and how Lynette and Aleena had touched him deeply enough to make him want to come to the hospital to see her when he'd heard about what had happened to her.

"I think he needs them, sweetheart. Not to replace what he's lost, but to know that life can go on."

Kenna nodded again, thinking that Lynette and Aleena could probably use a man like Clark in their lives as well. She had seen him that day and had watched how good he'd been with Aleena. Maybe there was hope there.

"Excuse me, Kenna. We need for you to come down to police headquarters so we can ask you some questions about what all took place here."

It was Reese who spoke up. "Ask her now, Steven, because when I leave here I'm taking her home. She's been through a lot, and I intend to make sure she gets some rest."

"I understand." Steven then asked questions, and she found the strength to relive those moments with Dr. Thomas only while securely held in Reese's arms.

It was an hour later before she was given the okay to leave. "I want to go check on Lynette before I leave, Reese."

"Okay."

Lynette had been taken to another floor, and the police officer guarding her door smiled and stepped aside when Reese and Kenna walked in. Clark was already there, along with Lynette's parents.

"I thought I'd keep an eye on her myself," Clark said, answering the questions he must have seen in their eyes. "Her parents said it would be okay and that they would appreciate me looking after her while she's here. Sort of like her bodyguard. That means I'll need time off work. "

Reese laughed. "You got it. Does that mean you plan to stick around Houston for a while?" he asked.

Clark smiled softly. "Yes, I think I will."

Reese and Kenna talked with Lynette's parents for a moment and with Clark again before catching the elevator to the ground floor. Not surprisingly, they discovered most of the Madaris family waiting on them. The women rushed over to hug Kenna while the men went to Reese to see if his version of what happened was different from what the media was broadcasting.

And Kenna thought the media was everywhere, being kept back beyond the taped area by police officers.

She glanced up when Alex, Trevor, Ashton, Drake and Tori stepped off the elevator and crossed the lobby to them and gave each man a kiss on the cheek before hugging Tori. "Thanks to all of you, for everything."

Then she was pulled into Reese's strong arms. "Don't I get something, too?" he asked, looking at her with a teasing grin.

"Most definitely," she said, smiling and looking up at him. "For the rest of my life I plan to make you the happiest man on earth."

"You already have, sweetheart." And then he leaned down and kissed her.

Two weeks later

Flanked by Ashton and Trevor, Sir Drake walked into a seedy-looking bar with a frown on his face. He glanced around. Amidst the smoke and dim lighting he saw the two men he'd sought by the pool table. A sinister smile touched his lips when he began moving in their direction.

Ashton Sinclair glanced over at Trevor. They knew there was no use wasting time asking Drake if he was sure about what he intended to do. They knew he was hungry for revenge. They knew if their wives had been decoys as Tori had been that night, they would be ready to kick somebody's ass as well.

One of the men was playing pool and had the cue stick in his hand when Drake reached out and snatched it out of his hand. The man, who was just as big as Drake, quickly swiveled around with a deep scowl. "What the hell?"

Instead of answering, Drake hauled off and punched him in the face. He dropped to his knees. The second man lunged toward Drake with his fist. In the blink of an eye, Sir Drake took the man's limb, and in one swift move you could hear the man's bone crack clear across the room. He yelled in pain before falling down to his knees as well.

Ashton and Trevor stood by, watching the entire thing. As far as they were concerned, the two men were getting just what they deserved.

"Who the hell are you?" the second man cried out, perspiration covering his face. "You broke my arm."

"And I would have blown your brains out that night if my wife hadn't stopped me."

Suddenly, it dawned on both men as terror filled the depths of their eyes. "Yes, that was *my* wife. And the two of you made a grave mistake by getting out of line with her."

"Hey, man, we didn't know she was your wife. We were just out having a little fun."

A crazed look appeared in Drake's eyes as he began rolling up his sleeve. "A little fun? Well, I'm about to show you what a little fun feels like so the next time you want to have *a little fun* you'll always remember it."

Twenty minutes later, Drake, Trevor and Ashton walked out of the bar, shrugging their shoulders to work the kinks out. Trevor and Ashton hadn't planned to get involved, but when the two men's friends decided to jump in, the two decided to sweeten the odds.

The bar was a total wreck. Ashton, Drake and Trevor apologized to the owner and left enough cash on the counter to rebuild the place, leaving seven badly beaten men littered across the floor. As the three were leaving, they were suddenly surrounded by several police cars with lights flashing. Officer Steven Byrd got out of an unmarked car, smiling and shaking his head. "We got the call. We also got word from the mayor and police chief that if you were here to pretend that we didn't see you at all."

Steven paused. "We're taking those two guys in for questioning. What they tried sounds similar to the M.O. in a couple of other rapes in the area. We think they might have been the two we've been looking for over the past year."

Drake nodded. "It wouldn't surprise me if they were," he said, working the soreness out of his fist. "I've done what I needed to do and now we're out of here."

As Steven and the other officers looked on, Drake, Trevor and Ashton got into Ashton's truck and drove off.

Epilogue

"You're supposed to shove the cake in his mouth, not feed it to him," Lee hollered to Kenna while the photographer snapped away, taking pictures of her and Reese feeding each other pieces of their wedding cake.

"Shut up, Lee. Your time is going to come," Reese said loudly to his cousin, so everyone could hear.

"Not on your life!" was Lee's response.

"Don't be too sure of that," Mama Laverne said to her great-grand, whose time she knew would be coming sooner than he thought. She stood watching Reese and Kenna and was thinking now what she'd thought when Reese had introduced Kenna to her years ago. *One day she will be his wife.* It had taken them long enough to figure it out.

Her attention was drawn back to Lee. He'd begun getting restless lately. His mother and his grandmother had noticed it. He had even mentioned taking a job abroad for a while. He was going to find out what others before him had learned the hard way. When it came to love and the woman who would eventually be your mate for life, you couldn't run away.

Reese glanced across the ballroom at the woman who could inspire so many emotions within him, and when he thought how close he'd come to losing her, he shivered inside.

"Hey, what's the frown for? It's your wedding day," Alex said, coming to stand beside him. "Kenna is a beautiful bride."

Reese nodded. "She most definitely is."

It had taken five months to pull everything together, and now Christmas was only a few weeks away. The wedding had been huge, with close to five hundred people in attendance, including many of Houston's finest. Their small wedding had ended up being large, but they hadn't minded, and the women in his family had been just tickled pink. And speaking of pink…

All the new babies in the family had been born. Blade and Slade's wives had given birth to daughters. Blade's daughter's name was Blair and Slade's daughter was Sierra. Ashton and Nettie had a daughter they named Ashlynn, and Clayton and Syneda had a son they named Caleb. And then last month Alex and Christy had announced they were expecting again, and Luke and Mac were becoming parents for the first time.

Reese's gaze traveled the ballroom, and he felt good inside when he saw Clark, Lynette and her daughter standing together at the punch bowl. Lynette had recovered nicely and Clark had continued to be there for her. They had built a special relationship.

Clark no longer worked for him, but had agreed to work for the local FBI office teaching classes and not going back out into the field. Everyone was glad and felt that his expertise in the criminal field should be shared.

"Time for me to cut in and dance again with my bride," Reese said to Alex, placing his champagne glass on a tray carried by a passing waiter. "They're playing our song."

And they were. Someone had asked the band to play "Inseparable," and he thought it was most appropriate. "I think this is my dance," he said to Emerson, and smoothly took his brother's place.

Kenna smiled as she blinked those beautiful dark eyes at him. As always, he was lost. He truly believed he'd gotten lost the first time he'd seen them. "Ready for our honeymoon, sweetheart?" he asked, pulling her closer into his arms.

She chuckled. "Yes, I'm more than ready," she said before resting her head on his chest. They would be flying to Buenos Aires for two weeks, and they planned to tango their nights away.

When the music ended the band immediately went into Argentine music, perfect for the tango, he laughed out loud and said, "Ready to get a head start and tango?"

She chuckled. "With you, always."

And then they showed everyone watching why they were so good together, the perfect couple, and indeed inseparable.

* * * * *